SAMANTHA SUTTON

and the
LABYRINTH OF LIES

SAMANTHA SUTTON

and the
LABYRINTH OF LIES

JORDAN JACOBS

sourcebooks
jabberwocky

Published by Sourcebooks Jabberwocky, an imprint of Sourcebooks, Inc.
P.O. Box 4410, Naperville, Illinois 60567-4410
(630) 961-3900
Fax: (630) 961-2168
www.jabberwockykids.com

Library of Congress Cataloging-in-Publication data is on file with the publisher.

Source of Production: Versa Press, East Peoria, Illinois, USA
Date of Production: August 2012
Run Number: 18434

Printed and bound in the United States of America.
VP 10 9 8 7 6 5 4 3 2 1

For my mom and dad

<u>Artifact/Specimen Inventory</u>

<u>Site Name</u>

Chavin de Huantar, Peru (CdH)

<u>Unit/Level</u>

N/A (Recieved by regular mail in Palo Alto, CA, USA)

<u>Find #</u>

SSFNb1

<u>Object Type</u>

Notebook (fragmentary)

<u>Measurements</u>

24cm x 18cm x 4cm

<u>Material</u>

Solid, unbleached card stock; paper; aluminum;
traces of cotton twine

<u>Description</u>

This is a small, reporter-style field notebook in very
poor condition. Most pages are loose from spiral binding,
others are highly fragmented. Several (most?) pages
are missing entirely. Water damage/ soil staining throughout.

<u>Context/Associations</u>

~~The recipient of this object knows it to be the~~
~~archaeological "field notebook" of Samantha Sutton, used~~
~~during her excavation of Chavin de Huantar in the~~
~~Summer field season of the year,~~

Please see attached document for detailed
contextual information.

[Out of sequence]

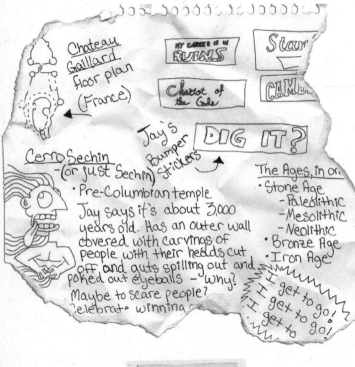

Chateau
Gaillard
floor plan
(France)

MY CAREER IS IN
RUINS

Staur

Chariot of
the Gods

CAMU

Jay's
Bumper
stickers

DIG IT?

Cerro Sechin
—(or just Sechin)
• Pre-Columbian temple
Jay says it's about 3,000
years old. Has an outer wall
covered with carvings of
people with their heads cut
off and guts spilling out and
poked out eyeballs — why?
Maybe to scare people?
Celebrate winning a

The Ages, in or.
• Stone Age
  — Paleolithic
  — Mesolithic
  — Neolithic
• Bronze Age
• Iron Age

I I I get to go!
I I get to go!
I get to

CHAPTER 1

Samantha Sutton jerked awake, her seat belt pressing uncomfortably into her cheek. She sat up as straight as she could and struggled to clear her mind of its strange, unsettling fog.

But when she cast her eyes through the dirty windshield, she immediately wished she hadn't. The road outside had grown narrow and rough, winding its way along a ledge carved into the cliff-face. Just inches from her side of the van, the ground dropped away into shadowy nothingness.

A careless turn would send them tumbling over; a fall would kill them all.

She forced her gaze back inside, bringing her hand up to ensure that her notebook still hung from her neck by its knotted length of cord. She could not remember falling asleep or even feeling drowsy. How long had she been unconscious?

Rubbing her bleary eyes, she turned to see her brother, Evan, snoring in the backseat, his headphones still on and his head lolling back. Her Uncle Jay was also sound asleep, his chin collapsed against his chest. To her relief, Osvaldo sat fully upright and alert in the driver's seat beside her, his smiling eyes fixed on the road ahead.

"Where are we?" she asked.

"Just past Huaraz, *pulguita.*"

Huaraz? She must have been asleep for quite some time. The barren mountainside outside the driver-side window glowed warm in the afternoon sun.

"What happened?"

Osvaldo laughed at her question.

"You passed out! All three Suttons, out like lights. But do not worry. It is the altitude, nothing more."

"I fainted?" she asked.

"Well, yes, in a way. At this elevation, there is less oxygen than you are used to. Your body did not want to work so hard, so it turned off for a short time."

She turned away, catching a glimpse of herself in the rearview mirror. The same dark braids framed the same elfin features, and the same freckles speckled across the same slightly upturned nose. But her large brown eyes were happy, and new life beamed from her pretty smile. She was fully herself somehow, now that her adventure had begun.

●●●●●

With her entire being, Samantha wanted to be an archaeologist, just like her Uncle Jay. On weekends, her parents would sometimes drive her from their home in Davis,

California, and drop her off at her uncle's university on the far side of San Francisco Bay.

Samantha and Jay would talk for hours, sprawled among his notes and photographs. Rubbing his rough, unshaven chin and excitedly smoothing his dark brown hair, her uncle would tell her tales of forgotten tombs, dangerous cave-ins, hidden cities, snakes, and scorpions.

But while Samantha adored these stories of adventure, she listened most closely when he described his ongoing excavations at Cerro Sechín, which bristled like some cornered animal against the desert bluffs of the Peruvian coast. She was drawn to the detailed note-taking the work entailed, the precise soil samples, and the careful analysis of bits of broken clay vessels, known as "potsherds." She loved the orderly elegance of test "units"—the perfectly dug squares and rectangles on which all excavations were based. Archaeology seemed to be a job for a very patient and organized mind. It seemed like something she could do.

And of course it was Jay who had given her the field notebook—a present for her twelfth birthday, back in January. Similar ones sat in disorderly piles on his book-shelves and in tumbled stacks around his office floor. But hers was clean, its unlined pages crisp, and Jay had passed a piece of twine through the tight spiral binding so it could hang from her neck like a pendant.

"Get used to writing everything down," he had com-manded when he presented it to her. "Things you read, conversations you have with people, ideas that come to you, even little details that don't seem to matter. You can sort out what's significant later."

He'd passed the loop of twine over her head.

"We archaeologists destroy what we study—that's just how it goes. If you dig something up, you're the first and last person to see it exactly as it was left. Everything comes down to what you observe at that moment and how carefully you record it."

She nodded, eager to show him that she understood.

"But that kind of observation takes lots of practice. And if you're going to work for me, I'm going to need you to be good at it."

"What?" she cried. "Work for you?"

"That's right. This summer. What do you say?"

But even in her excitement, Samantha had known that her say wasn't what counted. The decision would be up to her parents, and them alone. And while Raymond and Phoebe Sutton loved their daughter, they were far too busy with their careers to understand just how much archaeology meant to her. They had no time to ask her how she spent her afternoons at the library every day after school, or why she would whisper "Paleolithic, Mesolithic, Neolithic" to herself from time to time.

The previous spring, her parents had barely noticed when she constructed a model of the Chateau Gaillard in the shaded patio of the backyard—relying on her careful research to reproduce Richard the Lionheart's twelfth-century castle with cardboard, gravel, and glue. In their eyes, she was just a strangely serious little girl with a pretty peculiar pastime. Archaeology was just a phase, and she would surely outgrow it.

So when they finally said yes, Samantha was not surprised that their agreement came with a catch. Her brother, Evan, would accompany her to Peru.

She was much too young to traipse around South America looking for dinosaurs on her own, her parents had explained, confusing archaeology with paleontology for the millionth time.

"Who else will supervise you while your uncle works?" her father asked, not understanding that she wanted to be working too, right at Jay's side.

"The Archaeo Kid *is* much too little," Evan added, using the nickname he knew she hated. "Look at her! She's microscopic!"

Samantha realized she would just have to accept having Evan come along, and by the time Jay came back from Peru to retrieve them, she was nervous with excitement. All her hoping, all her pleading, all her months of research had finally paid off.

As Jay discussed the final details with her parents, Samantha wrestled her duffel bag out the door and into the back of her uncle's muddy pickup truck, distinctive for its solid layer of bumper stickers. Evan was already seated.

"Hey, Archaeo Kid!" he called through the open window. "Ready to be my personal assistant?"

But she barely registered the teasing. It didn't matter.

This would be the best summer of her life. She would be an archaeologist, at last.

As she opened the passenger door, Evan pulled his knees to his chin so that she was forced to slide into the cramped middle seat. He smelled like old pizza, and she was about to tell him so when Jay clambered inside and started the engine.

"Okay, guys. We have a flight to catch!"

"Where are we going?" asked Samantha, as her brother jostled her to fasten his seat belt. "Cerro Sechin?"

"No, Sam. Somewhere totally new. Well, *new* in a manner of speaking."

Jay pulled out of the driveway, grinning at his own joke.

"But you're going to love it. I met up with a couple of colleagues last year at a conference in Lima. We got to talking about a site where they've been working, and they invited me along. It's called Chavín de Huántar, and it's way up high in the Andes mountains."

The name seemed familiar, but Samantha was distracted by something else her uncle had said.

"So, it's not your project?" she asked glumly. If Jay wasn't in charge, she wondered how much she would be allowed to do.

He read the expression on her face.

"Don't worry, kiddo. I may be third in command, but I still got to pick a third of the team! When I arrived with my group a couple of weeks ago, we were welcomed with open arms. And you will be too."

"Chavín de Huántar," she said as they sped down the highway, letting the strange words roll from her mouth. "Is it Incan?"

"Oh, please," said Evan. "Of course not. All your research and you don't even know about Chavín?"

"Easy, Ev," Jay said, and then softened his voice. "Sam, remember how the Inca were around in the fifteenth century when the Spanish arrived? Chavín is much, much more ancient. In fact, it would have been older to the Inca than the Inca are to us. Not much is known about the people who built it, and that's why this summer is going to be so exciting."

"Unless I'm stuck baby-sitting *you* all the time," said Evan.

He reached for his headphones, and as soon as the muffled, tinny music of his handheld video-game system filled the cab of the truck, Jay whispered a half apology.

"I know you don't exactly love that your brother is coming with us, but it was the only way I could convince your parents to let you go. And besides, I can use his help. His Spanish is good, and we both know he's a smart kid."

But Samantha could not agree.

"He's not going to be any help on the dig at all," she muttered. "He's just going to torture me all summer."

"Oh, don't you worry about that, Archaeo Kid," Jay said, his smile sly. "You guys will be too busy to bother each other. I'll see to that. And maybe you'll be able to prove to him just how much you know."

She relented. Her uncle's enthusiasm was contagious.

"Besides, it's your help I need most of all," he continued. "In fact, there's a very important job at Chavín that only you can do."

•••●••

Samantha had not been on many airplanes in her life. Sitting by the window, she felt her heart race as the noise of the engine swelled and the plane charged down the runway to buck suddenly upward and into the twilit sky. Jay must have misread her excitement as nervousness because she soon felt his reassuring hand on her arm. To her relief, Evan—seated by the aisle on the other side of their uncle—seemed not to notice. By the time the plane had leveled its ascent, he was absorbed once again in his video game, *Pillager of the Past IV*.

Night had fallen outside her window, but Samantha was too excited to sleep. To pass the time, she examined her passport. Crisp, blue, and formal, it looked and felt like a new, exhilarating responsibility. She turned it over and over in her hands, then carefully examined the pages. There was her picture, taken at school, and beside it, in gravely serious print, her name: SUTTON, SAMANTHA ISIS. She couldn't wait until the passport was floppy and worn like her uncle's, and the pages filled with exotic stamps.

"We've got some time now, Sam."

Jay rustled for a moment in his knapsack and withdrew a stack of papers. They were photocopies of pages from his own field notebook, bound with a rubber band.

"Yours to keep. The field season has only been going for a couple of weeks, so you haven't missed too much. But I should catch you up with the rest of the team."

He laid the stack on her tray table. His handwriting was as bad as a little kid's, but his sketches and maps were expert and precise. Before her were pictures of snarling carved faces, majestic staircases, and pots with intricately engraved designs. Most exciting were Jay's diagrams of enormous stone buildings. They were zigzagged with a wild maze of passageways—called "galleries," strangely enough. Their tangled paths were hard to navigate, even in diagrammed form.

Questions came so rapidly to Samantha's mind that she was barely able to ask them.

"What is it? Who built it? What was it for? What are these…?"

"Hold on, hold on, hold on!" her uncle said, laughing. "Sam, there's one answer to *all* those questions—we don't really know. Archaeologists have been working here for decades, and mostly it's still a mystery. Hopefully, after this summer, we'll be able to come up with some answers."

With her uncle's notes before her, the hours passed quickly. Samantha did her best to absorb as much of the information as possible. She flipped through the stack again and again, and tried especially hard to commit one page—a map—to memory. A rectangular building seemed to dominate the area, with smaller buildings and imposing courtyards spread out before it. A river flowed north and south, marking the site's eastern edge. A second river flowed in from the west, meeting the first just above the site's perimeter.

But at the bottom of the page, something else caught her eye: a note, penciled in her uncle's hurried scrawl.

There may be some truth to the "Loco" rumors after all. Villagers extremely reluctant to discuss.

She nudged her uncle awake.

"What's this?" she asked. "What rumors?"

Jay glanced groggily at the page.

"That? Nothing for you to be worried about."

"But why is it in your notes?"

Jay rubbed his eyes, clearly eager to fall back asleep.

"It's kids' stuff. Nonfactual. Just a ghost story."

Samantha did not drop her questioning look, and Jay let out a semi-serious moan.

"Fine, Sam. The ruins are supposedly haunted, okay? Not by some ancient spirit or mummy's curse or anything like that, but by *el Loco*—a lunatic—who disappeared into the site many years ago and never came out. He is said to return to the valley in the moonlight, protecting some sort of treasure he left behind."

She nodded, committing the story to memory.

"It's no more than a legend, Sam, if you can even call it that. A rumor, like I wrote, spread by children."

He emphasized his point by pulling a pen from his pocket and scratching out the words completely.

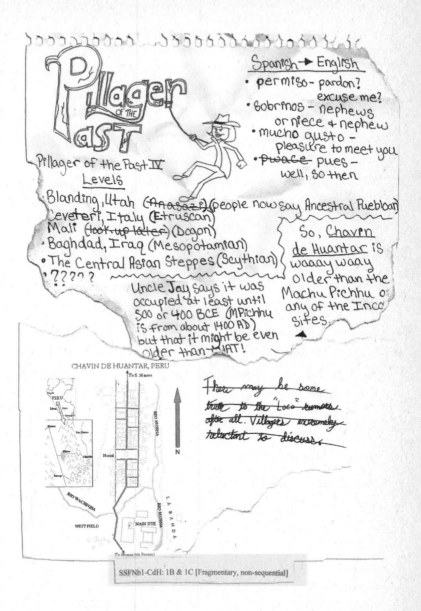

Pillager of the Past

Spanish → English
- permiso - pardon? excuse me?
- sobrinos - nephews or niece & nephew
- mucho gusto - pleasure to meet you
- ~~pwace~~ pues - well, so then

Pillager of the Past IV
Levels
- Blanding, Utah (~~Anasazi~~)(people now say Ancestral Puebloan)
- Ceveteri, Italy (Etruscan)
- Mali (~~look up later~~)(Dogon)
- Baghdad, Iraq (Mesopotamian)
- The Central Asian Steppes (Scythian)
- ?????

Uncle Jay says it was occupied at least until 500 or 400 BCE (MPichhu is from about 1400 AD) but that it might be even older than THAT!

So, Chavin de Huantar is waaay waay older than the Machu Pichhu or any of the Inca sites.

CHAVIN DE HUANTAR, PERU

There may be some truth to the "Loco" rumors after all. Villagers extremely reluctant to discuss.

SSFNb1-CdH: 1B & 1C [Fragmentary, non-sequential]

11

"Let's focus on the archaeology, okay?"

Samantha gave a cautious nod. In all the time they had spent together, Jay had never refused to answer a question that she had posed to him, even in a joking way. He hadn't even held back when they talked about his old site of Cerro Sechin—happily describing the gruesome carvings of dismembered human bodies, piles of heads, gouged-out eyeballs, and spilling guts that adorned its fortress walls.

From the aisle seat, Evan's video game beeped and chirped.

"Finally! Done with Africa!" he announced, as the small screen faded to black. "I just cleared the entire Mali board. Dug up and sold all three hundred terra-cotta statues."

The screen begin to glow again, and Samantha watched as a tiny character—the Pillager of the Past herself—jogged across a ruined road into what looked like a smashed and burning museum.

"Oh yeah," said Evan, grinning. "Baghdad! This level's supposed to be easy!"

●●◉●●

Samantha woke to the buzz of the television display embedded in the seat in front of her. It showed a map of the flight's progress, and the tiny plane symbol was just now inching across the equator. Through her window she could see nothing—just daybreak over a carpet of thick, dark clouds. Only when the plane banked to one side was the gray expanse broken by an endless chain of jagged white peaks reaching for unknown miles toward the horizon.

The Andes.

She was worlds away from her familiar life now. She would never spend another boring summer at home. Not when there were real adventures to be had.

At last, the aircraft eased through the clouds and Samantha saw a massive city spread out below her. This must be Lima, the capital of Peru, sprawling from the foot of the mountains to a dark and angry sea. Soon, she heard the landing gear unfold below her and the tremendous rush of air against the wings. With a thump and a lurch, they arrived.

●●●●●

For some reason, Samantha had expected Peru to *feel* different from the United States. She had thought the air itself would seem special, or that something inside her would be able to sense that she was in a new country, far away. But, as she marched down the metal stairway and onto the tarmac, she was surprised how familiar everything seemed. It was a little more humid than she was used to, but otherwise, it was like any warm, cloudy morning back home.

Following Jay's example, she slid her new passport across the desk to the stern, uniformed official and listened as he questioned her uncle in Spanish.

"He's asking what we're doing here," Evan translated in a low voice. "And uh-oh…this isn't good…"

"What?" Samantha whispered. "What's he saying?"

"They're talking about *you*."

"About me?" She twisted a braided pigtail nervously around her finger.

"The policeman says you're too ugly to come into the country. I think they want to send you home."

Samantha frowned. She didn't know any Spanish and instantly hated that she would be at Evan's mercy to understand everything that was said. As she heard the clank of the officer's stamp and retrieved her passport through the window, she decided to learn as much of the language as she could, as quickly as possible.

By the time they had collected their luggage and stepped into the heat of the parking lot, it was pouring. Steam rose from the swollen puddles, and raindrops the size of walnuts rapped against the roofs of cars.

The area beneath the concrete awning was crowded with taxi drivers jostling for passengers. Jay politely refused their shouted offers, leading his niece and nephew through the mob and toward a covered bus stop. While Evan and Samantha flinched and cowered as globs of water stung their faces, Jay strode on with his back straight, as if totally untouched by the rain.

Suddenly, though, he changed direction.

"Osvaldo?"

Repeating *"permiso, permiso"* and glancing back to make sure that his niece and nephew were following, he made his way quickly to where a man was waiting for them, his hand raised in silent greeting. Jay extended his own as they approached, and the two embraced warmly in the downpour.

"*Mis sobrinos, Evan y Samantha*," said Jay, proudly introducing his niece and nephew as they blinked in the pounding rain. "Guys, this is Professor Osvaldo Huaca. For most of the year he teaches archaeology at a university here in Lima, but he works up at the site for the rest of the time. He grew up near there, actually, and I think it's safe to say that he knows more about Chavín than anyone else alive."

The Peruvian man was short, shorter than Evan, but at least twice as wide. His wet black hair lay pressed against his head above dark, smiling eyes. While the taxi drivers nearby wore T-shirts and shorts in the warm weather, Osvaldo was wearing a thick sweater and jeans, soaked dark by the rain. A silver buckle glinted from his belt. His grin and demeanor were just like their uncle's—friendly, intelligent, and open—but there was also concern in the way he smiled and anxiety in the way he kept checking his watch.

"*Mucho gusto, Profesor Huaca*," announced Evan formally, in his crisp, junior-high-school Spanish. Then, turning to his sister, he hissed: "I think he's almost as short as you are, Archaeo Kid! Looks like you've got some competition for the World's Puniest Person award!"

Jay's face dropped, and he continued his introduction with quiet anger in his voice.

"Professor Huaca also happens to speak English. Probably better than *you* do, Evan." He turned to face his colleague. "I am so sorry, Osvaldo. These two have a bit of a rivalry going on, and sometimes they say rude and ugly things."

15

He flashed an angry glance at his nephew.

"Especially this one."

The Peruvian archaeologist's smile did not return. He coughed uncomfortably and shifted his weight on his feet.

"It is of no importance, Jay," he finally replied. "Children. What can be said?"

He met Samantha's nervous gaze.

"I mean no offense to you, of course, Samantha. I am sure you do not share your brother's manners."

"No, I do not, Professor Huaca," she stated emphatically.

Evan gave her a dark scowl, promising some form of revenge.

"Please call me Osvaldo, *pulguita*. We are all on a first-name basis on this excavation."

He said the last word as if it had an "s" or a "c" where the "t" went, and Samantha felt a wave of confidence. If "excavation" in Spanish was just *"excavación,"* maybe learning the language wouldn't be as hard as she'd feared.

"But Osvaldo, what are you doing here?" Jay asked. "We were going to just get an overnight bus through Huaraz. I thought it would be better to take it slow. Get these guys adjusted to the altitude."

"There is no time. We must get you back to the site."

Jay's face darkened.

"It's happened again?"

Osvaldo gave a quick nod, and even in their anger at each other, Samantha and her brother exchanged questioning looks.

Jay gave a long sigh. Water was coursing down his hat, streaming in thick rivulets from its broad brim.

"Okay, then. Evan, grab the bags."

Osvaldo, Jay, and Samantha trudged through the rain to a small white van, Evan trailing behind them with the luggage.

"Why don't you sit up front, Sam?" asked her uncle when they reached the vehicle. Then, indicating Evan with a joking frown, "I'll keep an eye on this one in the back."

Samantha could tell that her uncle was no longer mad at her brother. Jay could not be angry at anyone for very long. And yet, as he began to chat with Evan about the site, Samantha could detect something in her uncle's voice that she had never heard before. He seemed preoccupied and maybe just a little afraid.

••●••

The busy road from the airport wrapped around the city's center and through a landscape unlike any Samantha had ever seen. Covering the dry barren hills was an enormous sprawl of shacks built of plywood, sheets of metal, and corrugated plastic—stretching as far as she could see. As the van raced through the rain, Samantha could see where streams of brackish water had cut furrows in the dirt streets, flooding where they were choked with garbage.

"These are the *pueblos jóvenes*, the new towns," Osvaldo explained. "The people who live here have fled from the mountains."

"Why? What happened to them in the mountains?"

Osvaldo took a deep breath, weighing his words before he answered.

"It is a difficult life in the *montañas*, my dear. Little work. Very poor. And…*pues*, the Andes can be unforgiving in other ways. Terrible things have happened there in years past."

She nodded gravely, trying to absorb the news like an adult would have. But then Osvaldo leaned over her for the glove compartment, reaching for a map, and her eyes caught the cold glint of metal.

There was a gun inside, inches from her knees.

"Do not be afraid," Osvaldo soothed. "There have been some problems with *bandidos* on the road we are to take. But it has been a long time since I have had to use that."

Samantha did not know what to say.

"I am sorry." Osvaldo shook his head. "These are not things for a child to worry about."

She set to work on forgetting the horrible thoughts that filled her mind.

An hour later, they were out of the rain. As the van raced through a brown expanse of sugarcane, and as Jay and Evan talked loudly in the backseat, Samantha traced their route on the map spread across her knees.

The road to Chavín seemed to begin innocently enough, but soon the small blue line on the map would kink wildly back and forth, folding itself into the contours of the mountains. After the town labeled "Huaraz," the blue line gave way to a thin brown thread, and the zags and kinks became impossibly tighter.

Behind her, Samantha could hear Evan as he tried impatiently to teach their uncle how to play his video game.

"You have to hurry through the museum halls before the soldiers show up," her brother was explaining. "Clear out as many of the cases as you can."

"I'm just not a natural at this, I guess," Jay replied, stabbing at the buttons with his thumbs.

"What's this number?" Samantha asked, pointing to a figure printed alongside their route on the map. "Is that how many people live there?"

"4,700?" Osvaldo answered, "No, *pulguita*. That's the elevation of the pass in meters. About 15,000 feet."

Samantha was astonished. In California, her own familiar Sierra Nevadas were only around 6,000 feet above sea level.

The last of the sugarcane whipped past, and suddenly the Andes loomed before them. The map showed that the mountains were still a hundred miles away, but Samantha had to lean forward to see their summits through the windshield.

Soon, the van began its ascent. The deep ravines that gradually opened up on the left side of the car were spotted with flowering cacti. To the right, barbed-wire fences corralled goats and chickens and pigs into notches in the cliff-face. Patches of unpaved road became more and more frequent, and before long they were bumping along a wide earthen track. Here and there, small waterfalls coursed down the rocks, carving gullies across the road.

She could hear her uncle and brother laughing about something in the backseat, but she did not feel the slightest bit left out. These were the Andes unfurling around her, and she had the perfect view.

Until the formidable elevation sucked the oxygen from her body and plunged her into a dark and dreamless sleep.

●●◉●●

Now, Samantha sat up as straight as she could, determined not to let the altitude get the best of her again as she watched the landscape bounce past her window. But just as her mind cleared itself of thought, and just as she began to give in to her fatigue once more, Jay murmured something from the backseat.

"The looting," he said groggily over his nephew's loud snores. "Tell me what happened."

Samantha didn't move, knowing the conversation would end abruptly if they could tell she was listening.

Osvaldo exhaled.

"It's bad, *amigo*. Very bad. Many more test pits on the Temple's south side."

"You've reported it to the police?"

"Yes, of course."

"And…"

"And *nada*. They say they are doing what they can. In their opinion, the site's perimeter is secure. They say it is from animals rooting around."

"Ridiculous." Jay spat, no longer whispering.

"What's ridiculous?" Evan was awake now too, if only barely.

"Nothing, kiddo. Rest up. We're still a few hours away."

Samantha, too, fell back asleep. When she next awoke, the rocky cliffs had given way to a vast rolling grassland— the *puna* that she had read about in her books. Stepped ridges cross-cut the vastness, and distant white peaks poked up from the horizon. The van wound its way through rolling hills and around a small, clear lake—bright blue, even in the golden evening light. There were no other cars, no other people in sight. Just majestic scenery in every direction, as far as she could see.

Finally, after a long tunnel, the road began its descent. In the fading light, Samantha could make out a curtain of cliffs sweeping into the shadows below. The van crept downhill, the gravel surface crunching beneath its tires on switchback after switchback after switchback.

And then something emerged from the shadows before them and Samantha was too terrified to scream.

Map of Hostal Jato

Jay → Kitchen

Courtyard

→ Dining Room

→ Lobby

me + Evan

Business Card (Translate later)

HOSTAL JATO: OFRECE UN LUGAR IDEAL EN CONTACTO CON LA NATURALEZA, CON HABITACION CONFORTABLE, SIMPLE, DOBLE, TRIPLE, MATRIMONIAL—BAÑO PRIVADO, AGUA CALIENTE 24 HRS. PRECIOS COMODOS. PLAZA DE ARMAS.

Señora

weird teeth!

Ollantaytambo

This is an Incan archeological site down by Cuzco

MY trowel!!

Conquistador's account

Junto a este pueblo de Chavín hay un gran edificio de piedras muy labradas y de notable grandeza; era Guaca, y Santuario de los más famosos de los gentiles; como entre nosotros Roma y Jerusalen a donde venían los indios a ofrecer, y hacer sus sacrificios, por que le demonio de este lugar les declaraba muchos oráculos, y así acudían de todo el Reyno. Hay debajo de tierra grandes salas, y aposentos, tanto que hay cierta noticia que pasan debajo del río...
— Antonio Vázquez de Espinoza, 1622

The town is very small but really busy. There are always people out in the street, and tons of animals!

Translation →

crowded bus!

Next to this village of Chavín is a big building of very (??) stone of notable size. It was a Guaca (???) and sanctuary of the most famous of (??), like Rome or Jerusalem is for us, where Indians came to make offerings and make sacrifice because the demon in this place made oracles and all the reign came here (??). Under the ground are big rooms and chambers ... FINISH LATER

Tenon head

snot!

Spanish → English

• ~~Tran kee yo~~ Tranquilo — calm down
• Atras – back, or go backwards
• Dios mío – oh my god
• Mira – look at this
• ~~Quanto questa~~ Cuanto cuesta – How much does it cost?
• Para ti – This is for you
• ~~Ten queedaddo~~ Ten cuidado – Be careful
• Adentro – Inside

Isabel + Alejandro

SSFNb1-CdH: 2

22

CHAPTER 2

A bus lurched into view around the next corner, heading straight for them up the grade.

It was enormous, and a plume of smoky exhaust spurted dark and thick behind it. Its roof bulged, and as the two vehicles approached each another, Samantha could make out a series of lumps held tight to the top by a taut green net. They were sheep, she realized and—to her greater amazement—about a dozen people were seated among the animals, wrapped in blankets and hunched low beneath the covering.

But what terrified Samantha was the width of the oncoming vehicle. The road ahead was too narrow to allow the vehicles to pass each another. On the left, the craggy wall of rock loomed above them, and to the right, there was no rail to protect them from the thousand-foot drop.

Osvaldo would have to steer between the bus and the edge. But the oncoming driver was not slowing down.

Jay and Evan leaned forward between the front seats.

"We're not going to fit, *amigo*." Jay's voice was hushed but tense.

The bus, belching its smoky exhaust, was now so close that Samantha could read the faded sign for HUARAZ in its windshield.

"Osvaldo, the road's not wide enough."

"*Tranquilo*, Jay. *Por favor*."

Loud blasts came from the bus's horn now as the gap between the vehicles closed.

"Get to the right!" Jay put his hand out as if to reach for the steering wheel.

"I am as far to the side as I can go!" Osvaldo cried, pushing him away. "This *chupado* needs to give me room!"

The distance was closing fast and became too close for Evan to bear. From behind her, Samantha heard him throw open the van's sliding back door.

"Evan, no!"

Jay flung his arms around his nephew and wrestled him back inside, the gaping door showing only the blue-black emptiness of the void.

Samantha was thrown forward in her chair just as a frightening combination of sounds erupted at once: the barking squeal of the bus as it ground to a stop, the halting screech of the van's own brakes, and the soft crunch of metal as the two vehicles made their soft collision.

"*¡Atrás! ¡Atrás!*" shouted Osvaldo through his open window, and the other driver quickly followed his instructions, reversing the hulking bus down the slope toward a wider section of road. As Osvaldo hit the gas, the van lurched violently and something clattered out the sliding back door and over the cliff. It was Evan's video-game system, spinning off into space. For several seconds, the Pillager of the Past was left alone to face a hoard of Scythian mummies before smashing on the rocks far below.

"Let's move, Osvaldo! Come on!"

Muttering an oath in Spanish, Osvaldo again stomped hard on the gas pedal, and after a terrifying instant, the van tore forward. Finally, solid earth was visible below Samantha's window, and all four wheels were planted firmly on the road.

They were safe.

Samantha peeled open her clenched fists, rubbing where her fingernails had dug into her palms. In the same instant, Jay and Osvaldo erupted into howls of laughter.

"Every time, *amigo*! Every time something like this has got to happen!"

"We are some very lucky *hombres*, my friend," Osvaldo gasped between hoots. "*¡Dios mío!*"

Leaving Samantha and Evan silent and shaken inside, the professors made a quick inspection of the van. The damage was slight, and after a laughing handshake with the equally relieved bus driver, both vehicles went on their way.

The descent took another hour, and Osvaldo negotiated the final switchbacks with his head lamps on their brightest setting. Finally, at long last, a scattering of lights peeked up at them from the valley depths.

"There it is, guys," announced Jay from the backseat. "Chavín de Huántar!"

Samantha turned around in her chair, and Evan's sleepy eyes met hers. For just a moment, they exchanged eager and elated grins.

●●◉●●

She awoke this time to the sweet smell of roses. A blue, early-morning light flooded through the window above her pillow, and it took her a moment to recall that she was not in her own bed at home but in a faraway country on the underside of the world.

The previous night was a blur of memories. She could remember the road making S-shapes along the valley floor, the gurgling of water as they crossed bridge after bridge, the crunch of gravel and the barking of dogs as they entered the small town, and the feeling of tired relief as they finally came to a stop in front of the whitewashed walls of the Hostal Jato—yellow under a lone streetlight. There had been a flurry of words in Spanish and a weary struggle up a steep set of tiled stairs. She had barely pulled the soft, brown blanket up to her chin when she fell into a deep and dreamless sleep.

Now she rolled onto her stomach, brushed aside the curtain, and gazed through the dusty window at her first sight of the village.

The valley in which Chavín was situated was very deep. From her bed, she could not see the tops of the mountains opposite. Below her, across the smooth dirt road, stretched the main town square—the Plaza de Armas—a large expanse of cracked concrete and patches of soil, spotted with cacti and bright pink flowers.

The entire scene was alive with motion. A group of children made their way noisily up the road, their backpacks bouncing against their school uniforms. Nearby, two women splashed water across the street's dirt surface in order, Samantha guessed, to keep the loose dust from blowing into their storefronts. In the center of the square, a mustachioed man in a trim blue suit was attaching a red and white Peruvian flag to a flagpole, and Samantha watched as it climbed slowly upward and unfurled.

Evan was still in his bed: a snoring lump under a heap of sheets and blankets. But as Samantha rustled in her suitcase for fresh clothes, the snoring stopped abruptly, replaced with a long, low moan. The moaning continued as she braided her hair into pigtails and tiptoed to the bathroom to get dressed. When she came out, Evan had emerged somewhat from beneath the sheets, propping himself up with one hand and cradling his head with the other.

"My...head...hurts...so...bad..." he whispered, his eyes still pinched tightly shut.

Samantha picked up the bottle of water their uncle had left them the night before and offered it to her brother. After a few moments, his eyes opened to a painful squint, and he grabbed it roughly from her hand.

"You're welcome," Samantha muttered. As soon as the words were out of her mouth, her brother yelped in pain.

"Don't talk so loud!" he hissed, squeezing his eyes shut. "For once in your life, Samantha, could you just try not to make any noise?"

She sat down in a chair to lace up her hiking boots, only a little more loudly than she needed to. If only Evan's admirers could see him now. His brother's lean, strong physique, dark brown hair, and the glint of naughtiness in his deep brown eyes made him one of the more popular eighth graders at Emerson Junior High. But now here he was—soccer-team captain, class president, King of the Winter Dance, first-chair trumpet, and *jefe* of the Spanish Club—reduced to a sniveling mound.

They were startled by a loud pounding on the door, and Evan retreated whimpering beneath the covers.

"How's everybody feeling?" boomed their uncle, striding into the room.

He seemed taller than Samantha had ever seen him. He held his satchel, clanking with tools, and his hat hung on his back from the strap around his neck.

"I'm okay," Samantha said with a shrug. "But Evan seems to be dying."

"You all right, kiddo?" Jay asked with some concern, addressing the twitching lump of bedding.

"I hate this place," came the whispered response.

Their uncle's wide grin returned.

"It's just the altitude, Ev. Lots of people get headaches

when they first come up here. Drink a lot of water, take things slow, and you'll feel better as the day goes on."

He turned to face his niece.

"In the meantime, Sam, *you* come with me."

They stepped into the hallway and down a staircase into an outdoor courtyard. The sun was already bright and hot. The smell of flowers grew stronger, and Samantha noticed a bed of beautiful red roses against the courtyard's opposite wall.

"*Buenas, señora*," Jay said, as an old woman stepped from the door of the *hostal*'s office, wiping her hands on a white dish-towel.

"*Buenos días, Samantha*," the señora said, crouching to Samantha's height. Samantha fought a gasp of surprise when the woman's lips parted in a smile, exposing teeth unlike any she had ever seen. The front teeth, top and bottom, had been filed flat on their faces, and small panels of abalone shell were affixed to them so they glittered silver, pink, and green.

"*Buenos días*," Samantha replied after a pause, matching the old woman's greeting as best she could.

A man and a woman descended the stairs behind them, weighed down with backpacks and canteens. They were speaking in a language that was neither English nor Spanish.

Jay tipped his hat to the duo.

"*Buenas.*"

"Are they with us?" Samantha asked her uncle.

"No. We didn't rent out the *whole* hostal! Chavín gets a small trickle of tourists—it's a good jumping-off point for a lot of long mountain treks. Some folks come from Europe, some from Lima, a couple from the United States now and then. It's good for the town, and the entrance fees go a long way in protecting the site."

The señora ushered the two tourists through the small lobby into the hotel's sunny dining room, leaving Jay and Samantha in the courtyard alone.

"Okay, Sam. Time for you to make a big decision."

Across a nearby bench lay a line of tools. Each had a triangular blade fitted to a wooden handle by an angled piece of metal, but they were all slightly different. There were variations in the width or length of the blades, for instance, or in the particular angle of their sides.

Jay cleared his throat.

"Now, many years ago, on my very first real dig, in the Colorado Plateau…"

"In Woods Canyon," Samantha corrected him, her eyes still scanning the tools before her.

"Right, Sam. In Woods Canyon—which is *in* the Colorado Plateau—my professor presented me with a choice very much like this one. The trowel I chose, he told me, would be the most important decision I'd ever make."

Samantha giggled skeptically.

"Sam, listen. This is very important. You're about to choose the tool of your trade. It's like…"

He struggled to find the right comparison.

"It's like a wizard's magic wand."

Samantha laughed aloud. Now she could tell her uncle was mostly kidding. He knew how she felt about those kinds of books, no matter how many times her parents had given them to her as presents.

"So go ahead, Sam! Pick them up. See how they feel."

Samantha went down the line of trowels, squeezing the handles, comparing the weight of each as she flexed her wrist, tossing them lightly from hand to hand. Finally, she made her decision. The trowel's handle was made out of a smooth yellow wood, and she liked how it pinged when she rapped it against the bench.

"Great choice. And…"

Jay knelt in front of her, grabbed her by the shoulders and spun her around.

"…since you're an archaeologist…"

In a swift, single motion, he dropped the blade of the trowel into the back pocket of her jeans, so that the handle angled out and up.

"…you should carry your trowel like one."

She noticed a similar handle emerging from under the back of Jay's red flannel shirt—worn, pitted, and streaked with mud.

"The Archaeo Kid!" he announced mischievously. Samantha answered the hated nickname with an exaggerated scowl.

Her uncle examined his handiwork, wiping the dust from his hands.

"Now all you have to do is excavate something."

With the handle of her new trowel bouncing against her lower back, Samantha hurried up the hard-packed dirt road, trying to keep up with her uncle's long, enthusiastic strides. She could feel the altitude as she jogged and soon she was almost out of breath. Evan trailed several feet behind them. He had chosen his own trowel unceremoniously as they left the hostal but had refused the small packet of food the señora had offered them. His stomach now sloshed with water and painkillers.

The sky was a deep and solid blue, and Samantha tried to absorb the sights of the town around her. A cluster of young women stood on the broken sidewalk. They were clad in brightly colored dresses and brimmed hats—much like the ones Samantha had seen worn by men in old movies. Farther along, Jay exchanged nods with a small company of soldiers that strolled toward them wearing dark green uniforms with floppy red berets. They seemed very young to be soldiers—maybe just a couple of years older than Evan—and heavy guns hung across their chests on long braided cords.

A few dogs, large and small, followed for short distances, sometimes barking before turning onto side streets or stopping to scratch against a step or doorway. With each bark, Evan grimaced from the noise and brought his hand back to his throbbing forehead. He caught his sister's glance back at him and met it with an angry "Be quiet!"

"I didn't even say anything."

"Well you did now, so shut up."

A five-minute walk and the road slanted upward, grew bumpier, and left the buildings behind. This was the road on which they had entered the night before, and Samantha was eager to see what she had slept through. Slender eucalyptus trees and coarse bushes sprouted from the tall yellow grass in the embankment. Here the valley narrowed, and without even turning her head, she could see both mountainsides to her left and right, covered with a patchwork of steeply sloping fields.

The air smelled of dust, animal dung, and the exhaust of the few old trucks they had seen bouncing and jostling through the town's narrow streets. Soon, they heard the sound of rushing water and came to a wooden bridge, rough and rickety, over the Rio Wacheqsa. The river itself was now a small and noisy trickle, but from the height of the riverbanks, Samantha could tell that it swelled enormously for at least some of the year. High above the town, a group of llamas grazed in the dry grass.

Finally, the site came into view. Situated on the left-hand side of the road, it was protected by a tall stone wall, reinforced with concrete and whitewashed, the words *Monumento Arqueológico Chavín* painted bold and black upon it.

As the Suttons approached, a boy and a girl bounded toward them, blocking their path. It was clear from the way they began joking and laughing with her uncle that he knew them. When they noticed Samantha, though, they redirected their energy to her.

"*¿Líticos, señorita?*" the small boy asked her, looking up at her through warm brown eyes. Put off by the formal-sounding "señorita," it took a moment for Samantha to glance at what the boy had cupped in his hand. He held a small flat stone, and she caught the hint of an intricate web of designs before the boy was roughly brushed aside.

"*No, no. ¡Mira!*" the tall, skinny girl elbowed herself in and extended a flattened palm. "*¡El Lanzón!*"

She grinned eagerly, revealing a large gap between her two front teeth. The stone in her hand was wedged into a disc of cardboard to stand upright. It was a slender rectangle with a square notch cut from one corner. The whole thing was etched carefully with clear, curving lines, but it took a moment for the design to make any sense. Slowly, Samantha could see the swirls and spirals as a fanged mouth, flared nostrils, and a pair of angry eyes. It was a monster of some sort—something old and angry.

"*¿Cuánto cuesta?*" Evan asked. He produced a fistful of American currency from his pocket, and Samantha didn't need to understand his question to know his intentions.

"Evan!" Samantha whispered. "You can't buy that! It's an artifact!"

"Who cares?" said her brother. "I like it. And I bet it's dirt cheap!"

Her uncle's calm voice eased her fears but vindicated her brother as well.

"It's okay, guys. These aren't artifacts, they're

reproductions. In fact, the artists of these masterpieces are right in front of you."

"See?" Evan sneered at his sister. "You can't even tell an artifact from a fake!"

"It's on me, Ev." Jay flipped the tall girl a pair of shiny *un sol* coins. "Here you go, Isabel. *Para ti.*"

Isabel flashed her gap-toothed smile and gave a giggling curtsy before handing her small sculpture to Evan.

"And you, Sam? What do you think of Alejandro's craftsmanship?"

Samantha eyed the young boy's cruder version. She was still smarting from her brother's insult, but she was polite enough to compliment the rough carving with smiles and close examination before shaking her head no.

"Okay, then," said Jay. "*¡Adiós, amiguitos!*"

He strode toward the gate, Evan trudging behind him. But as Samantha made her way to follow, she felt Alejandro's small hand on her elbow, holding her back. He met her eyes in a determined squint, then pulled her close to whisper in her ear.

"*Ten cuidado. El Loco está adentro.*"

She pulled away from him.

Loco.

That word again. Madman. The ghost story mentioned in Jay's notes.

But the boy's warning was urgent and firm. This was not just a story, at least not to him.

"Samantha, let's go!" Jay called. "Time's a-wasting!"

"Um, okay." Samantha fumbled. "And Alejandro, I like your carving. Maybe next time?"

But the boy surprised her by pressing the trinket into her hand. It was a gift.

"Oh!" Samantha started. "*Gracias!*"

"*De nada,*" he replied, his face still filled with concern. Then he and Isabel scampered away up the road, leaving the Suttons to enter the site at last.

●●●●●

There was a pleasant smattering of "*holas*" as the Suttons passed a group of policemen leaning against the ticket office, chatting with the woman inside the booth. But Samantha could not find her voice to answer.

Chavín de Huántar. This was a place of awesome mystery. Archaeologists were baffled by their findings here. Her hands were shaking at her sides.

But Samantha was crushed by what she saw. The ancient site didn't seem mysterious at all. She had expected a great stone temple, deep excavation trenches, computer stations, and tables spread with amazing finds, but before her was nothing but a low grassy hill. While she had imagined the busy noise of work crews and cries of discovery, the only sound was the intermittent buzzing of lazy black flies.

"This is it?" Evan groaned, staring at the squat mound of dirt and grass.

"This is it!" Jay answered, slapping his niece and nephew on the back before quickening his step.

When they reached the mound he veered to the left, and his pace increased to an eager jog so that Samantha and Evan had to run to keep up. Another, larger mound appeared before them, and as the ground sloped gently downhill, the embankment seemed to grow. It was the height of a two-story building when they reached its end, turned to the right, and stopped.

Samantha's disappointment vanished.

This was it. This was definitely it.

Before them lay the Plaza Mayor, an immense plaza sunken into the earth in a perfect square and stretching into the distance in the direction from which they had come. The low hill they had passed around—and which now loomed above them on their right—was one of two that flanked the broad courtyard. From this vantage point it was clear that these grassy mounds were not simple heaps of earth but structures of massive stone blocks, overgrown and buried by the centuries. From each, a series of graceful staircases cascaded into the plaza.

Nearby, just beyond the courtyard's eastern edge, the Mosna River churned and seethed in full force, charging to meet the Wacheqsa just down the valley. It was choked with boulders, and the water bubbled white and frothy as it found its way northward.

However, it was what dominated the courtyard's western side that filled Samantha with the greatest awe. A broad stone stairway led up from the plaza to a flat terrace, from which rose a second staircase to a second terrace. And there—dwarfing everything—loomed the Temple itself.

She could tell it was big, but without anything to compare it to, she could not get a clear sense of its size. Her perspective was jolted when she made out a wheelbarrow parked at its base, tiny beneath the massive stones. The Temple must have been at least four or five stories tall, covering the area of two city blocks.

"What is it?" Evan asked, the words tumbling from his mouth, "Who built it? What was it for? What are those…"

"I'll give you the short version," Jay said, smiling. "Sometime about two thousand years ago, a group of people organized themselves and began to build this place. They didn't build it all at once, though. Different parts were added over the course of several hundred years."

"Now what's it for?" he continued. "That's what we're trying to figure out! We're pretty sure it had a religious function. Actually, it seems to have been the religious capital for an enormous region. Chavín's influence can be seen in sites north, south, and all the way to the Pacific coast. Whatever was going on here was very, very powerful. Beyond that, there's not much we can say."

Following Jay's lead, all three Suttons bounded down the stairs and into the majesty of the Plaza Mayor. On two sides, the flanking mounds rose impressively, their hewn stone staircases a solemn gray through the dry grass that covered them. The mass of the Temple towered over everything, promising mystery, wonder, and adventure.

They climbed the wide staircase and into the shadow of the Temple itself, coming to a stop where a trio of rectangular blocks rested on the grass, carved with ferocious faces. Each was a little bit different, but all featured sharp, pointed fangs around an angry grimace, with enormous eyes that bulged from their sockets.

These were "tenon heads," she remembered from her uncle's notes, named for the long stakes of stone that had protruded from the back of each. Only broken stumps of the tenons remained, but Samantha could imagine how the heads had been stuck to the outer walls of the Temple, like giant thumbtacks, all the way around.

She pointed at one of them, to where carved tubes emerged slug-like from each nostril.

"What are those supposed to be?"

Jay's grin was as mischievous as ever.

"What do they look like?"

Samantha risked the obvious answer.

"Snot?"

"You agree with the experts, then, Sam. It's a very old sculpture of a very runny nose."

"The Archaeo Kid happens to be an expert on the subject herself, Uncle Jay."

But Samantha was too excited to pay Evan's comment any attention.

So *this* was Chavín. Her first site. An ancient temple, a mysterious religion, and a very, very puzzling series of artifacts. This was going to be the best summer she had ever had.

She sat down, stretching out on the grass to take everything in.

"Don't get too comfortable!" Jay shouted, and she could hear the smile in his voice. "There's so much else to see!"

"If *she* gets to lie down, then *I* get to lie down," Evan insisted. But he had forgotten that he had copied his uncle and sister by sliding his trowel into his back pocket. As he flopped himself down, his satisfied sigh became a howl of pain, thundering through the valley.

When his moaning subsided, Evan eased himself to his feet. A small splotch of blood was already seeping through the seat of his pants.

Jay brushed the dust from his nephew's shoulders.

"Okay, Ev. Let's take a quick detour to the first-aid kit so you can patch yourself up."

Samantha swallowed hard.

"Can I stay here?"

Her uncle shot her a look of surprise but quickly suppressed it.

"Sure you can, Sam." The pride in his voice was unmistakable. "We'll be back before you can say 'Ollantaytambo.'" Samantha had read enough to recognize the name of a major Incan archaeological site.

Moments later, they had disappeared around the bulk of the Temple Complex, and she was completely alone. She gazed over the site in silence. A cool breeze had picked up, and looking across the valley from where she sat, Samantha noticed a sinister bank of fog inching over the lofty rim like a thick wall of mud. She shivered, pulling her hands into the sleeves of her sweatshirt. Beside her, the carved heads that she had found so amusing only minutes before seemed to stare at her, all three of them, with a look of hateful possession. As the thick sludge of fog flooded over the cliff-face, rolling over the river and across the square plaza to envelop her, she could almost hear the carvings growl.

And then Samantha started. Because it wasn't her imagination. There was a noise—a real noise—breaking the silence. She heard a series of metallic scrapes, mixed with a string of deep animal grunts. With horror she realized that it was coming from high above her, behind her, from within the Temple walls. And it was getting louder.

She straightened and swiveled around.

And that's when something shiny and sharp whizzed past her head and pierced the earth near her feet.

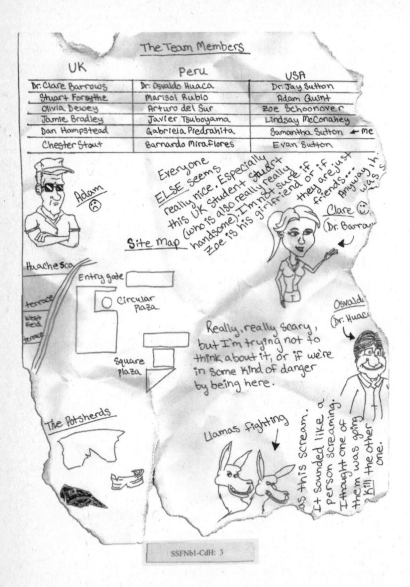

Chapter 3

The object that sliced through the air beside her ear was a trowel, and the menacing ping of its impact punctured the muffled silence of the mist-choked valley. Samantha spun around to scan the sheer face of the Temple behind her, her heartbeat thumping behind her eyes.

Through the fog, she saw something moving high above her—wriggling snake-like from the wall of stone. A sickly feeling of unease rippled through her as she made out the head and shoulders of a man, his face toward the sky, pushing himself backward out of a small hole in the Temple's eastern face. He gave out an angry groan as his hands sought holds above the opening, and then he used a pair of long, powerful arms to pull himself free and drop with a heavy thud a few yards from where Samantha stood. The man swore, uncoiled, and heaved himself to his feet.

It was clear that his trowel had not been meant for her. He had probably tossed it out behind him without looking to free his hands and ease his exit. But even so, some deep instinct told her to avoid this man, to disappear into the fog before he spotted her.

She turned on her heels and took a few hurried strides in the direction that her uncle had gone. But it was too late.

"Hey! Hey, you!"

The voice was deep and hoarse.

"*Hey!*"

She heard a string of muffled bad words, and then a strong hand was on her shoulder and pulling her around.

The young man before her was flushed, out of breath, and irritated. She recognized him in a vague sort of way as one of her uncle's students, someone she had seen in the halls of the Anthropology Department during her visits to the university. His cropped blond hair was powdered with dust, and a smear of coarse whiskers darkened his throat, chin, and cheekbones. The taut muscles of his arms and neck were those of a young athlete, but the twisted scowl of his mouth seemed to belong to someone much older. There was something sinister about him, and she wished that her uncle would return.

The stranger whipped a crumpled hat from his back pocket and pulled it low and tight onto his head. It was a military version of a baseball cap—square-shaped, army green, and streaked with sweat and dirt.

"You're Professor Sutton's kid?" he asked gruffly.

For a moment, he peered at her through eerie, dark eyes, their pupils lost in the blackness of his irises. But then, to

Samantha's relief, he pulled a pair of sunglasses from his pocket and put them on.

"I'm not his *kid*," she answered, getting hold of herself. "I'm his *niece*."

The stranger snorted.

"Your uncle mentioned he'd bring back visitors. Strange place for a vacation, I think."

"I'm not on a vacation."

He bent to pry his trowel from the earth and spun it between his fingers like a gunslinger.

"Wait. Your uncle isn't going to let you help out with the excavation, is he?"

She nodded, growing angrier.

"Fantastic," he snapped. "Just what we need."

She could almost hear the thoughts swirling behind his glare—worries of slowed schedules, interruptions, tantrums. She chose her next words carefully.

"Sounds like you could use all the help you could get, with the looting that's going on."

He stared at her for a moment, then dismissed her comment with a grunt.

"I'm looking for Dr. Sutton. You know where he is?"

It was with utter relief that Samantha made out the sounds of a rapid discussion coming toward them through the fog. It was the voice of her brother, clearly recovered, describing the forthcoming *Pillager of the Past V*.

"Oh, good!" said Jay, as he and Evan came into sight. "Samantha, Adam, I see you two have met."

"We were just introducing ourselves, Professor," said Adam, his tone changing. "It's very nice to meet you, Samantha Sutton."

He thrust out his hand for her to shake, and she noticed the pronounced veins rising from his muscular forearms. Even with her uncle looking on, she hesitated before extending her hand, and cringed as it disappeared in his burly grip.

"And this is Evan, my nephew."

"I'm Adam Quint."

"Hi."

Adam turned to Jay.

"I've been looking all over for you."

"We just had a slight family emergency," said Jay, laughing. "Sorry to have kept you waiting."

"We need to talk."

"Well, I was going to let these guys meet the rest of the team…"

But Adam cut him off.

"My unit was looted last night."

Jay's face fell.

"Looted?"

Adam nodded gravely.

"The new unit?"

"Yes, the two-by-one. There's something strange going on here, Professor. It was only yesterday that I finally found anything…anything that a looter might want."

Jay ran a hand through his hair, clutching his hat with the other.

"Is the unit salvageable?"

"No. Totally destroyed."

Samantha's mood darkened further. Something serious was happening—something bad.

"All right," her uncle said, stroking his chin. "I'll call a team meeting."

"Dr. Huaca already did." Adam replied. "Everyone's by the unit, waiting for us."

They made their way toward the entrance gate, using a small path between the Temple and the fence on the site's southern perimeter. Jay led, lost in thought, with Adam and Evan right behind him. Samantha didn't like the way Adam moved: a little too quickly and a little too smoothly, like a snake.

But she had other things to think about. The looting made her anxious. It was scary to think that there were thieves around. Who knew how desperate they were, or how dangerous? She caught glimpses of her uncle's worried face as they walked and saw that the issue was on his mind, as well. Still, the site's other mysteries held the greater part of her thoughts. Where had Adam come from so suddenly? That hole in the face of the Temple—where did it lead?

What was within the massive structure? When would she get a chance to take a look inside? And who was this Madman that the boy Alejandro had warned her of and whose mention her uncle had so uncharacteristically scratched from his notes?

They came around the Temple's western face to find

a group of students gathered around the rectangular hole that was Adam's unit. Samantha straightened and tried not to look nervous. If the other students were all as rude and resentful as Adam, she wanted to make extra sure that they knew she could be taken seriously.

"Good morning," Jay said as they joined the larger group. "Everyone, I'd like you to meet Evan and Samantha Sutton, who, if you couldn't guess, are my unfortunate relations. Guys," he said, turning to his niece and nephew and indicating the group before them, "this is the team."

Samantha looked over the face of each person as they introduced themselves. She counted about twenty of them—young men and young women, eager, healthy, and strong. She took special note of the fact that while a few were American—students of her uncle—some were from a university in England, and others were studying under Osvaldo in Lima. Each met her gaze with a smile or extended a hand to shake.

So Adam was clearly an exception, she realized, feeling better. She looked to where he leaned sullenly against the Temple's wall, watching the introductions in cold silence. Above him, Samantha noticed for the first time a single tenon head that jutted from the smoothness of the Temple's wall. Its frown matched Adam's exactly.

Two more people came to join them, speaking in English, then Spanish, then English again. One was Osvaldo, who smiled when he saw her. Like her uncle, he seemed taller and more full of life this morning, even under these circumstances, as if returning to Chavín had restored a missing piece of himself.

With him was a woman, lean and tan and uniquely beautiful in an effortless kind of way. Her light brown hair was pulled into a tight ponytail, and her sunglasses rested on the top of her head.

"And this is the excavation's other co-director," Jay continued, "Professor Barrows."

"You must be Evan and Samantha," she said in a warm British accent. When she held out her hand, Samantha shook it eagerly.

"Dr. Clare Barrows?" Samantha whispered in awe.

"You can just call me Clare. All of us use our first names here."

"I…I read your book about the Inca."

In fact, Samantha had read the book many times and had creased the binding of the library's copy with her use.

"Oh, did you?" asked the professor. "It's already a little outdated, I'm afraid."

"I read it too." Evan lied, putting himself between Samantha and her hero. "It was absolutely fascinating. A real page-turner. Enthralling from beginning to end."

Clare gave him a skeptical but amused look before turning back to Samantha.

"More importantly, though, what are your first impressions of Chavín?"

"It's incredible!" Samantha replied, her confidence returning.

"Well, good," said Clare with a smile. "I think you'll find it's the kind of place that just gets more and more incredible as you get to know it."

Introductions complete, the group turned to examine what was left of Adam's unit. Near the surface was an exact rectangle, as if someone had used a giant cookie-cutter to remove a perfect block of earth from below the Temple's face. But farther down, the even walls had been hacked away, and rough cavities pitted the unit's floor.

"I had just started uncovering a stirrup-spouted vessel yesterday afternoon. Remember, Dr. Barrows? The one I was telling you about at dinner?"

Samantha thought it was strange that Adam used Clare's formal name to address her, as if he refused the casual friendliness she offered. But the famous archaeologist just nodded as Adam continued his explanation.

"From what I'd exposed, it seemed to be intact. And when I came back this morning, it was gone."

"How about you guys?" Jay asked the other students, with Osvaldo translating for the benefit of the Spanish speakers. "Your units all okay?"

His question was met with solemn nods.

Osvaldo rubbed his brow.

"I will speak with the site police. Maybe they can add one or two guards for the nighttime shift."

Samantha watched as Jay addressed the crowd.

"Everyone, please listen up. This is important. The excavation itself is at risk."

All signs of his warmth were gone.

"Now, I'm not saying anyone did anything wrong. But let me repeat something we told you all at the very beginning. Do not, *do not*, talk about your finds in town. Not at the disco, not at the bodega, not out on the street. An intact Chavín pot will sell for hundreds of dollars on the antiquities market, which is more money than most of the people here could earn in an entire year. Word can spread fast in this valley, and sooner or later it's bound to reach someone who is willing to take the risk, loot the site, and sell whatever they can get their hands on."

"Wait a minute," Adam spat, getting redder. "How stupid do you think I am? I didn't say anything to anyone."

Jay's voice softened, and he was himself again.

"Let's just all be cautious. That's all I'm asking."

From behind the crowd of students, Osvaldo's deep, accented voice broke the embarrassed silence.

"Jay, with respect, I do not think it was someone from the town. If the units are looted, the site is ruined. If this site is ruined, the tourists will not come. If the tourists will not come, the town will lose money. The people who live here know this. They have always known this."

"Fair enough. We shouldn't jump to conclusions. Still, let's just try to keep our finds confidential until they're safely out of the ground and behind a locked door, okay?"

The meeting was over and the group dispersed, leaving only the Suttons and Adam around the ruined pit.

"So, what's the plan?" asked Adam. "What do I do with the unit?"

"We'll come back to it later in the summer if we have time," Jay said. "For now, I want to open up the West Field. I'll have you start this morning by putting in a new unit over there."

He turned to his niece and nephew, his smile returning.

"Evan and Sam, why don't you two give Adam a hand?"

"Both of them?" asked Adam.

"Both of them," Jay replied. "Let's just see how it goes."

•• ● ••

But as soon as Jay gave the order, it was obvious how things would go in the West Field.

Muttering something about "baby-sitting," Adam stomped his way to a small shack beside the main gate. He threw open the storage shed, thrust some tools and a couple of buckets into Evan's waiting hands, and grabbed a wooden stepladder before slamming the door hard enough to rattle its hinges.

They walked past the small museum and out the site's main gate, then crossed the road through the dusty wake of a passing truck. When they reached the tall stone fence that enclosed the West Field, Adam heaved the ladder against it, stomped up, and leapt to the ground on the opposite side. Evan elbowed his sister aside and followed with a muffled thud.

When it was Samantha's turn, she paused at the top of

the ladder to look out over the field before her. There were no temples here—no plazas or staircases or tenon heads. It was simply a wide, barren pasture, tucked below the steep inclines of the valley's edges and sloping gently upward toward its southerly end.

Only two things in the field seemed to be man-made, and they were not very spectacular. The gradual slope was interrupted by a pair of stone walls, holding back the earth above them so that the field was separated into three broad terraces. The fence she was sitting on wrapped around all but one of the sides, while to her left the uphill, southern boundary was marked by a line of ramshackle homes.

She removed the trowel from her pocket, jumped cautiously to the ground, and ran uphill to where the other two were waiting.

Adam spat a wad of phlegm into the bushes.

"Okay. Surveying. I'll dumb this down as much as I can. We have to find a place to put in the new unit. Even though archaeologists have been working in Chavín for decades, no one has bothered to work in the West Field before. This will be the first time, and we want to pick somewhere that will give us a good idea of what might be over here."

"How do we do that?" Samantha asked, undaunted by the resentment in Adam's voice.

"He's *trying* to explain!" hissed her brother.

Adam continued to speak directly to Evan, as if he had asked the question.

"Well, we can just pick a spot and get a random sample

that way. Or, we could see what kinds of artifacts are on the surface. Sometimes, but not always, that helps tell you what's beneath."

He paused, considering the choice.

"That's how we'll start."

From his satchel, Adam produced a bunch of small flags—floppy bits of blue plastic fixed to short metal wires.

"Put one of these next to anything that you think might be an artifact."

Adam barked more instructions, and they spaced themselves evenly in a row along the sloping length of the field. Samantha took the uphill position, just beside one of the retaining walls that divided the field into terraces.

They moved slowly forward, stooping to scan the ground beneath them. From her research, Samantha was very familiar with many kinds of artifacts. Still, it was hard to find them among the weeds and natural stones. What at first she thought was a bone was in fact a small dry root, bleached white in the sun. Another potential find turned out to be a clump of soil and disintegrated into dust between her fingers. Risking a glance downhill, she saw that neither Evan nor Adam had planted a single flag. Her brother had paused to throw dirt clods at a large brown bird.

As soon as she refocused on her task, something caught her eye. In their discussions, Jay had once explained that while amateurs said "shard" to describe a broken bit of pottery, real archaeologists—for unknown reasons—used the word "sherd." And now one lay on the ground before her:

a sherd—pink, smooth, and slightly rounded, the same thickness all around. She placed it back exactly where she had found it and eagerly planted a flag.

Two more potsherds caught the sweep of her gaze. One was a shiny black, and she made out the imprint of a fine design on its face. The other was a matted tan, and from its one smooth, rounded edge she could see that it had once been the lip of a cup or bowl.

More sherds—tan, black, and gray—lay flat on the surface or protruded from the ground from beneath tufts of grass and piles of dehydrated animal droppings. Here and there, tiny flakes of a black, glassy stone flecked the soil as well. These, Samantha knew full well, were obsidian, used to make razor-sharp blades. The surface of the West Field was littered with flakes, and she planted a flag next to each.

Down the slope, Adam was making rapid progress across the field. He was clearly experienced. He held his whole body rigid and tensed, with everything focused on the task. Closer to her, Evan was also making finds. With each flag he planted, he gave a triumphant "yes!" A few times, Samantha caught him eyeing her progress competitively. She tried not to care. This was archaeology, not some sort of Easter-egg hunt, and if Evan wanted to turn this into a competition, that would be up to him. She would move as slowly as she needed to and put the importance of science over her eagerness to find more than her brother.

Several minutes later, they had reached the other side of the field and were looking back over the clusters of flags. Adam's face showed a dark, deep concentration as he scanned the landscape with what was clearly an expert eye.

"There."

He pointed to a clump of Samantha's, nestled against the retaining wall.

"Let me make something clear before we get started," he said. "I'm not going to put up with any whining. This is not going to be like anything you've seen in the movies, I can tell you that now. We're not going to find any gold. We're not going to find any mummies. We're not going to find any chests of buried treasure. Got it?"

Samantha stayed silent, thoroughly annoyed by Adam's tone.

"With the big landslides this valley gets and all the plowing there's been in this field, there's no telling what the stratigraphy—the layers—will look like down there. There's no guarantee that there will be anything here at all. Can you both handle that?"

Evan and Samantha nodded.

"So no complaining?"

They shook their heads.

"No running to your uncle if we don't find anything you think is exciting?"

They shook their heads again, just eager to get started.

"Okay then. Let's get to work."

And with that, Adam heaved the heavy pickax over his shoulder and brought it crashing down in a violent arc.

It was if the pick had pierced the body of a living

creature. As soon as the tool struck the earth, they were startled by a reverberating scream that grew louder and more ghastly as its echo beat between the valley walls.

As Samantha and Evan flinched, and as Adam swore and stumbled backward, two llamas charged from among the rickety buildings on the slope above them. The animals were in a frenzy, wrapping their long necks together and snapping at each other's exposed throats. As they staggered toward the archaeologists, it was clear that the larger, darker animal was winning. Blood coursed from the other's throat in two lengthening stains. Trying to escape from its opponent with a violent twist, it screamed again, sounding almost human in its anguish.

And then the fight ended—as abruptly as it had begun. The animals uncoiled their necks and parted warily. The darker llama shook itself, its wool spilling dust, and trotted back uphill from where it had come. The wounded opponent stood for a moment, its wounds brown and wet, then gave a bleat and followed—leaving Adam, Evan, and Samantha rattled and alone.

Adam found his voice.

"Well, that was interesting," he grumbled, clearly embarrassed that he had been so startled.

They regrouped, setting their equipment down beside the site of their new unit. Still, as her two partners set about unloading papers and tools from Adam's satchel, Samantha could not shake the sound of the llama's scream. It had been a cry of wild terror or of sharp, unbearable pain. She knew the thought was ridiculous, but the scream had seemed almost like a warning: a desperate plea to leave this place alone.

She twisted a pigtail between her fingers. What, exactly, was she about to uncover? What was waiting for her under the surface of Chavín's West Field?

Señora's parrots: they can talk but they always yell "¡Corre!" (Run!). They kind of creep me out!!

Stuart

Zoe

Jay says none of the stories are true, but I wonder if they are. At least a little bit. Either way, Adam hates me already.

He's s

Evan is totally obsessed with trying out for the soccer team. I told him it's a bad idea. He's good at soccer of course, but he's so out of breath up here tha

SSFNbl-CdH: 4

CHAPTER 4

"*Corre, corre, corre!*"

From their cage dangling high in the corner of the Hostal Jato's dining room, a duo of ill-tempered parrots cut through the dinnertime bustle with shrill cries of alarm. But the archaeologists below them paid little attention. Crowded onto benches around the long, low tables, the team chatted happily as the señora bustled merrily about, refilling steaming bowls of soup and heaping plates high with rice, eggs, potatoes, and fried bananas.

Squeezed between her uncle and her brother on the narrow bench, Samantha glanced at the large frosted windows, noticing how quickly daylight was sliding into dusk as the sun dipped behind the valley's western cliffs. It was, Samantha was discovering, her favorite part of the day. Even as the team laughed and gossiped and told bad jokes in two languages and an assortment of accents, real information was also being shared. In the comfort and relative privacy of the dining room, the archaeologists spoke openly about their work, and Samantha focused on absorbing everything she could.

The eager enthusiasm among the team was helped in that there had not been any looting in the site since Adam's unit had been destroyed. Over the past few days, the three professors had had several tense conversations with the police who guarded the site and one with Chavín's mayor. All had quickly agreed to increase security at the gate and elsewhere around the site's perimeter. They had also ordered the archaeologists to be vigilant.

Now, with the danger behind them, the team was eager for the work ahead. There were data to be collected, discoveries to be made, and everyone was anxious to move forward.

"*¡Corre, corre, corre!*"

Again, the parrots' screams broke through.

"You'd better listen to them, Archaeo Kid," said Evan.

Samantha knew enough to ignore him.

"What are they saying, Uncle Jay?"

"*Corre* means 'run' in Spanish," he explained.

"Yeah," said Evan, eager to finish his earlier insult, "as in 'Run, run, run, that weird little girl Samantha is coming.'"

His uncle gave him a disapproving look.

"The local soccer club comes here to watch the professional matches on TV. The parrots seem to have picked up what they yell when their team has the ball."

"*¡Goooooaaaaaaaaaal!*" screamed the larger parrot, as if in response.

"There's a local club?" Evan asked.

"So I hear," Jay confirmed. "See what you can find out about it."

But Samantha's attention was caught up in the happy voices around her—American, Peruvian, and British. The three groups of students seemed to be loosely divided among two teams. A friendly rivalry had sprung up between them, and the students bragged in English and Spanish of their finds.

One group worked under Osvaldo's supervision within an area known as the Circular Plaza. Inside it, they were uncovering evidence of a small settlement that had sprung up long after the people who built Chavín had come and gone.

The other students, supervised by Clare, worked along the Temple's western side. These units were already very deep, and yet to everyone's surprise, the wall of the massive structure still continued, down, down, deep into the earth. This meant, Clare had told her, that the Temple must have towered over the surrounding ground, looking even more imposing than it did today.

Now, Osvaldo and Clare each sat among a mixed cluster of students. But a larger group was eager to speak to Jay. His work was still in its planning stages, but something about it was thrilling and mysterious. Samantha had overheard several students speaking softly about how much they wanted to work with him when his project was finally under way.

She was proud of her uncle, of course, but worried that

all this excitement was ruining her chances. If Jay's work was so exciting, it would be hard for him to choose his niece—a beginner—over the more experienced members of the team. She would be stuck with Adam and Evan forever.

"*¡Corre, corre, corre!*"

Samantha poked at the hunk of chicken on her plate, trying to follow Jay's animated conversation. He was discussing the Spanish conquest of Peru and the conquistadors' first impressions of Chavín. But as the exchange slipped from Spanish to English to Spanish again, she soon lost its thread.

Evan nudged her hard to get her attention.

"Are you planning to *comer tus plátanos?*"

"Am I what?"

Evan reached his fork over her plate, speared her two remaining slices of fried banana, and popped them into his mouth.

"I asked if you were planning to eat these," he said, chewing loudly.

She gave him a hard look.

"Oh, you were? Want 'em back?"

He opened his mouth wide, showing the yellow paste inside.

"Gross, Evan."

But it was, by the measure of his recent behavior, a mild annoyance. Things were not going well in the West Field. From the moment Samantha had seen Evan waiting in Jay's pickup truck, she had feared for her summer, knowing that her brother would be what he always was, the center of attention. And all her worries seemed to be coming true. Evan was stealing her adventure like a forkful of fried bananas.

As they had set to preparing their unit over the last few days, she had realized with much discomfort that Adam was actually warming to her brother. She watched as he taught Evan to plot out a unit using tape measures, a bubble level, and string—marking a perfect rectangle in the earth. Samantha sat on the retaining wall while her brother got to use high-tech surveying equipment to mark the new unit's exact location for plotting on the official excavation map.

Through it all, Evan and Adam joked and laughed, sometimes speaking in Spanish that she could not even begin to understand. All she could do was fill her notebook with her own thoughts and diagrams, hoping that one day she could use the information for herself.

Still, she was determined to stick it out and not to bother her uncle with her troubles. At least for now.

"¡*Corre, corre, corre!*"

"Do as you're told, Archaeo Kid," Evan sneered. "Run along!"

Elbowing her brother hard, Samantha freed herself from the bench to sit at the far end of the room, alone now but for the two European tourists wedged around a small table in the corner. She listened as they spoke their own unfamiliar language and ordered their meals in strained Spanish. They had a map spread out before them, planning some trek into the mountains.

"Samantha Sutton, isn't it? The Archaeo Kid?"

It was Stuart, one of Clare's students. He put down a fragrant cup of *manzanilla* tea and slid onto the bench across the table.

"Please don't call me that," Samantha said, trying to smile. "It's just something my parents called me once, and now my brother uses it all the time to annoy me. My uncle, too, sometimes, but only as a joke."

"Gads, I'm such a goon," Stuart said, his Scottish tenor seeping through the room's activity like a calming salve. "I should have guessed as much. Your brother said you preferred it."

"I told you so," said Zoe, one of Jay's students, as she settled next to Samantha on the bench. Zoe had the elegant bearing of a ballerina, and even her simple act of sitting was full of grace and refinement.

"Well," Stuart went on, "we just came over to say hard luck."

"Yeah, Samantha," said Zoe, offering her own condolences. "It's too bad."

"Too bad about what?"

"Getting stuck with Adam," said Stuart, his sunburned face showing genuine sympathy. "I wouldn't wish it on my worst enemy."

"Me neither." Zoe shuddered. "Ugh."

Samantha cast a glance to the opposite corner of the room where Adam sat alone, hunched over his bowl of soup. The brim of his cap was pulled down low on his brow, and his mirror-like sunglasses hid the direction of his chilling gaze. He could be staring right at them, but neither Stuart nor Zoe seemed to mind.

"Too much of a big man to eat with the rest of us, I reckon." Stuart groaned, and Samantha caught sight of his muscular forearm as he pointed across the room. "Look at him over there, with that hotshot hat and those hotshot aviators and those hotshot muscles. I've decided to call him the Gorilla Guerilla."

Samantha liked the nickname, but she liked even more how the "r's" tumbled from Stuart's mouth like a babbling brook.

"I think we're all a little afraid of him, to be honest," Zoe whispered, but she modified her statement in response to Stuart's disapproving frown. "I mean, all of Dr. Sutton's students, at least."

"Why?" Samantha asked.

"He's a TA," Zoe began, but realized that Samantha might not know the term. "A teaching assistant. He's a graduate student who grades papers and exams, leads your uncle's classes once in a while—that sort of thing. People just don't like him."

"He's a bit intense, isn't he?" asked Stuart. "And more than a little bit full of himself."

"He's horrible. He's condescending, rude, intolerant of people who have their own opinions. But it's not just that." Zoe's eyes darted left and right. "There are *stories* about him."

"What kind of stories?" Samantha asked.

"Oh, there are tons. They can't all be true, I guess, but the ones I've heard make you wonder. Like, you know where he got that hat?"

"Oh, I heard this one." Stuart butted in. "Wasn't he on some survey project in Guatemala? Somewhere in the Western Highlands?"

"Lake Atitlán," Zoe confirmed.

"Right. He's on the shores of Atitlán. The team is spread out at kilometer intervals, so Adam's all by his wee self—probably muttering to himself like he does."

"And frowning," Zoe added, with a grin. "And swearing a lot."

Stuart chuckled.

"Anyway, some *bandido* jumps out from behind a rock, swinging a machete, meaning to rob him. Maybe worse."

Stuart took a sip of his tea to draw out the pause, then dropped his playful voice for dramatic effect.

"Our Gorilla Guerilla takes one look at this chap, plucks the blade out of his hand, knocks *him* unconscious with the butt of it, then throws him over his shoulders and pitches him into the lake. The *bandido* drowns. Dead. Then and there. Adam just picks up the man's hat and goes on with the survey."

Zoe was ready with another story about Jay's top student.

"I heard he was thrown in jail in Oaxaca, Mexico. He got arrested for trespassing up at Monte Albán. It took three policemen to bring him in."

"Is that true?" Samantha asked, reaching nervously for one of her braids.

"I believe it," said Stuart, blowing on his tea.

"And then there's what happened last summer," Zoe continued, "when we were down with your uncle in Sechin. One day, deciding he's too good to work, Adam goes off to explore Chankillo, this big fortress way out in the desert. Anyway, he has some miscommunication with the taxi driver, and at the end of the day the guy doesn't show up. So Adam hikes ten miles through the desert to the Pan-American Highway and hijacks some truck—*makes* it take him back into town. Then he tracks down the taxi driver and beats him up. Puts him in the hospital. In a coma."

"He's a bit of a thug, all right," Stuart said.

Zoe nodded in agreement.

"I certainly wouldn't want to work with him."

"And with the looting? In his unit?" Stuart whispered. "I wouldn't be surprised if he…"

But he was interrupted by one of Osvaldo's students, who clapped him hard on the back.

"*¿Qué tal, amigo?*" Stuart's glorious burr was apparent even in his Spanish.

The Peruvian student winked at Samantha, and she smiled back.

"*El Cóndor. ¡Vámanos!*"

Zoe and Stuart excused themselves to get ready for a night of dancing at El Cóndor, Chavín's sole nightclub, and Samantha was left alone with her thoughts. Surely Adam was an unlikable character, but was he really dangerous?

Was he someone who would try to attack a police officer, hijack a truck, or throw an unconscious man into a lake to drown?

Dinner was cleared, and the room had emptied but for the few archaeologists. Those who had chosen not to visit El Cóndor were sipping big mugs of manzanilla tea, reading books, writing in their field notebooks, or chatting quietly over board games. While Osvaldo and Clare sat at their laptop computers, engrossed in their analysis, Jay was playing chess with a Peruvian student named Marisol. From across the room, Samantha watched as the pretty young woman called out "*jaque mate*" and knocked over his king. Jay extended his hand for a congratulatory handshake. Then catching Samantha's glance, he waved her over.

"What's on your mind, Sam?" he asked as she took Marisol's seat. "You seem a little *preocupada*."

"It's Adam," she said, after a pause, "I just…do you trust him? Is he…dangerous?"

Jay raised an eyebrow, and Samantha found herself explaining, unable to stop as the stories poured out of her. Her uncle listened quietly, an amused smile on his face, until Samantha told the story of the hijacking. At this, Jay roared with laughter, somehow upsetting the chessboard and sending chessmen clattering all over the table.

"Adam Quint?" he gasped. "*Our* Adam? Hijack a truck?"

"That's not what happened?" Samantha asked, picking up a fallen bishop from the bench.

"Not even close! It wasn't a *hijacking*, it was a *hitchhiking*! Poor Adam waited on the side of that road for six hours, running out of water, baking in the sun. The only car that took mercy on him was a truck full of chickens. You should have seen him when he finally got back to town! He was covered in feathers and droppings and sunburned to the edge of his life. I can assure you, he was in no condition to hunt down the missing driver. He could barely move!"

"And the Guatemala story? And what happened in Oaxaca?"

"Oh, Sam. Sam, Sam, Sam." Jay wiped tears from his eyes. "You're thinking like a historian."

Samantha didn't know how to respond.

"What I mean is that you can't put so much stock in stories like these," Jay continued, setting up the righted chessmen for another game. "They're tall tales. Exaggerations, if anything, spread around by people who don't like him."

Jay moved a pawn forward two places on the board between them.

"Look. Adam is very good at what he does. I've never had a student as talented. And yes, it's true: he's not the most likeable guy. Some people can't stand him, some people envy him, and the combination can lead to all kinds of stories. But it definitely doesn't mean that any of them are true."

Samantha moved her own pawn forward. She felt embarrassed, but when Jay spoke again, his voice was soft and kind.

"Think like an archaeologist, Sam. Work from hard data. Get evidence before deciding what did or did not happen."

Samantha tried to take his words to heart and to focus instead on the chessboard in front of her. Stories were stories, after all. But in contemplating the rumors about Adam, another thought had wriggled from its place at the back of her mind.

Did she have anything to fear from the Madman story? Alejandro had seemed so firm. But she didn't dare ask Jay again. Especially not now.

"*¡Corre, corre, corre!*"

As she and her uncle took turns moving their chessmen across the board, the birds continued to scream above them. At last, the señora emerged from the kitchen to throw a blanket over the cage, extinguishing the parrots' prophetic warnings with artificial night.

●●◉●●

The next morning found Samantha trudging up the road alone, the figures of Adam and her brother disappearing around a bend up ahead.

She and Evan had made their regular call to their parents, and because of the time difference, they had once again left several minutes after the rest of the group. But Samantha had let herself fall even farther behind. Despite her uncle's assurances, the stories about Adam had left her uneasy, and she needed a chance to think things over.

There did seem to be something sinister about Adam

Quint—some dark purpose in his glassy gaze and a suspicious secrecy in how he double-locked his door and refused to let anyone near his room. Jay was probably right—the stories of jail, hijacking, and murder had to be exaggerations, rumors, or outright myths—but they bothered her all the same.

She passed the last of the rustic homes and storefronts, catching surprising glimpses through open doors of well-appointed living rooms and flickering computer screens before crossing the bridge at the Rio Wacheqsa. The road angled upward, and she could feel her pace slow and a rising burn spread throughout her lungs. By the time she drew even with the site's main gate, Adam and Evan had already retrieved the day's equipment from the storage shed and were heaving it over the West Field's wall.

A herd of cattle overtook her, cutting her off from the others with a sudden rush of moos and clanking cowbells. She stepped to the side of the road to let them pass. As she cast her eyes over her shoulder, where the grassy shoulder of the Temple could be seen through the site's main gate, a powerful longing came over her. She wanted to know—*needed* to know—what secrets the structure contained. When Jay was not busy, she promised herself, she would ask him about it. And maybe he would take her inside.

When the last of the cattle had passed, she was surprised to see that they were tended from the rear by someone she recognized. It was Isabel, the girl who had sold Evan his carving some days before. She lugged a heavy bucket as she followed the enormous animals and in her other hand clasped a long stick, swatting at the flanks of the rearmost bull.

"*Buenos días*," she lisped as she drew near, giving Samantha a gap-toothed smile.

"*Hola*," Samantha replied, proud she had used some Spanish at last.

But when she eyed Isabel's bucket as it swung by her, she stifled a gasp. Inside, three stacked sheep's heads stared back at her. Their eyes were half open beneath lazy lids, and their ragged necks were caked with hard, crumbly blood. Long gray tongues dangled between their slackened lips, gathering flies.

By now, Adam and Evan had disappeared over the wall. Samantha crossed through the dusty wake of the cattle herd, climbed the rickety ladder, and pulled herself over to land with a thump in the West Field. She adjusted her notebook on its string around her neck and, steeling herself, walked the several yards to the unit.

Over the last few days, Samantha had watched as Adam and her brother had stripped off the scraggly covering of grass and thorny brush in a perfect rectangle, and the exposed soil now lay ready to be cut into with their tools.

She eyed Adam as he arranged the materials into a tidy pile. There was a weird mismatch between the Gorilla Guerilla of the stories and the expert archaeologist that had laid out the orderly unit before her. The unit was exacting in its neatness. Beautiful, almost. Its angles were true, its sides straight and clean. Such skill showed a reverential respect for the science. How could such a person be dangerous?

"Come on. Let's go," said Adam, and he and Evan began to clear the surface of the leaves that had been blown into the unit overnight. Samantha tried to help, picking out a loose tuft of grass from the unit's clean surface, but Adam stopped her, shoving a clipboard into her hands.

"If you want to play archaeology, you can start by filling out these."

Beneath the heavy metal clamp were a unit form, a level form, and a feature form. She had no idea where to begin.

"Just do the top part. Date and unit number. Think you can handle that?"

She tried to banish the anxiety from her voice.

"I know how to write, if that's what you mean."

But she had just put her pen to the paper when the clipboard was plucked from her grip, replaced by the handle of a shovel.

"Get up. Quick."

Something had caused Adam's sudden change of heart. It was her uncle, coming into view over the wall. She reluctantly accepted the shovel, knowing that Adam was merely trying to appear to have included her in the work.

"Everything mapped out?" Jay said, grinning, as he reached the unit. "Seems to have taken a little while, but Adam has taught you well."

Samantha almost corrected her uncle—Adam hadn't taught her anything. And the reason it had taken so long was just as much because of his frequent breaks as her brother's short attention span. But she remembered her promise to herself not to trouble her uncle with her problems. With a little effort, she even managed a weak smile.

"Looks good, guys," he said before addressing his niece. "Sam, you want to get started?"

Exhilarated by the chance, she strode to the middle of the unit and stomped down hard on the shovel, stinging Adam and her brother with a spray of loose gravel. It was an accident, but it was still satisfying to see each raise his arms to protect his face.

Samantha looked at the shallow divot she had just made in the field's dry surface. It wasn't much of a hole. Again, this time with all her weight, she jumped down hard on the blade, pushing all her strength through the soles of her feet. But still there was not much to show for her efforts.

Jay hefted a pickax from the pile of tools.

"Let me show you how it's done."

He took his niece's place in the unit and, with the smooth motion of someone who had done it a thousand times before, plunged the pick head into the earth.

"Somebody toss me a bucket," he commanded happily, and Adam put one just outside the unit's string border.

Jay pounded away, again and again, his arcing strokes even, controlled, and each of identical depth. Then, like a surgeon asking for a scalpel: "Shovel!"

Samantha placed the handle in his outstretched hand. In a single movement, he scraped the blade under the loosened chunks of soil and tossed the shovelful into the waiting pail, without a single pebble or clod of dirt landing outside it. Slide, scrape, toss. Slide, scrape, toss. In seconds, he had cleared the unit of its clumps and stones, leaving a perfect rectangle—dark with the moisture of the newly exposed earth.

"Adam, Evan…screen this please?"

With a grunt, Adam lugged the full bucket to where a wooden contraption lay collapsed and folded on its hinges among the array of tools. He barked some orders and Evan wrestled it upright. In its open position, it reminded Samantha of a table, but with two hinged legs instead of four stable ones. Where the tabletop would have been was an open box with a fine metal grid—like a screen door—as its bottom.

Adam emptied the bucket onto the screen, and Evan followed his instructions by vigorously shaking the whole mechanism back and forth. Loose soil rained through the bottom of the screen, and Samantha smiled as a billowing cloud of dust enveloped Evan completely, turning his whole self a grayish shade of brown.

"Shall we?" Jay asked Samantha, and they approached the screen together. At first, all she saw was a mass of small pebbles and clods of earth, intermingled with a broken network of dried roots. But when Jay reached into the tray and plucked out a shiny black chunk of pottery, she began to see the artifacts among the rubble. Evan's glare followed her hand as she removed another sherd—this one beige—and then another of the black variety. When she opened her hand to display the finds, Adam grabbed them from her outstretched palm and slid them into a labeled plastic bag.

But that was not all the screen had caught. Resting the screen on his thigh, Evan pulled out—one by one—a degraded green rubber band, a warped and rusted bottle cap, and a dirty metal coin—which, when Jay cleaned it off with a spit-moistened thumb, revealed a date of 1989. Evan flashed a skeptical look at Adam and dropped these items in the plastic bag as well.

"Is this really what we're looking for?" Evan snorted. "Little bits of trash?"

"Some would say that's what archaeology is all about, Ev," said Jay, laughing. "But I know what you mean. We're going to need to dig through the modern deposits before we hit anything related to the people who built and used this place in its earliest years. And then, of course, we need to consider the *Cataclismo*."

"What cataclysm?" Evan snapped to attention.

"An enormous landslide that swept through this part of the valley some decades ago."

"Did it *kill* anyone?"

"Yes, Evan. It was one of the worst tragedies this region had seen in a long time. Damaged the site pretty badly too."

He cleared his throat.

"Anyway, we don't know how far down this disturbance goes. That's one of the reasons that we keep everything. Even the little bits of trash."

Jay handed Samantha the pickax.

"Adam, let's take the unit down 20 centimeters and see what happens. Do watch for changes in soil color and consistency, of course, but let's try to keep it moving. Okay?"

"Sure, Professor."

"And let's keep assignments as they are for the rest of the day. Sam, you stay in the unit. Evan will screen. Adam, keep an eye on things. But please let them get the hang of it themselves. It'll help them learn what they need to know for the rest of the summer."

As her uncle disappeared over the stone fence, Samantha raised the pickax above her head and plunged it into the gravelly earth at her feet. The heft of the tool, the way it arced over her head and sank deep into the soil: it all felt good. And it felt even better when, out of the corner of her eye, she saw her brother disappear into another choking cloud of dust.

while Evan plays a more managerial role.

Evan, it looks like you will be able to take the CollegePrep course before school begins. I had to tell a little lie--that you will be in eleventh grade next year, and not ninth —but it shouldn't be a problem. Samantha, we will want to begin conversations with a college application advisor as soon as

Osvaldo and Clare don't trust him at all and I don't either. If he wasn't stealing it, then what was he doing?

→ Make co

A snuff tube made from a birds bone (for tobacco?)

Veruga is this reall. bad disease, but Jay says it isn't a problem at this altitude.

Tourists (from Germany?)

Inca Cola

English ← Spanish

- Kee-yare ace Quieres- you want
- Propio – own
- Tra-ba-ho Trabajo – work
- Tengo tay que – I have to
- Nos vemos – see ya
- Que dices – what do ya say
- Fantasma – ghost

..kes me so angry. They don't take me seriously at all, and Evan is the one who gets all the credit for

SSPNb1-CdH: 5

79

Chapter 5

"Mom? Dad?"

Pushing the phone hard against her ear, Samantha couldn't make out more than a faint, distant whisper. Perhaps her parents were having trouble hearing her on their end too, as they drove through the predawn darkness on their early-morning commute, five thousand miles away.

But then her father spoke up, his voice lively and clear. "Yes, sweetie, we can hear you just fine."

She relaxed her grip on the receiver. Over the past five minutes, she had spoken nonstop, detailing the kindness of Jay's colleagues, the closeness of the team, and how exciting it had been to make her first few finds. As always, she had picked her words carefully, omitting any detail that might alarm her parents and cause them to bring her home.

But maybe she hadn't needed to be so cautious. As Evan entered the hostal's tiny office, eager for his turn on the phone, she identified the tinny background noise as her parents' car radio. It was not a weak connection but the morning business report that explained why they had not responded to a single thing she'd said.

Once again, she had competed for their attention and lost.

"Samantha?" her mother said. "This student of your uncle's—Aaron? The one who's looking after you?"

"Adam?"

"Right. Do be sure to get his contact details before you leave. He may be a good reference for your college applications when the time comes."

"Okay, Mom. I will."

Evan snapped his fingers and motioned for the receiver.

"And be careful down there, Samantha," said her father. "We want our little Archaeo Kid to come home safe."

Samantha passed the phone to her brother and stepped into the hostal's courtyard. The nickname irked her, and the one-sided conversation had left her glum. But it had been comforting to hear her parents' voices and reassuring to catch them in the midst of their regular routine. She was surprised how much she missed them.

She sat beside the señora's fragrant rose beds, her notebook open on her knees, to wait for Adam and her brother. She was proud of their work in the West Field so far and the part she had played in their progress. After more than a week of digging, the unit was now exactly one-and-a-half meters deep. Every level had provided a perfect, representative sample, able to withstand the mathematical probing that Osvaldo, Clare, and Jay would subject it to as they tried to reconstruct what had happened in this valley so many years ago.

She heard a door open and close and, expecting Adam, stood to alert her brother. But coming into the courtyard was one of the European tourists who stayed at the hostal, using it as a base for lengthy treks through the surrounding mountains. When his clear blue eyes met hers, they exchanged a friendly smile.

"*Guete morge*," he said. "*Was schriibsch du do?*"

She felt herself blush.

"I'm sorry," she said, pointing at herself. "Just English."

The man's twinkling eyes forgave her.

"You…work…in this place?" he asked. He was concentrating hard. It seemed a struggle for him to dredge up each English word, and an almost visible ripple of pain moved across his face with every effort.

It's okay, Samantha thought. I don't speak your language either.

"Yes," she said aloud. "I am helping at the site. You know, archaeology?"

"*Ach, ja,*" he said. "*Dinosaurier.*"

"No, not dinosaurs," she said. "Archaeology. Here. I can show you."

She lifted the notebook's string over her neck and handed it to him. He turned slowly through the pages, scanning her careful notes and diagrams with polite concentration.

"*Guet,*" he said at last, passing it back to her. "*Merci.*"

Samantha smiled. She was flattered by his curiosity, especially after her parents' lack of interest.

"Have you been to the site?" she asked.

"Site? *Nein, nein.* Another time, yes. But now," he indicated his hiking poles, "*Ych bi do fuer zum wandere.* To explore only…the mountain passes."

The other tourist entered the courtyard now—a tall, thin middle-aged woman, loaded with the gear they needed for a lengthy trek.

"*Muesch si nit aarede, Papa!*" she admonished the old man, and Samantha realized she was his daughter.

It's no trouble, Samantha wanted to explain. Archaeologists have a responsibility to educate the public. But before she could decide how to express such a complicated message in simple English, the two had departed, trundling out the door and on their way to some far and mountainous trail.

Minutes later, as Samantha led Adam and her brother up the road to the site, she wondered at the type of person who would come all the way to Chavín for its natural beauty alone, with no interest in its archaeology whatsoever. Yes, the valley would be an excellent base for the snowcapped mountains nearby, with their sweeping vistas and challenging ascents. But Chavín de Huántar was special and the valley's most obvious draw.

There are all kinds of people in the world, she decided, and let the matter rest.

●●◉●●

The afternoon sky was bright and a warm breeze swept across the West Field, carrying with it the cleansing smells of eucalyptus and woodsmoke. A pair of courting llamas stampeded this way and that at the top of the slope. As Adam filled out paperwork and Evan waited at the screen, Samantha filled another bucket with loose earth from the unit's floor. Except for a few protruding roots, each wall was as flat as a concrete slab.

"Could you hurry up a little?" said Evan, groaning.

He was realizing, slowly, that real archaeology wasn't exactly *Pillager of the Past*. So far, most of their finds had been dull, nondescript sherds of pottery, and Evan had grumbled at each broken fragment that needed to be cleaned of its mud casing, cataloged, and bagged.

Though she would never admit it aloud, a very small part of Samantha understood her brother's frustration. No matter what questions the tiny fragments could answer about time period, technology, or trade, a little excitement would be nice. Heaving the bucket into her brother's waiting hands, she allowed herself a glance over the fence toward the Temple and wondered again what secrets it might contain.

And then she thought of the warning Alejandro had given her at the site's gate and the vague explanation Jay had offered on the plane when she had spotted the word in his notes. *El Loco*. The Madman.

If some strange mystery haunted the massive Temple

building across the road, it intrigued her. It excited her. But it also cooled some of her eagerness to plumb its secrets—at least until she could learn more.

And anyway, it felt good down here under the surface of the West Field. The air was cool and the smell of earth was comforting. The shovel cut into the damp soil as smoothly as a knife in a stick of butter. She sent shovelful after shovelful into the waiting bucket in graceful arcs. There was a kind of peace in the process, and as she worked, she found herself settling into a kind of a trance.

A shadow fell over the unit.

"*Buenas tardes*," said a voice, and Samantha squinted up into the sun. It was Isabel, grinning widely. She held a bottle marked "Inca Kola" and was sipping the bright yellow liquid through a straw wedged in the gap of her teeth.

"You'd better leave," said Evan.

Adam was more direct.

"*¡Fuera de aquí! Scram!*"

Isabel ignored them both entirely.

"*¿Quieres?*" she lisped, holding out her bottle to Samantha.

Samantha smiled graciously and took a tiny sip. It tasted like bubble gum, and its syrupy thickness slowed the bubbles in her mouth. As she was trying to decide whether or not she liked the unexpected taste, she realized that Isabel had lowered herself into the unit to more closely study Samantha's handiwork.

"Would you like to take a turn?" Samantha asked, offering her the shovel.

"*No, no,*" she said, pulling a half-finished carving from her pocket. "*Tengo que hacer mi propio trabajo.*"

With her own important work to do, Isabel didn't have the luxury of hanging around for long.

"*Hasta luego. Nos vemos—*"

Isabel could not finish her farewell. She was suddenly swinging by her arm in the air, struggling in Adam's fearsome grip.

"*Vete,*" he hissed, setting her down roughly. "Out."

Spitting insults in Spanish and Quechua, Isabel ran from the unit, but not before smacking Adam in the chest with her empty bottle. He snatched it up off the ground and hurled it back, missing her by a large margin.

"You," he said, noting Samantha's defiant scowl. "Back to work."

●●◉●●

Slice, slide, scrape, toss. Slice, slide, scrape, toss.

The hours passed to the soothing rhythm of Samantha's method, a layer of upthrown soil caking her clothes and skin.

At the bottom of the unit, dust seemed as plentiful as air. After two weeks of the excavation, every pore on her arms and legs was a dark freckle that no amount of soap could remove. Streaks of mud developed wherever sweat and soil could mingle. Even the smallest movement released a swirling brown cloud, and blowing her nose left an earthy black sludge in the tissue.

Early in the summer, Samantha had scrubbed herself pink. But by now the irremovable dirt had become a source of pride, evidence of a hard day's work.

Slice, slide, scrape, toss. Slice, slide, scrape, toss. Slice, slide, scrape, toss.

And then something delicate and white popped loose at her feet, just at the crease where the unit's wall, or "profile," met its floor. She listened to make sure that Adam and Evan were still by the screen, but they seemed too deep in Spanish conversation to notice the pause in the sounds of her shoveling, and she knew she had a few moments to examine the object in peace. She stooped to retrieve it, and the damp clods of mud caked around it disintegrated in her hands.

It was a bird's bone, its outer surface gleaming white in places through its coating of mud. Copying a method she'd seen Adam employ on potsherds, she spat onto her fingertips and used the saliva to wipe the object clean. With each swipe of her thumb she revealed an intricate lattice of finely etched grooves, dark brown with the soil embedded within them.

From the shape of the bone and the slight depressions in each end, Samantha could tell that the object was hollow. She used the pen from her notebook to gently push out the cylindrical clog of mud in a single piece. What now lay across her palm resembled a drinking straw, adorned with the careful designs of an expert artisan.

She heard the tromping sound of approaching boots and laid the artifact in Adam's outstretched hand.

"Where did it come from?"

"The profile."

"Show me."

Samantha obeyed, pointing at the wall of the unit where the bone tube had dislodged itself.

"Great." Adam snarled. "When I told you two not to pick at the profiles, I meant it. Without knowing where this comes from—*exactly* where it comes from—it's practically worthless."

Samantha felt her anger returning.

"But I *do* know where it came from. I saw exactly where it fell out."

"That's sloppy," Adam shouted over his shoulder as he walked away. "Bad archaeology."

She paused before going back to her digging, watching what Adam did next. She followed his movements as he slid the artifact into a new plastic bag, gave a furtive look around, and slipped it into an outer pocket of his satchel.

Immediately, Samantha knew that something was wrong. This was not how things were supposed to work. The site's artifacts were to be bagged by level and unit, and at the end of the day, they were sorted into careful piles in the team's field laboratory, safe behind a locked door off the hostal's dining room. There they awaited a preliminary examination by a rotating crew of students before the entire haul was sent down to Osvaldo's university in Lima.

It was a lot of work, and it was important: some of these

steps had been put in place by Peruvian law. Forms had to be completed, photographs taken. Samantha could think of no reason that this artifact should be treated any differently, and she could come up with no logical explanation for why Adam would take it for himself.

A rustling in the grass brought her attention around.

"*Buenas, amigos.*"

Samantha could not have been happier to see Clare and Osvaldo coming toward them through the weeds. Osvaldo gave her a wink as they drew nearer.

Adam was cool to their arrival.

"Dr. Barrows. Dr. Huaca. Can I help you with something?"

"Just checking up on how things are going out here," answered Osvaldo coolly. His voice was more jovial when he turned to Evan.

"*¿Qué dices tú?* Anything *interesante?*"

Evan cocked his eyebrow.

"Interesting? Here? Maybe. If you're the kind of person who likes broken dishes."

"What about you, Samantha?" Clare asked, kneeling a few feet back from the unit's rim. "Any finds?"

"Um. Yeah, actually." she said, summoning all the courage that she could. "I found some sort of carved bone."

"Oh? Wonderful! Can we see?"

She looked up to see Adam staring at her with unmistakable menace.

"Adam's got it," said Evan, coming to her rescue. "He stuck it in his bag."

Adam's face went from red to white. He rose awkwardly, produced the artifact from his satchel, and handed it to Clare.

She and Osvaldo exchanged confused looks before sliding the bone from the plastic bag and holding it to the light.

"Snuff tube?" Clare asked.

"*Definitivamente*." Osvaldo agreed. "Where was this found?"

"It…it was from the profile." Adam stammered. "I left our profile bag at the lab. I was going to put it in as soon as we got back"

"But you've mapped it, at least? Plotted it on the level form?"

"He didn't do any of that," Evan said, surprising Samantha again. "I was watching."

Adam was growing angry.

"No, I didn't. Not for a profile find. That's not how we do things."

Clare's response was steady, but its curtness revealed the annoyance behind her words.

"Sorry? Not how *who* does things?"

"Professor Sutton's team."

Osvaldo folded his arms.

"Is that right?"

"*Sí, señor*." Adam voice had hardened again. "That's not our methodology."

Clare's answer was matter-of-fact.

"Adam, I think it's time I explained something to you. We—Dr. Huaca and I—are this project's co-directors, and what we say is law. Peruvian law, really, since the government has approved our work here, and since we hold all the licenses and the paperwork is in our names. And I don't care if it's you or Jay or anyone on this team—violating our practices means a long bus ride down the mountain and an early flight home."

Adam was doing his best to appear calm, holding back his anger as the truth sank in.

"Whatever you say."

"Good. Let's get to work, then."

Osvaldo and Clare watched as Adam measured the location of the artifact's discovery. He acquiesced silently to their few words of instruction, holding the tape measure and dangling the plumb-bob with hands that quaked with rage. Finally, when the item was plotted out to the satisfaction of the two professors, they rose, leaving Adam to fill in the necessary paperwork. As they passed Samantha, Clare leaned in to whisper in her ear.

"Keep an eye on things, Sam, would you?"

Osvaldo echoed this request silently, using two fingers to point at his eyes and then at Adam. The gesture would have been understood anywhere on earth: "Watch him."

As Samantha again took the shovel in her hands, she felt vindicated. No matter his skills as an archaeologist, Adam Quint did not have the professors' trust. She had allies now—important ones. Perhaps there was justice in the world.

Now, she just hoped he wasn't dangerous.

●●●●●

While the next few days of work bled one into the next, the return of Evan's bad mood could be dated to a single afternoon.

It had taken him some effort to ferret out the practice schedule of the local soccer club, and when the day arrived he hurried to the field after work, a borrowed ball in hand. He stood on the sidelines, juggling the ball with his feet, head, chest, and knees. But none of the tricks he performed seemed to impress the locals. After several minutes, he was finally told that *el equipo está completo*—that the roster was completely full. He trudged home to the hostal dejected.

And then the shower exploded.

The hostal's water supply led back through a eucalyptus-fueled water heater and then all the way to the Rio Wacheqsa, somewhere up the valley floor. As Evan stood in the shower mourning his athletic rejection, the flow slowed to a dribble, the nozzle clogged with leaves and twigs. And suddenly, with a hiss and a bang, the rising pressure exploded through the knobs, rifling them into Evan's back and sending him out the door, down the stairs, and into the courtyard, a towel hastily wrapped around himself and twin welts rising on his back. As the story circulated among the team in the days that followed, Samantha could not help but feel sorry for him.

Her own efforts to adjust to life in Chavín were less dramatic but may have been just as frustrating.

Applying bug repellent all the time was a chore, but she knew it was hugely important. Flies, fleas, and mosquitoes seemed to linger only near the valley's livestock, but Jay's description of the effects of *verruga* was enough to convince Samantha not to take the chance. The disease was as ugly as it sounded. As Jay described it, people bitten by *verruga*-infected insects were likely to notice a gradual tightening of the muscles in their cheeks and around their eyes, until their features grew permanently distorted.

"It's too late!" Evan would say whenever the topic came up. "Look at her face! She's already caught it!"

But water was the biggest hassle. Her uncle's friendly but stern advice had taught her to be careful about what she drank or used to brush her teeth, and how to purse her lips when she washed her face or took a shower. To buy a bottle of water meant stepping into one of the town's few bodegas and enduring the curious stares of other shoppers as she blurted out *"Una botella de agua, por favor"* in her uncertain Spanish. She had bought enough *botellas* from a kindly store owner to last her a few weeks. But soon she noticed that her stockpile was rapidly shrinking as Evan helped himself to her supply.

Samantha did her best not to let the challenges of Andean life get to her and focused instead on being an active part of the excavation team.

And that was why she was now making her way through the golden light of evening to Chavín's fanciest restaurant. She had volunteered for the job of collecting the mail, which was delivered to El Ficho along with the rest of the village's letters and parcels. She had grown fond of the short walk through the Plaza de Armas and north along the main thoroughfare to the restaurant's grand doorway, and she enjoyed the responsibility of bringing the team their important correspondence from home.

She stepped into El Ficho's tiled lobby, hearing the whir and ping of a microwave as the cooks prepared one of the frozen American pizzas that made the restaurant so popular. The smell of pepperoni wafted from the kitchen as the young woman behind the desk handed Samantha the day's stack of mail, bound with twine. Beneath the pile of postcards and envelopes was a package, and Samantha started when she saw her own name scrawled across it, along with her brother's, in their mother's precise script.

She sat at an empty table in the elegant dining room, eager to open the package and know its contents before her brother could get his hands on it. It clacked enticingly as she set it down.

What was inside? Perhaps her parents had sent her the water filter she had asked for, or maybe they had finally caved in to her request for a camera.

But what lay beneath the brown paper wrapping was not a present but a chore. The letter inside explained everything, written in the strange, formal way of people who spend their free time reading books like *You! Can! Manage! People!* and *Even More Little Secrets to Big Business Success*:

Dear Evan and Samantha,

We miss you both very much and we hope that the project is proving to be successful.

We would like you to do something for us. Evan, before you get upset, please remember that you are part of a family, and even when you are on vacation, your primary obligations are to those who put food on your table. Besides, it's only a small favor, and we don't think it will take too much time away from your uncle and his dinosaur bones.

A client of ours is interested in market strategies in Latin America, and because you now have access to a valuable customer network in Peru, we have told them that you are willing to help. We would like you to please distribute the enclosed products as widely as you are able, along with the attached survey.

Samantha, because these products are directed to a female clientele, it would be most appropriate for you to physically distribute them while Evan plays a more managerial role...

Samantha sighed. This was not the first time her parents had asked for her help in their work. She remembered quizzing snickering classmates about their favorite flavors of cough syrup and questioning her gym teacher, Mr. Baskin, about how he and the rest of the Physical Education department decided what brand of dodgeball to purchase.

But this new assignment was different. It would be humiliating—what would Stuart think, for instance?—and it would take hours. This summer was supposed to be her time, and she had far better things to do.

She cast the paper aside and tried to make sense of the contents of the box. It was filled with small plastic disks, and it took a while for Samantha to recognize them as makeup compacts. Each was imprinted with a name in gold lettering, like *Latina Lavender* or *Tegucigalpa Tea Rose*.

She dug her hand into the box, picking out *Peruvian Pink*. But as she flipped open the lid, the makeup slid out in a chalky disk and crumbled on El Ficho's ceramic tiles, leaving behind only the compact's tiny mirror. The product had somehow been destroyed en route—a fact Samantha confirmed with a glance into Andean Apricot and Mayan Magenta.

She had been freed from her burden almost as soon as she had been saddled with it. But still she was downcast as she trudged home, carrying the clattering box of ruined makeup under her arm. No matter how good an archaeologist she became this summer, her parents would still see her as a child, a little girl with a hobby, the "Archaeo Kid." She was useful for their simple assignments but incapable of any serious work of her own.

She would just have to prove them wrong.

Spanish → English

- Que tal - what's up?
- cosas de oro - gold things
- Tumba - Tomb
- almacena - keep or store something

the "action figure" - it's so detailed. I wonder how it got here...

The Circular Plaza

Screening stuff is the worst! The mud is so sticky you kind of have to jam it through the screen with your trowel (or use your hands)!

Lanzon

Laberintos

temple map →

Lanzon!

It is so so so so amazing. It's like a monster, and it's just kind of waiting there in the dark until someo...

haunted? I mean obviously not, but is there really a legend about a ghost in the temple? I don't want to ask Jau because he'll...

Dijota & Chimay

Chapter 6

Samantha clenched and unclenched her fingers, then rubbed the new lines of calluses that burned across her hands. A condor circled above her, borne high aloft by the swift Andean winds and scanning the ground for carrion. She took a moment to watch the enormous bird as it wheeled away, up and over the valley walls.

Two more days of digging had brought them to a depth of two meters, about six feet if she remembered her math right. Here they had encountered a thick layer of Chavín clay, and its heavy consistency made it reluctant to give up its secrets. Each heavy bucket-load strained the screen so that it sagged from its wooden frame and gummed up the screen's metal lattice. The only way to determine each bucket's contents was to go through it by hand, clod by stubborn clod.

Evan had taken a turn, but after just a few hours, complained of his throbbing fingers.

"This will destroy my trumpet career, you know," he

explained, "and as first chair in Concert Band, I do have certain responsibilities."

It made no difference to Adam, who operated the screen. He had been quieter since the incident with the carved bird bone, wary of the Sutton siblings and following the professors' methodology with exacting precision. Still, Samantha could sense a simmering rage within him, apparent in the way he slammed down his tools or hurled stones at the pair of llamas when they came too close to the work area.

But most of Adam's time was spent elsewhere. He would disappear for minutes or hours, returning without explanation and meeting Evan's cheerful banter with stony silence.

So it was no surprise that the burdensome screening duty fell on Samantha alone. Resting the screen against her hip, she sliced into another clod with her trowel and pulled it apart with her fingertips. Nothing. She tossed the smaller bits back onto the screen and pushed them through the metal wires with the flat of her trowel.

"Another bucket, coming right up," Evan said, and Samantha braced for the heavy load, grimacing as the screen dug into her hip with the weight of the clay. She gave it a quick shake and set to investigating the bulky clods that were left behind.

"Hey!" her brother cried. "Look at this!"

Emerging from a damp glob of soil was a very small ceramic foot. Evan pried away the mud casing to reveal the rest of a leg, the length and width of his little finger.

"Here's more!" Samantha said, ripping open another damp clump to expose the leg's pair, as well as a tiny torso.

They arranged the pieces in Evan's outstretched palm. Each leg was delicately fashioned, complete with a knobby knee and delineated toes. Samantha could see that a fine string could be threaded through a hole at the hip to attach to the torso piece, allowing the legs to swing free.

"It's an action figure." Evan whispered, and Samantha laughed.

"Or maybe a doll," she said.

"No, definitely an action figure."

They worked quickly to break apart the remaining clumps, exposing a single, delicate arm and what may have been a fragment of the head.

A rustle in the grass brought their attention round. It was Adam, returning from another unexplained absence and flinging his heavy satchel to the ground.

"Look what we found!" Evan called out, and Samantha was surprised that he had allowed her an equal share of the credit. But if Adam were impressed, he didn't show it. He just slipped the four components into a labeled plastic bag and placed it into the larger paper sack that held the rest of the level's finds.

Watching these movements closely, Samantha was relieved to see that Adam had followed the proper protocol. But then she noticed that her uncle was approaching through the weeds and wondered if Adam had seen him first.

Jay was grinning.

"I hate to interrupt," he said, "but I was wondering if I could borrow my niece."

•••••

Samantha kept breathless pace with her uncle up and over the West Field wall, across the road, through the gate, and around the grass-covered temple buildings into the Circular Plaza. There, the scene was bustling. Several units lay open before them, and small teams of students shoveled, troweled, screened, and bagged with practiced proficiency.

"Come on, Sam," Jay urged. "There's someone I want you to meet."

She scanned the activity around them. There was Osvaldo picking his way among the units, examining finds and offering critiques in English and Spanish. Zoe was here too, hard at work exposing a pair of masonry walls. There were no strangers here. Who was she supposed to meet?

"*¿Qué tal, Jay?*" said Osvaldo, and the attention of the excavation team turned toward the new arrivals.

"*Bien, amigo,*" Jay answered. "Just making some introductions."

Osvaldo smiled widely, and there was a smattering of conversation among the students.

"Samantha," said Zoe, with a hint of a shudder. "Pass along my regards."

Samantha followed her uncle between the units. She had never examined the Circular Plaza before, but what she saw now amazed her.

The courtyard was partly encircled by a low wall, and she could see that it might have once extended around the entire circumference. Fantastic carvings lined the surface of what was left. At floor level was a line of snarling ghouls, their open mouths lined with wickedly curved fangs and their bodies spotted like those of jungle cats. At chest-height marched a stately procession of monstrous men— one clutching a bristling staff, while another raised a giant seashell to his grimacing lips. The ghoulish parade came to an end where a majestic stairway entered the plaza, hinting at something powerful up the steps.

Jay and Samantha made their way slowly upward until, midway up the Temple's face, they zagged to the left, following the length of a terrace to where a gaping opening awaited them. The darkness of the Temple's interior was absolute. The doorway seemed like a toothless mouth, the air it emitted stale and earthy.

Jay slipped a flashlight into Samantha's hand and pushed her gently to the threshold.

"I'll wait out here."

"How will I know where to go?" she asked, annoyed at the quaver in her voice.

"Oh, I think you'll find him," Jay said, "if he doesn't find you first."

Samantha smiled wanly, gripped the flashlight, and took her first steps inside the ancient Temple of Chavín de Huántar.

The passageway veered immediately to the right, and

Samantha was relieved to see a weak glow in the middle distance. She made her way toward it, running her hand along the rough-hewn stone walls to keep her balance as the sounds of the plaza outside faded to a stony hush. The dim shaft of light entered the Temple by way of a small rectangular hole, just where a second passageway opened up to her left. After a brief hesitation, she turned, creeping deeper into the Temple's interior.

Samantha had never been afraid of the dark, but this was something different. Her steps slowed, anxiety clawing at her ankles. She found the flashlight's switch and was relieved when its powerful beam slashed through the gloom. Still, the corridor's end lay beyond the flashlight's reach. She could feel someone waiting for her in the hollowness ahead. Someone old and angry.

She gave one last thrust against her fear, forcing herself forward to where, at last, the passageway opened into a cramped, cross-shaped chamber. Then, as she made sense of the shape that loomed in the center of the room, she took two rapid steps backward.

It was a monster. A pillar of living stone.

It took up most of the room, reaching high above her head so that even the chamber's lofty ceiling seemed barely able to contain it. But it wasn't its size that held her petrified gaze and clamped her teeth together. Every inch of the pillar was intricately carved, and its effect was terrifying. Here was a tangled web of snakes. There a clawed hand. And over there a pair of dead, soulless eyes. Each component came together to form a terrible whole: a demon, a fiend, an otherworldly horror.

It took a breathless moment for Samantha to realize that she had seen it before in the form of Alejandro and Isabel's tiny carvings. This was *El Lanzón*—the "lance"—what Chavín was all about.

She stayed in the chamber as long as she could stand, recording her thoughts in quaking handwriting by the beam of the flashlight. But her crawling feeling of unease grew too much to bear, and before long she was scrambling for the exit.

She emerged, blinking, to the team's raucous applause. It had been a test, she realized, a modern rite of passage at the site of ancient ceremonies. And she had passed.

Jay's face glowed with unmistakable pride.

"And now, Sam," he said in a low voice, as the archaeologists returned to their work. "I want to offer you a job. Something that only you can do."

•••●••

She was giddy as they climbed the rest of the way up the fog-dampened staircase to the Temple's grassy, uneven roof, coming to a stop where a low mound concealed another opening. Here a steep, narrow staircase descended into another chamber within the Temple's black heart.

"This is the *Galería de los Laberintos*, the Gallery of the Labyrinths. Stay close in this one, Sam. It's…well…a bit of a maze."

He ducked to enter the doorway. A thrill of adventure passed through her, and she did not hesitate before plunging into the darkness behind him.

The stairway turned and twisted, cutting into the Temple like a screw. The sounds of their footsteps were swallowed up, and Samantha could hear nothing but the pounding of her pulse.

Down, down, down.

Would the stairway never come to an end? She wondered how far they were beneath the entrance, or if they had descended even deeper, below the surface of the ground outside. With no windows, the blackness was total, and for a few dizzying moments, the beam from Jay's flashlight disappeared from view. But then they were on level ground at last and she was once again in control.

The steps had led them to a tight corridor with a smooth, mud-packed floor, and it turned right, left, and left again as they crept deeper—through doorways and up and down interior stairs. Occasionally, her uncle's light caught small openings in the walls—ventilation holes—leading along twisting paths to the outside. But still, the air was thick and damp, and she could taste its mustiness as she breathed.

At last, they turned another corner, and the corridor came to a sudden end. Some time ago—maybe ten years, maybe five hundred—a part of the ceiling had caved in, and now their way was blocked by a mass of rubble and stone.

"This is it, Sam."

He extracted a piece of paper from his satchel, shining his light on it so she could review it.

"This is what I've been working on," he began. "A map—what's known about Chavín's galleries so far—compiled by generations of archaeologists."

Samantha looked over the document, locating both the Lanzón and Laberintos galleries among other tunnels and chambers.

"But it's not complete. Far from it. Most of these measurements are rough estimates, and there are many, many other galleries that have yet to be systematically explored."

Samantha looked up, fiery excitement blazing within her as he continued.

"When I accepted their invitation, I proposed to Clare and Osvaldo that the Temple Complex be mapped in its entirety, once and for all. I hope to come back with some very precise instruments to help me plot it exactly. It will be a huge project. It'll probably take me years. But I want to start this summer by getting a fuller idea of what's here, in order to decide on a strategy for the work ahead."

Samantha understood what he had in mind. She also understood the whispered excitement among the archaeology students that had accompanied any hint at Jay's research plans in recent weeks. This work would plumb Chavín's innermost secrets. It would be the most important job of all.

"But why me?"

Without a word, Jay swung the flashlight around, focusing its beam on a shadowy opening in the gallery's earthen floor.

It was small. Very, very small. Getting on her hands and knees, she saw how it curved sharply downward, but the angle of the curve and the shadows of the walls made it impossible to see what lay beyond the turn.

"You want *me* to go in *there*?"

"There, and a bunch of other places, Sam. There are openings and passageways like this all over the Temple Complex that we're not going to be able to explore without the help of someone your size."

Jay's voice was serious.

"But that doesn't mean you have to do it."

She swallowed hard.

"I'd understand if you say no, Sam. But think it over. For my sake."

She nodded, stood, and followed her uncle out of the Temple and into the comforting light of day.

●●◉●●

Chavín's night brought a different kind of darkness.

It was the tender variety, magical and soft. Each evening the sun plunged behind the western cliffs, and after the briefest of dusks, the narrow band of sky above was spangled with a band of stars as dense and white as a shattered bowl of sugar. Samantha would sometimes pause in the hostal's courtyard to gaze at the unfamiliar constellations of the Southern Hemisphere, pondering the people who had seen the same stars thousands of years before.

Tonight, as she made her way with Jay, Clare, and Evan

downhill from the Plaza de Armas, what little artificial light there was filtered through the shuttered windows or emitted dull and yellow from the widely spaced streetlights. They were silent as they crisscrossed from one patch of light to the next, each of them faltering once or twice over the potholes and ruts in the unpaved road. Here and there, Samantha sensed an animal of some kind beside her. At other times, she felt the coarse fabric of an Andean shawl against her bare arm as she was overtaken by unseen villagers—whose lifetime knowledge of the road's unique dips and furrows enabled them to stride as quickly and surely as if they were on a midday stroll.

Evan was not nearly as graceful, and when his elbow clashed sharply with Samantha's, he gave her a nasty shove, sending her a few sidestepped paces away.

Stealing through the night, she considered her uncle's invitation to work with him inside the Temple. The darkness of the galleries was one thing. But the thought of a collapse, of being pinned deep underground or crushed outright by ancient masonry brought a twist in her gut. And something else gnawed at her too. Something deeper. A sense that the Temple's secrets might better be left alone.

A slight stumble brought her mind back to the road, and finally Samantha could see the brightly lit front court of the high school. The deejay was still setting up, and there were quick blasts of music from a pair of mounted speakers as he tested and adjusted the wiring. A clump of teenagers was lined up before him, and Samantha heard her brother's footsteps as he distanced himself from her and the two professors to enter the dance alone.

As they came through the tall iron gate and into the high school's concrete courtyard, they were met by Osvaldo's booming voice.

"*¡Amigos! ¿Que tal?*"

He had separated himself from a cluster of partygoers, leaving them laughing and slapping each other's backs over a joke he had just told.

"Samantha! Your first *jarana*," he said, smiling. "You are in for a quite a good time!" More townspeople streamed in behind them, and the party took on a festive air. Little boys chased each other in their pressed trousers and dress shirts. Little girls joined in, some in lacy dresses and others in more traditional high socks, skirts, and woolen coats. Their parents stood beside long plastic tables, laughing, talking, and clucking at their children as they ran by. She saw Stuart across the courtyard, flirting with a young woman in dangling earrings, and Zoe beside him, laughing sweetly with a pair of girls in wide-brimmed hats.

Chavín's teenage population arranged itself around the speakers as they waited for the music, acting just like any teenagers would at a party back home. Samantha suddenly felt self-conscious about her appearance—her small elfin features and her pale, freckled skin. But Evan headed straight for where a thin, acne-scarred young man was chatting with the spiky-haired deejay, and she watched as he extended his hand, said something funny, and immediately won them over.

Typical. She had neither the confidence nor the Spanish it would take to approach the few girls her own age, most of whom were standing quietly with their families.

The volume of the party was starting to build, and finally, music sputtered from the speakers at full volume and in the middle of a song. The singer's voice could barely be heard over the distorted sound of trumpets, panpipes, and heavy electronic drums. She glanced again at her brother, whose subtle head-bobbing exactly matched that of the Peruvian teenagers around him.

The song came to a sudden end as the deejay tapped the microphone.

"*Atención, por favor. Señores y señoras, su atención.*"

It was in Spanish, of course, but with a little concentration, Samantha found herself able to understand almost every word.

"A good, good, good, good, evening, ladies and gentlemen. And now, an announcement from our *alcalde*."

"The mayor," Osvaldo whispered in her ear, as a dignified figure strode to the microphone. The man was wearing a striped suit and a thin black tie, and sported a mustache as thick as a broom. He smoothed the bristly mass with a pair of fingers, ran his other hand through his diminishing gray hair, and addressed the village.

In a deep voice, he gave some remarks in rapid Spanish that Samantha could not follow, but she could see that he captivated the crowd with his quiet power. He turned to where most of the archaeologists had clustered and transitioned to English without interruption.

"As mayor of the *pueblo de* Chavín, I give a warm welcome to the esteemed archaeological corps. *Doctores Huaca y Barrows*, we are honored by your return to our village and are eager to continue our relationship with you and your students. Doctor Sutton, I extend the same welcome to you, your students, and your family."

Samantha smiled politely, but her smile faded as, across the courtyard, Evan gave a deep, sarcastic bow. The deejay and the other tittering teenagers around them seemed to like it.

"And if I may add," the mayor continued, "I am not only the *alcalde* of Chavín, but the *custodio* of the site of Chavín de Huántar, an irreplaceable part of the heritage of all *chavinos*, all *peruanos*, and all the world. It is with the utmost respect that I have entrusted your team with a share of this burden. May we all prove our worthiness in this respect."

Samantha followed the mayor's gaze and saw that it had locked with her uncle's. A smattering of whispers broke out around her, and she felt relieved when, with a final "*gracias*," the mayor left the stage.

The deejay bounded back to his station, and soon music thudded again from the speakers. When he grabbed the microphone, his next words were greeted by excited applause.

"*Señores y señoras*, ladies and gentlemans: *El Huayno.*"

The crowd broke into a frantic rush for dance partners. Jay, who had been standing beside her, was suddenly gone, and Samantha spun around to see him leading Clare, arm in arm, into an open space in the courtyard's center. When the new song began a moment later, Jay began to stamp his feet, his hands behind his back. Clare did the same with equal gusto. Soon, like the other couples crowding around them, they were whirling, then facing each other, swaying and stamping to the music.

"Shall we?" Osvaldo offered his hand, and Samantha gave him a horrified look.

"No, my dear, not to dance," he said, chuckling. "Just to get a better view!"

They joined the crowd that had encircled the two archaeologists.

"Imagine," Osvaldo sighed. "My whole life in Peru and none of your uncle's ability at dancing the *huayno*."

"Ability" was not how Samantha would have described it. Her uncle was moving with confidence but without much skill, and it was obvious that he knew only about half the moves. Clare was better but not by much. It hardly mattered. The two of them were enjoying themselves so much that their spectators began to cheer them on, clapping to the rhythm until the music faded completely into a ten-year-old American hit and the floor was flooded with teenagers.

"Uncle Jay?"

Samantha felt her brother shove past her, followed by his two new friends.

"These guys wanted to meet you."

Jay held out his hand, which both teenagers grasped firmly in turn—the second more firmly than the first—as if to prove their strength.

"This is Chimay," he said, indicating the thin boy with a constellation of angry pimples across his oily cheeks and forehead. His baseball cap advertised the name of a Peruvian beer.

"And this is Dijota." The deejay was broad and tall, by far the largest person Samantha had yet seen in Peru.

"We've met before," Jay said, a slight edge to his voice. "I believe Chimay is up from Arequipa for the summer, managing the video arcade while the Fuentes are away. And Dijota is the deejay at El Cóndor, if I'm not mistaken."

"And he's on the soccer team," Evan added. "He's going to see if I can be an alternate."

Both boys nodded and right away launched into a series of questions in Spanish:

"*¿Hay cosas de oro en las ruinas?*"

"*¿Usted ha encontrado una tumba?*"

"*¿Dónde se almacenan los artefactos?*"

With a little concentration, Samantha could tell they were asking if the archaeologists had found gold objects or a tomb, and where they were storing the artifacts.

"Look, guys," Jay interrupted, and again Samantha sensed something anxious in the way he answered. "You heard the mayor. I really can't talk about our finds. But if you have any general questions about the site, I'll be happy to…"

Dijota gave Chimay a short nod, and without a word to Jay they dejectedly slunk away. Evan turned to follow, but his uncle held him back.

"Evan," he said in a low voice. "Be careful what you talk about with those two."

"Yeah. I know."

"I certainly don't mind you making friends with them, but just remember that we really can't be too careful up here, especially given what's happened."

"Yeah, Uncle Jay." Evan sounded annoyed. "I know. I'll be careful."

But as he, too, disappeared into the crowd, Samantha was sure that he wouldn't be.

Dijota put on a new song, and Samantha watched more of the dancing. Someone had filled a large plastic tub with cool water, and bottles of Inca Kola floated inside. Sipping the syrupy liquid, she realized that a pack of children her own age had gathered around her. She was relieved to see Isabel and Alejandro among them.

"*Hola*," Alejandro said. He wore a dark red sweater with a patch on one of its elbows and the other showing signs of needing one soon.

"*Hola*," she responded, surprising herself with the confidence in her voice. That seemed to be all that was needed to break the ice, and suddenly she was surrounded by the entire group, as if she was just one of their group of friends.

Samantha bit her lip and resolved to attempt some Spanish. These kids seemed friendly enough.

"The sculpture you gave me…*el lítico…es muy correcto.*"

"*¿Cómo?*"

Alejandro had not caught her meaning, but he leaned his tiny frame closer, concentrating, ready to try again.

"Um…*El Lanzón…tu Lanzón…es muy correcto.*"

His look of concentration dissolved into a smile.

"*Aaaah, ¿sí? ¡Gracias!*" He beamed, and she could tell he had gotten her meaning. "*Nunca lo he visto.*"

"What?" It was Samantha's turn to concentrate. "Sorry, I…"

"*Yo…*" the boy pointed to himself, vigorously shook his head, "*…no…*" then pointed south up the valley, in the direction of the site, "*…lo he visto.*"

Samantha wasn't sure she'd understood. He had lived here all his life, but he had never seen the Lanzón?

"Why not?" she blurted out, but then she remembered how her brother had said it earlier in Spanish. "*¿Por qué no?*"

Isabel pushed him out of the way before he could answer.

"*Él,*" she pointed at him, "*tiene miedo.*"

To indicate her meaning, she threw up her hands as if to protect herself and made a face of absolute horror. The kids around her giggled, and Samantha understood. Alejandro was afraid.

"Of what?"

Alejandro shrugged off the laughter of the other children, then dropped his voice to a whisper.

"*¿Has visto el Loco?*"

Samantha's eyes snapped toward him, his warning at the main gate coming back to her in a rush of unease.

Working through his question helped her to calm herself. Already, she had come to realize that many words in Spanish sounded like similar words in English. *Has* sounded like "has," without the "h" sound. *Visto* sounded like it probably had something to do with seeing. And she knew *el* was one of the ways to say "the."

So…had she seen the Loco? Had she seen the Madman? Beside her, Isabel snorted.

"*Pues, yo no tengo miedo a nada,*" she boasted with hand gestures to show how brave she was, and Samantha believed her at once. Probably nothing on earth could scare this girl. Isabel looked completely unflappable. "*Pero, no hay ninguna persona que vive dentro.*"

"*¡Vive, no! ¡Es un fantasma!*" Alejandro shot back defensively, and the argument exploded into taunts. Just then, Osvaldo interrupted them, swaggering into their midst with a wide grin.

"*¿Qué tal, niños?*" he boomed. "Everyone having fun?"

"*¡Bueno!*" shouted Isabel. Like everyone else in town, she seemed to know and like Osvaldo.

"Were you able to talk with them, Samantha?" Osvaldo asked when the group of kids had disbanded into the crowd. "Is your Spanish improving so quickly?"

Samantha opened her mouth, a flood of questions ready to spill forth. But she held back. If the Loco was just some dumb story, passed around by the village's children, she didn't want to embarrass herself in front of the important professor. So instead, Samantha merely explained that they had been asking her about the site, but that she had remembered Jay's admonitions and had not answered them.

"Oh, do not worry too much about that, *pulguita*. I feel that your uncle is a little paranoid on this point. The people here are protective of the site. They wouldn't loot from it. And besides, who are we to keep secrets from the people who live around the site? These children are just like you. Of course they are curious!"

She bit her lip, then decided to take the risk.

"Osvaldo, there's nothing bad inside the site, is there? Nothing I need to be worried about?"

The Peruvian professor gave her an odd look but responded in the same gentle voice.

"All old places have old stories, Samantha. But not all of them are true."

Samantha smiled. And only after Osvaldo walked away did she realize that he had not answered her question.

The evening turned into night, and still the party continued. She was enjoying herself, joining a game of tag on the edges of the courtyard, flitting through the shadows to escape or pursue. But when the fiesta dwindled to an end, and she made her way with Clare and Jay up the darkened streets to the hostal, the thought of the galleries came back to worry her. Even in the excitement of her first visit inside the Temple's corridors, she had felt some unspecified terror within them. And tonight, Alejandro had deepened this gnawing apprehension.

El Loco. The Madman.

Her usually skeptical mind adopted an irrational, nighttime logic. Did someone live inside those darkened chambers? Were they haunted by some ghost?

When, hours later, Samantha was stirred from her sleep by an exchange of loud farewells on the street below her window and jarred more awake by the groan and slam of the bedroom door, she felt relieved to know that Evan was back and safe, and that she was no longer alone.

Spanish → English

- Adónde vas — Where are you going?
- Tiene miedo — Be scared!

Drugs!!!!!
Coca is just a leaf, and people chew it.

Coca leaves

San Pedro Cactus makes you hallucinate, and your ey...

Llama 5½ - 6 feet

Vicuña — like a sheep

Alpaca 4½ - 5 feet

H told him not to try to be on the soccer team! And now he's so embarrassed th...

Map of valley

monoliths?!?

Río Mosna

Fútbol
Sunday Soccer

View from cliff ruin

Ruinas —

Road

Caballeros - IIII

horrible accident. As I'm writing this, we don't even know if they're still alive.

CHAPTER 7

Nightmares were a common aggravation in Chavín. Everyone got them, Clare reassured her. It had something to do with the altitude. But this was little comfort to Samantha. She had been plagued by them ever since she had entered the Temple a few days before, and now they weighed gloomily on her as she considered the assignment her uncle had offered.

Each night, her dreams were awhirl with unsettling images and sounds, and they haunted her for hours after she awoke. Adam would flit across her mind's eye as she slept, his cruel face half given over to the graven horror of the Lanzón. She would see the leering features of the tenon heads, their stony mucus flowing in liquid curls around her feet. She would feel herself tripping down some unseen staircase and tumbling into the Temple's depths. And then she would be running through the twists and turns of the galleries, fleeing the lurching clutches of the Madman.

"Samantha. Hey, Samantha!"

There was a rumble, growing louder and more deafening as something approached. It was another landslide, she knew in her delirium, a second *Cataclismo* to bury them all.

"Wake up!"

Her brother's harsh whisper yanked her from her sleep. She peered through heavy eyelids to see him at the foot of her bed, shaking her mattress with his dirty boot.

"Hey, Archaeo Kid! Come on! Let's go!"

It was morning, or was about to be. Dawn was just beginning to cast its blue light through the curtains of their room. Trying to shake off the anxiety of her nightmare, Samantha realized that it was Sunday, the team's day off.

Something unusual was going on, she thought blearily. Her brother would never be out of this bed this early under normal circumstances. But at least Evan's gleeful expression told her that there was no cause for concern.

"What time is it?"

"Almost six," he answered. "Come on. Get up. I've got a surprise!"

She swung her legs out from under the blanket and sat up. "For me?"

"No, not for you. For Jay. But you get to tag along."

Samantha and Evan waited for their uncle in the courtyard downstairs, watching as the European tourists left the hostal for some dawn trek, their enormous backpacks clanking. When Jay emerged some minutes later, he seemed pleased by his nephew's initiative.

"Okay, Ev. What's up?"

The sky was clear, the day beginning, and it was exciting to be up this early, before the village's commotion began. Evan led them across the Plaza de Armas just as Jay's watch chimed six. They followed him north, past the high school and El Ficho, and into the northernmost reaches of the village.

It was more rundown out here, far away from anywhere a tourist was likely to go. Chickens and pigs rooted in heaps of garbage on the roadside. Littered shreds of plastic bags stirred noisily in empty lots. The three Suttons were treated occasionally to the pungent odors of rotting fruit and dirty diapers.

As they made their way through the village's northern extreme, a line of large stones barred their way, cutting across the dirt road and extending to the left, up the steep slope of the valley wall.

"Are these old?" asked Samantha, surprised to see such large chunks of masonry so far away from the site.

"As old as things come around here," said Jay. "We think that this wall controlled the flow of people through the valley floor, even before the Temple Complex was built. And," he leaned close, "there are rumors of a gallery running beneath it."

Samantha felt a thrill run through her. There were still so many secrets to uncover.

But then, much to her dismay, she noticed Chimay and Dijota waiting for them ahead, leaning up against the wall of a low-slung building. An extinguished neon sign in the window—SALON DE VIDEOJUEGOS—identified it as the village's video-game arcade, and the handwritten sign taped crookedly beneath it—DE CHIMAY—announced its current manager to the world.

"Did you invite them, Evan?" Jay asked in a low voice, his calm tone failing to hide his irritation.

"They told me they wanted to show us something."

The teenagers were laughing as the Suttons approached, and Evan engaged both of them with a handshake surprisingly intricate for their short acquaintance. When they gave Jay a polite nod, Samantha saw that her uncle's response was minimal, verging on complete disregard.

"What are you going to show us?" Jay asked Chimay stiffly. The teenager had a cigarette dangling from his skinny lips, and as he answered, its end glowed a brighter orange.

"*Otro sitio.*"

Jay raised an eyebrow.

"Another site?"

"*Sí.*" Dijota cut in with the booming voice of his profession, then switched to accented English to sweeten the deal. "Very beautiful. Many old things."

"Is it…*cómo se dice…*" Jay was searching his mind for the right word. "Looted? *¿Saqueado?*"

Both boys shook their heads.

"*No, no, señor. Es intacto.*"

Jay sighed, and the two teenagers interpreted that as assent. But just as they were about to move, Isabel's gangly figure appeared in a doorway opposite the arcade. She saw Samantha and waved enthusiastically.

"*Buenos, Samantha*," she said. "*¿A dónde vas?*"

Samantha didn't know how to answer and instead just pointed to the path that zigzagged almost vertically up the slope before them.

"*Bueno*," Isabel said, smiling and stepping into the road to join them.

Chimay spoke up to protest, shooing the young girl back inside. But Isabel's mind was made up, and she responded with such a vehement string of insults in Spanish and Quechua that the teenager shrank away from her.

"Chimay and Isabel are cousins," Jay explained to his startled niece and nephew.

"*Sí, somos primos*," Isabel confirmed. "*Soy cinco años más joven que él, pero tiene miedo de mí.*"

Samantha watched as Chimay rubbed his cigarette out in the dirt, keeping a wary eye on his little cousin all the while. Isabel was right. He did seem scared of her for some reason, even if she was five years younger.

"*Vengan.* Come," Dijota beckoned impatiently, and the group began to move slowly up the slope.

"Have you been up this trail before?" Samantha asked her uncle.

"No, actually, and I've been meaning to. It's an ancient path, Sam—an old pilgrims' route to the Temple, maybe— and it goes deep into the mountains. There are a few small towns farther along. Several still have no electricity or running water, and this trail is the only way to reach them. The señora from the hostal is from up here somewhere."

As he went on to describe these isolated villages, Samantha had a hard time picturing them. Somewhere high above them were places so remote that they took a full day to walk to, but they still relied on Chavín for its shops and supplies. These were places that even Spanish had yet to penetrate, where the Incan language of Quechua had been the only tongue spoken for hundreds and hundreds of years. She wanted badly to see one of these towns but, as Jay explained, the journey would take days for someone unaccustomed to the altitude.

And indeed, some five minutes later, Samantha was already feeling woozy. Her lungs seemed wrapped in a tight scratchy bag, and her heart thumped behind her ears. She wasn't the only one having trouble. While Jay and Chimay took long strides, and Isabel's legs beat the ground like pistons, Evan and Dijota were having the worst of it. Dijota's misery matched his heavy build. But Evan—who ruled Emerson Junior High School's soccer field—was a tremendous athlete, and it was jarring to see him struggle. Samantha reminded herself of what her uncle had told them—there was no way of predicting who would be affected by the altitude and who would not.

It was mid-morning now, and Samantha turned to take in the view of the valley. It was amazing how high they had already climbed. The town, tiny below them, had begun to stir. Trucks lumbered down the main road and the barks of dogs echoed off the hillsides. On the far side of the Plaza de Armas, families entered the church for the morning's service. On the near side, the mayor was raising the Peruvian flag into the golden morning light.

To Samantha's alarm, Chimay pulled another cigarette from behind his ear, lit it, and sucked in a long noisy breath. But Dijota had another idea. He waited until Jay had continued up the trail to produce a small plastic bag from a pocket in his sweat-drenched shirt.

"*Amigos*," he announced, dangling a small plastic bag, "some energy from *los Andes*."

Inside were a small film canister and a thicket of gray papery leaves. The two Peruvian boys each grabbed a clump. Chimay wet each leaf with his tongue, sprinkled it with a dash of white powder from the canister, and wedged the entire stack into his cheek. Evan had raised his own disorderly pile of leaves to his lips when Jay's stern voice rang out from up the trail.

"Don't even think about it, Evan."

"Huh?"

"Throw it away."

"Why?"

Jay ran a few steps back down the steep hill.

"Because that," he said, snatching the dry wad of leaves from his nephew's hand, "is a drug."

Samantha felt her eyes go wide. A drug? Being used right in front of her? Jay caught her horrified expression.

"The leaves, Sam. They're *coca*. The white stuff's just baking soda to draw out the narcotic."

He threw the papery wad into the scrub.

"Coca's been used in these mountains for hundreds of

years. It's not the really dangerous processed stuff you see on TV, but even with the raw version it's easy to get hooked."

"And our parents would kill you," Samantha added.

"Right," Jay concurred.

"Well, he didn't say it was a drug!" Evan cried, red from both embarrassment and exertion. "How was I supposed to know?"

They continued upward. Dijota's speed had indeed picked up, his breathing had slowed, and he occasionally raised a hand to rub at the tingling bulge in his cheek. He and Chimay took the lead while Jay hung back with his ailing nephew. Samantha walked at Isabel's side, marveling at how, with each stride, the steepness of the trail brought her toes to the level of her opposite knee.

"Uncle Jay! Look at this!"

Evan had dislodged a chunk of something from the road's embankment and held it triumphantly for all to see.

Samantha groaned.

"That's just a piece of plastic."

"*Es plástico*," Dijota repeated, and he and Chimay snickered.

"Hey, Archaeo Kid," said Evan. "How about you be quiet and let the real archaeologist take a look?"

He dropped the object into their uncle's waiting hand.

"Well, this is interesting," Jay said, after a moment. "And no, Samantha, it's definitely not plastic. It's porcelain. This glazing here shows that this is the outer surface. And from this edge here you can see where the lip was."

Evan's excitement was growing.

"What is it?"

"Toilet bowl fragment." Jay grinned, letting the shiny chunk fall to the ground. "We'll just leave it to the archaeologists of the future, shall we?"

Ten minutes passed. Then twenty. Twice, Samantha stepped to the side to allow strangers to overtake her on the trail, each with the speed and tenacity of someone walking on flat ground. One, an old woman, carried a load of firewood on her back as big as a haystack, bound to her by a strap she wore across her forehead. Samantha wondered how many years she would have to live at this altitude to build up that sort of stamina.

She was really feeling the elevation now, and to the visible displeasure of the Peruvian teenagers, she accepted Jay's more regular offers to stop and rest. Isabel happily matched Samantha's pace, while Dijota and Chimay left the Suttons behind to charge ahead.

"Come on, Samantha," her brother gasped from behind her, between ragged breaths. "You're slowing us down."

As they climbed higher, Samantha fought the impulse to turn and look behind her. She wanted to save the view for the end, when she knew they would go no farther. Finally, she spied Dijota and Chimay sharing another noxious smoke where an almost imperceptible path led off the main trail to the left.

"*¿Aquí?*" Jay asked, now panting himself.

"*Sí, señor.* Very near."

And now Samantha turned, gazing upon the wide

apron of the Cordillera Negra stretching below her into the valley. They had climbed much higher than she had thought.

"*Miren*," Isabel said with a wave of her hand, proud to show the Americans the beauty of her home.

Across the valley and above the steep brown hill, the frosted peaks of Cordillera Blanca towered high—their snowcapped summits giving little clue of the lava that churned inside many of them. The landscape dwarfed the massive structures of the Temple Complex, clearly visible up the valley to the right. It was no longer any wonder that the European visitors who shared the hostal with them had come from so far to explore this incredible terrain.

Relieved to be on flat ground, the group moved rapidly along the path in single file. They hugged the steep hillside as they picked their way between the tall, dry stalks of one unknown crop and then another.

They were almost parallel with the Temple Complex below them when the trail finally deposited them onto a wider ledge, and they were met by a scatter of collapsed masonry and bleached white bones. Samantha scanned her uncle's face for a reaction, with the thrilling realization that, together, she and Jay were seeing a site for the first time.

Chimay and Dijota watched as Jay strode to the center and knelt to pick up a potsherd.

"Huh."

His expression was blank, and Samantha wondered what he was thinking.

Evan's reaction was easier to read.

"Uncle Jay! Do we get to name it? Can it be 'Sutton Ruin?' Or maybe something in Spanish—'*El Castillo de Evan*'? Oh, wow! *Are those human bones?*"

"Sam?" Jay asked, without turning around. "What do you think?"

"They're way too big to be human. They're camelid, I think. Llama, alpaca, maybe vicuña."

"No, I meant the site. Any thoughts?"

She scanned the pitted ground around them, casting her eye over the coarse craters and furrows.

"I'm not sure. It just seems a little…messy?"

Jay rose.

"I think 'looted' is the word you're looking for, and you're right. Completely picked over. Destroyed. Not even worth our time."

He took a final look at the potsherd in his hand before chucking it casually down the hillside.

Samantha traced the potsherd's arc, watching from her vantage point as it fell in front of the azure sky, the white Cordillera, and the brown grasses of the valley's opposite wall. But then her eye lit on something she hadn't noticed before. Across from them—beyond where the Rio Wacheqsa seethed from the hillside, beyond the broad sweep of the West Field, beyond the cattle-choked road, beyond the site's entrance, the storage sheds, and the Temple itself—there, sitting just on the opposite side of the Rio Mosna, were three enormous stones: "megaliths,"

130

if she remembered the term correctly. They sat in a crude corral, propped up lengthwise to tower above a scattering of what looked like pigs and horses.

"Let's head back down," Jay said, starting toward the trail.

But Chimay stepped quickly in front of him. Dijota moved into position beside his friend, standing firmly in the professor's way.

"*¿Perdón? ¿Señor?*"

"What?"

They held their ground and Chimay extended an upturned palm.

Jay snorted.

"You want a reward?"

"*Sí, señor.*"

Jay pushed the hand aside and shoved angrily between them. The teenagers made as if to follow, but Isabel said something biting and they decided against it, speaking in low tones as they readied new quids of coca for the descent.

As her uncle disappeared along the ridge, Samantha raised her notebook from where it hung around her neck and started to sketch the monoliths. She was careful to draw how they lined up perfectly with the Temple Complex across the Mosna, and how the enclosure's tall stands of eucalyptus blocked any view of them from the site itself. She made sure to add the details of the expansive compound that sat nearby—a series of low buildings and courtyards, propane tanks and wrecks of cars—noting how some panels of its corrugated roof had rusted red.

She was penciling in the line of pigsties that lay between the monoliths and the house when the notebook was ripped from her hand, her pencil scratching an ugly gash to the edge of the page and the string pulling painfully against the back of her neck as it went up and over her head.

"Give it back, Evan!"

Her brother's crimson flush revealed his motives. He was humiliated—Jay had not been impressed with the site, and his two new friends had not been given the reward that he clearly had promised them. Samantha provided a ready target for his frustration.

"What do you need to take notes for?" he spat, venting his rage. "He said this site is useless!"

She ran at him, but he nimbly stepped away.

"Give it to me!"

"Give you what?"

"My notebook!"

Their uncle was out of sight now.

"You must not be talking to me, Archaeo Kid, because I don't even have it anymore."

As he spoke, he thrust the notebook into the arms of startled Chimay. When Samantha stepped warily toward him, he hastily pitched it over her head toward Dijota. From where she stood nearby, Isabel's reaction was swift, and she managed to knock the notebook off course and into the weeds at the edge of the precipice. Both she and Dijota lunged for it.

But as Isabel snatched it up and cradled it close, Dijota's

foot caught in the rubble of the looted ruin. Unable to stop himself, he fell. His massive weight passed over his trapped ankle with a crunch and a pop, sending him sprawling and roaring among the bones and brambles.

●●◉●●

Hours later, Samantha and Isabel sat with their backs against the cinder block wall of Chavín's high school, watching as Evan stretched and preened along the chalk sideline of the soccer field.

The injured Dijota had spoken to the team's manager about letting the young American serve as his substitute for the day, and now Evan looked ridiculous in the deejay's enormous, bloodred jersey, so broad that its shoulders sagged in large folds across his back. Still, Samantha appreciated the insignia on the left breast, a stylized depiction of a tenon head with the team's name—Chavín Ruinas—embroidered below it. Evan had negotiated a shiny pair of cleats from Chimay, trading away his half-functional headphones in the process. But it was not much of a sacrifice—his only use for them had been to play *Pillager of the Past*, which still lay shattered in some canyon far above them.

Beside her, Isabel muttered something, and Samantha turned to see Chimay enter the soccer field through the gate in its chain-link fence, an unsteady Dijota trailing on his crutches. These had been provided by Jay, who had grudgingly ordered them from the same man who fashioned the excavation team's screens and shovels. The accident hadn't been her fault, but Samantha was still afraid that Dijota would somehow blame her for it. She watched him settle dejectedly to the ground on the opposite side of the field, dolefully accepting the lit cigarette offered by his comrade.

Evan scanned the assembling crowd with his hands perched brashly on his hips, making sure he would have an audience for the game ahead. While his new teammates and their opponents stretched in small groups among the few school buildings, or chatted with family and friends, he warmed up in full view, starting with a few high-step jogs in place before targeting a scruffy tuft of grass for a practice kick, sending it sailing. After dropping onto his hands for some push-ups, he rolled over for a series of jerky stomach crunches. When he finally rose to his feet, his face was red and his chest was heaving—his pregame warm-up unaccustomed to the thin Andean air.

Samantha slumped lower against the wall. She had seen the full routine before. At games back home, she would sit between her mother and her father on Emerson Junior High's bleachers, and she knew that Evan and his teammates would follow the kicks, push-ups, and sit-ups with what he called a "pre-victory lap" around the field, their names announced over the loudspeaker as they crossed the half-line one by one. As captain, Evan always had his name read first and it was met by a chorus of screaming female voices, which sounded again and again throughout the game as he invariably scored goal after goal after goal.

But here in the Peruvian Andes, no one was screaming for Evan. Around her, picnic lunches were being unpacked, babies tickled, hands clapped together in happy greeting. No one seemed to be paying Evan any attention whatsoever.

Jay was nearby but occupied—chatting with town officials and the two or three British students who had decided to devote their Sunday to the soccer game. The two other professors and the rest of the excavation team had joined a half-empty bus of tourists for a twisting, turning drive to the neighboring village of San Marcos.

Spectators continued to gather, and Samantha was surprised by their number. The visiting team, the Caballeros, came from high above the valley, from one of the small villages Jay had mentioned that morning. They had walked to the game with their families along this ancient route, camping for a night on the way. A cowboy on a rearing horse was emblazoned in blue across the chest of their jerseys, which many wore over stiff pairs of jeans.

A referee entered the field and summoned both sides to its center. A shiny *un sol* coin was flipped high in the air, and soon the teams were in place, ready to begin, with Evan poised for the kickoff.

As soon as the ball left his foot, it seemed, the other team had taken possession and was racing full tilt for the goal. Chavín's defenders blocked the first shot but could not reach the second, and already the score was one to nothing.

As she saw Evan grimace, primed for revenge, Samantha's ear caught something from among the crowd noises around her: a voice, in English, speaking in an animated tone.

"No," Jay was saying, jabbing a finger at a person who Samantha could not see. "No way."

Samantha craned her neck, but the movement in the crowd around her continued to block her view. At last, she caught sight of the green military cap and the glint of mirrored sunglasses, and heard the low raspy voice. The target of Jay's anger was obvious.

"It's an opportunity, Dr. Sutton," Adam said. "Once in a lifetime."

"Forget it."

"I need this. You know I do."

Jay shook his head.

"Adam, if Dr. Barrows or Dr. Huaca heard that I was even considering this, we'd be shipped out of here before you could say 'Jiskairumoko.' You, me, my entire crew."

Isabel gave Samantha a nudge.

"Tu hermano tiene la pelota."

Samantha turned to see her brother accelerating down the field, dribbling expertly around the defenders. One of the Caballeros attempted a vicious slide-tackle, but Evan evaded it with a last-second hop. As Samantha watched him arc his foot back to shoot, however, he was suddenly enveloped in a cloud of dust. And when it cleared, he was lying flat on his back, his chest heaving. On the other side of the field, the Caballeros had scored another goal.

Again, Adam's voice penetrated the hoots and grumbles of the crowd.

"Dr. Sutton, you don't even need to be involved."

"You listen to me." Her uncle chose his words slowly and dropped his voice so low that she could barely hear him. "You're *my* student. I *have* to be involved. You even mention this to me again, and it'll be *me* sending you out of here."

As the referee readied the ball on the center line for the third kickoff, Samantha could see Evan say something to the short-statured opponent in front of him. Her brother's face had taken on a look of dark frustration, and Samantha could guess that Evan was issuing a challenge, an insult, or worse. The whistle blew, and as the ball sailed downfield, Evan found himself again on his back, this time holding his knee, grimacing, and rocking from side to side.

"*¡Cálmate, joven!*" someone yelled from the crowd.

"*¡Tranquilo! ¡Tranquilo!*" called someone else, as Isabel laughed merrily.

But Evan would not calm down—which was unfortunate, given how hard his lungs were working for oxygen. During the fourth kickoff, the Caballero said something to Evan, something that was then echoed with added laughter by all the Caballeros within earshot of the center line.

When Evan received the ball from his teammate, he rocketed into them, his shoulders low and his elbows swinging sharply. And yet again, he found himself on the ground, clutching at a line of new bruises from his ankle to his hip. Another goal had been scored, and the Ruinas players were shaking their heads in frustration.

"Hear me out on this," Adam was pleading now. But Jay wouldn't budge.

"Let me make myself perfectly clear. You do this again and I'll go to the police."

With an oath, Adam pushed his way roughly through the crowd and away from the school grounds, leaving a trail of angry spectators.

As the ball was brought back to the center line, Evan's chest was heaving, his grimace of pain cloaking a deeper, growing fatigue. It was even more obvious when he trotted into position and put his hands on his knees for a moment as the ball was reset. The Caballero forward issued another insult, prompting more laughter, and when Evan received the kickoff pass, he went flying down the field, his face as deep red as his borrowed shirt.

"¡Páselo! ¡Páselo!" Isabel cried.

But Evan approached the goal without passing and ignored the waving hands of his teammates. This would be his point to score, as it was his point to prove. He brought his foot back, took a last look at his target, and collapsed in a heap.

By the time Samantha joined the throng that had formed around her brother, he was conscious again and trying to get back to his feet. But his teammates were concerned for his health and wouldn't let him. He caught sight of his sister and waved her away.

"Samantha, get off the field." he wheezed. "We're in the middle of a game!"

But the referee had fished something from his pocket and was now holding it aloft. A red card. Evan was expelled.

"*Por tu salud, niño,*" the referee explained apologetically. Evan groaned and pounded his fist into the ground.

"For my health? Are you kidding me?" he spat. "I can look after myself!"

Even so, he allowed Samantha to help him to his feet. They made their way through the crowd to Jay, who stood waiting with a bottle of water for his nephew.

"What was the other team saying?" Jay asked, as Evan drained the container. "What was getting you so mad?"

"How should I know?" Evan growled. "You think I speak Quechua?"

Samantha eyed her uncle carefully. Nothing in his face or bearing betrayed his conversation with Adam. It was as if it had never happened.

Samantha said good-bye to Isabel and followed her uncle and brother up the road toward the Hostal Jato, the game still raging on behind them. Her uncle, it seemed, was capable of his own dark secrets. And in Samantha's opinion, Chavín had far too many secrets already.

● ● ● ● ● ●

The señora met them with news of the crash.

Somewhere between Chavín and San Marcos, where the valley narrowed into a deep canyon, a bus had turned too widely, tipped, and tumbled over the edge. There was no news of the rest of the archaeological team. Stone-faced, Jay sat with his niece and nephew in the late-afternoon shadows of the hostal's courtyard. They waited in unbearable silence, gazing anxiously through the gate and toward the small group of townspeople assembled in the Plaza de Armas. These were the families of others who had made the trip to San Marcos that day, Samantha realized, finding quiet comfort in each other's fellowship.

For the Suttons, the wait was over within the hour. Osvaldo rounded a corner and came into view, leading the pack of students as Clare brought up the rear. Samantha and Evan rushed to meet them and listened as a shaken Stuart explained what had happened, welcoming Zoe's frequent interruptions.

By chance, the group had decided to come back between the scheduled bus services, borrowing a van from an acquaintance of Osvaldo's. A different vehicle had met its demise on the road from San Marcos, and all the team was safe.

But as they entered the hostal and the sounds of their happy homecoming erupted through the building, Samantha turned to look outside. What she saw bewildered her. As the last of the students trailed into the courtyard, Jay remained behind. He gave a furtive look around, took a few running steps forward, and lifted Clare into an adoring embrace of utter relief.

And beyond the secret couple, the anguished families

sat in dazed silence, awaiting news of their loved ones and ready to continue their vigil deep into the night.

CHAPTER 8

Samantha knelt in the unit, finding solace in the sound of her trowel as it scraped against the hard, packed clay. It was cool down here. The unit's high sides—its "profiles"—created a pleasing pool of shadow. Only when Samantha stood to pass a full pail of soil to her brother could she feel the sun's harshness across her face.

Still, the events of the previous day unnerved her, and the details of the accident still rang in her ears.

The tragedy had not been as far reaching as first was feared. The doomed bus had held only the driver and his elderly sister, hurrying back to Chavín for another load of passengers to take to San Marcos's popular Sunday market. But both victims had been well loved, and Samantha could sense sadness among the people of the village.

So that the guards could attend the funeral, the main site had been closed for the day, and there would be no work for most of the team. To Samantha's disgust, a few members of the team had actually cheered when Osvaldo broke the news at breakfast. Evan took things further. When he found out that work in the West Field would carry on unaffected, he let out a dramatic groan, and Samantha cringed as she saw Zoe and Marisol shaking their heads in disapproval.

Her uncle had seemed somber—mournful even—but in her dark mood Samantha had wondered if he was secretly pleased. With the galleries off limits for the day, he could while away the hours with Clare.

But as loath as she was to admit it to herself, there was a small part of Samantha that was relieved by the main site's temporary closure. It meant that she could put off her decision on Jay's offer for another day. After Sunday's tragic events, she was not ready to face the unsettling dread of the Temple's galleries. She was happier in the quiet of the West Field, alone with her thoughts and feelings.

With Adam unaccounted for, Samantha and Evan made their way unaccompanied to the West Field, lugging the spare equipment from the hostal's lab. Evan was crankier than ever. Word of his athletic misadventure had traveled fast, and as the two struggled uphill, they were met with grins from the villagers. Samantha felt some consolation in this. At least the story of Evan's performance on the soccer field was bringing much-needed humor as Chavín began to grieve.

Despite the circumstances, they were making good progress in the unit that morning. Evan had uncovered the dual tubes of a stirrup vessel's spout—broken, but lined with a delicate design. Samantha herself had found a flat, disc-shaped piece, perhaps the bottom of a bowl. Every couple of minutes, Samantha would stand and call to her brother, who would reach down and pluck from her outstretched hand a potsherd or a flake of sharp obsidian. Then she was back to her knees, scanning the smooth earth for another piece of the past.

Isabel had joined them some hours into the day, taking a break from her own responsibilities to watch with bemused curiosity as Samantha labored away on what could only seem like a silly task.

They chatted happily, though neither understood most of what the other was saying. But Samantha was grateful for the company and found herself even more focused on her work with Isabel's eyes upon her: cutting the soil loose with greater care, brushing it into the dustpan, and pouring it into the metal pail—"peeling it back from the corner," as her uncle liked to say. Again, she stood and hoisted the bucket by the handle, and Evan skulked over from the screening area to retrieve it.

"You're going way too slow, Archaeo Kid. Your little friend here is killing us. Tell her to leave if she's distracting you."

"Stop rushing me," Samantha shot back, emboldened by the presence of her friend. "This is science, not some stupid race."

Evan ignored her.

"And would it kill you to leave some of the sherds in the

bucket? There's nothing left to screen by the time I get to it. I'm dying of boredom over here."

"You should have brought a soccer ball to play with," she snapped. "You could sure use the practice."

Evan yanked the bucket from Samantha's hand, and she settled back into her work. Her forearm was sore from troweling. In fact, her whole body ached. There were cuts on her fingers and a bruise the size of a fist above one knee where she had hurt herself coming over the West Field's wall. And now, without warning, Evan sent the empty pail past Isabel to come crashing down into the unit, scratching Samantha's elbow. She placed the bucket upright and set to work again.

But when Samantha sank her trowel into the ground a new sound rang out—the sharp zing of metal on granite. Isabel leaned in close, and Samantha used her tool's sharp tip to poke at the corner of the unit. Thin rolls of earth pried loose, revealing cold gray stone beneath it. She used the coarse hand broom to sweep aside the unfixed clay, then her trowel to probe for the rock's periphery.

Suddenly, the trowel's tip caught an edge, extending faintly across the unit at a slight diagonal. But as she tried to trace its outline, she realized that it wasn't an edge of a single stone, but a narrow space between two. And then, with a few more strokes of her trowel, another line appeared parallel to the first, so that the flat surfaces of three large stones were visible across the unit's floor.

"*¿Qué es esto?*" Isabel whispered, transfixed.

For a moment, Samantha considered waiting for Adam to return from wherever he was lurking to assess her discovery, but she decided his more experienced opinion wasn't needed here. She had seen massive stones like these before: on the other side of the road, capping the pitch-black corridors of the Temple itself.

She called her brother over in a shaky voice, and a dopey grin stretched across his face as he confirmed her appraisal. In a matter of seconds the three of them were laughing—bounding down the road and through the mournful town—racing to be the first to tell the professors that a new gallery had been discovered in Chavín de Huántar.

●●◉●●

They found Jay, Clare, and Osvaldo in the laboratory off the hostal's dining room, meeting with the rest of the team. The siblings' lungs were blazing as they burst through the door, and they struggled to announce their news. Within minutes an eager line of archaeologists was streaming out the gate and through the town, Isabel and the Sutton kids leading the charge, eager to show off their discovery. But when Samantha hurried up the West Field's ladder and landed with a thud, she was dismayed to see Adam waiting by the hole, as if he had been working with them all along.

The students jostled for space around the unit's edge, knowing enough to leave a couple of feet to prevent the profile's collapse. Samantha cast her eyes upward and for the first time noticed a ring of Andean vultures circling high above their heads.

Clare was all smiles.

"You came down right on the roof, Sam."

"Beginner's luck," Osvaldo added with a wink.

There was silence as Jay lowered himself into the unit and traced the clean lines between the three giant stone blocks. The ancient masons had done careful work. The stones fit together with only the smallest of gaps. Jay's expert use of the hand broom soon had the stones completely exposed.

"What's underneath?" Evan asked. "One of those passageways?"

"Could be," Jay said, clasping Adam's hand and climbing out of the unit. "But maybe it's a drain of some kind. Or there's nothing below, and it's just a masonry floor."

The grin spreading across Jay's unshaven face betrayed his excitement.

"But there's only one way to find out."

●●●●●●

A single stone would be pried free, the professors decided, and whatever lay beneath would be explored and recorded.

But the unit needed to be readied before giving up its secrets. With Jay now supervising, Adam was back at the unit and working hard. Meanwhile, Clare and Osvaldo fanned out across the village, looking for workmen to hire. The stones were enormously heavy and would have to be removed with practiced care. So, for the rest of the day and most of the next, there was nothing Samantha could do but watch as measurements were made, forms completed, and photographs taken of the unit and the masonry within. Evan used this time to hurl pebbles at the pair of woolly llamas down the slope.

Finally, over the wall came Osvaldo, Clare, and six burly men. Each of the hired workers wore sturdy boots and a cowboy hat, and carried thick coils of rope looped across their muscular chests like bandoliers. The file of students that followed them seemed almost frail in comparison and gave the men a wide space as they set to work.

It was another couple of hours until the stone was at last dragged clear. The crowd of students closed in on the unit, with Samantha and Evan in front.

At first, nothing could be seen through the dust that swirled in the bottom of the hole. But it spiraled upward and dispersed when Osvaldo lowered himself in. As Jay and Clare watched intently from above, the Peruvian professor unfastened a small flashlight from his belt loop, twisted it on, and cast the light downward.

When the beam lit the exposed cavity, its contents were greeted by the astonished words of three countries.

"Oh, wow."

"That's brilliant. Absolutely brilliant!"

"*¡Mira, chato! Causa, ¡que paja!*"

The crowd of students pushed closer to the unit's edge, craning for a better glimpse.

"*Soporten detrás, por favor*," Osvaldo ordered. "Everyone. Please. Stay back."

But from her position, Samantha could see it all perfectly. The light of the flashlight had fallen on the mouth of a dried-out human face, turned upward so that it seemed to be screaming at the sun.

It was a skull, or just about. A taut layer of skin still remained down one cheekbone and across the top of the head so that it looked like it had been partly wrapped in a brown paper bag. The mouth hung gapingly, unhinged at the jaw. Fine black braids extended from the skin of the crown, framing the face. The rest of the body—or what could be seen through the hole in the gallery's roof—was tucked up in a ball, swathed in a coarse brown fabric. The bundle completely blocked the view of the gallery, so that it was impossible to see how far it extended in any direction.

Osvaldo pulled a pair of blue latex gloves from a pocket. Very gingerly, he ran a hand along the topmost edge of the cloth garment and slowly produced two ornaments of a greenish metal, still tied with twine around the body's neck. He held them in his open palm, allowing his colleagues a glimpse.

"Well?" Jay whispered to Clare, as the murmuring around the unit grew louder.

"Post-Chavín, without a doubt," she answered. "Inca, almost certainly."

Osvaldo climbed from the unit so that Jay could take his place. He flashed his niece a quick smile but was soon all business again, directing students to form small groups in order to peer at the burial a few at a time and answering each of their questions in Spanish or English.

Samantha remained at the unit's edge. She had seen pictures of dead people in books before—unwrapped Egyptian mummies with their blackened skin, leathery "bog bodies" from Britain, the embracing skeletons of Herculaneum, the contorted corpse of Otzi the Iceman found in the Alps.

But this was the first she had seen in person, and it unsettled her. All her excitement had evaporated, and she tried to fight back the rush of new emotions.

"It's a classic Inca burial," Jay explained. "Crouched into a sitting position and—that way is east—facing the rising sun."

Adam pushed his way through the crowd to take a long look at the body and let out a long string of swearwords. Then he wheeled around and vanished among the cluster of buildings to the south.

"We'll need to sex the burial more methodically before we can say for sure," Jay was explaining now, and Samantha could hear her brother snicker. "But I'd say from her hairstyle and facial structure that she's a female."

Samantha felt a tear well up, hot and unwanted, and she hurried to wipe it away with the back of her sleeve.

"No, not mummified in the sense you're probably thinking," Jay was saying, "None of the embalming or other preparation you would see in Egypt or in some Chinese examples. This is just natural desiccation, the body drying out from the environment and altitude."

Samantha realized what was bothering her—what was taking her away from the thrill of the discovery. There was someone's body before her, all that remained of a human life. Was this right? Samantha asked herself, hearing the remaining cluster of students ooh and ah. Shouldn't they just leave this body in peace?

As the final two students disappeared over the West Field wall, Evan clambered in beside his uncle and peered into the empty eye sockets. Jay was using a gloved finger to show Evan a gap in the dried skin across the scalp, through which a jagged line could be seen extending down the center of the skull.

"This shows that she's a pre-adult, Ev. A kid. Somewhere between ten and fourteen years old at the time of her death."

Samantha brought a hand to her own face, seized by a sudden urge to verify that her skin was still smooth and warm, and that her eyes still had their lids. The coincidence was not lost on Evan either. He pulled himself up the edge of the unit so that he could sit with his legs dangling.

"Look at her, Archaeo Kid! She could be your twin. The sister I never had."

Samantha's boot shot out before she could think, delivering a sharp kick to Evan's thigh. He cried out and dropped back into the unit for cover, knocking soil and pebbles loose from the profile and onto the bundled body of the girl.

"Hey! Stop it!"

The infuriated cry startled her, and she took a few steps backward. Jay glared up at her from the unit.

"Listen to me, and pay very close attention," he said coldly, sounding like a stranger. "There is no excuse for being reckless around a unit, especially one with something so delicate exposed. Whatever little disagreement you two are having, fix it. *Now.* Once we dig something up, the information we can get from it is gone. It cannot be replaced. You owe it to the site, to me, to the people who live here, and to *her,*" he pointed downward, "to take this seriously."

Evan quietly climbed out of the unit, muttered an excuse, and exited, leaving Jay and Samantha alone in terrible silence.

"I'm sorry," Samantha murmured at long last, lowering her eyes.

Jay let out an extended and exasperated sigh.

"I know, Sam. That was very unlike you. But we're here as guests. If we get sloppy, we're abusing our privileges. We have to be as careful and responsible as possible."

"Sorry," she said again, with the full weight of her guilt.

"It's not the end of the world. We'll straighten it out and keep going. Now get in here and take a look."

Her reluctance must have been obvious.

"It's okay, Sam. You made a mistake."

She didn't answer.

"You don't want to?"

She shook her head.

"There's no smell."

"It's not that," Samantha said. "I just feel kind of bad for…for digging her up."

"Oh, Sam." Jay's voice was soothing and strong. "I know exactly what you mean. And in some ways, it never gets easier. No matter how many burials you excavate, you still find yourself thinking of all the people you know who have passed away, or about how we all have to die at some time or another."

He put out his hands, and Samantha allowed Jay to lift her down. He gave her a moment as she studied the bundled skeleton in the opening at her feet. She struggled to find the right words.

"It's like we're *taking* something from her."

"I know, Sam. I really do. But we can't really take away from who she was. We're *never* going to know her. Not like you know your friends at school or like you know me. We might be able to figure out how this girl died, if she ever was really sick or hurt, if she was poor or rich, and maybe even what she liked to eat. But we won't ever know her name or anything about her friends or her dreams or what she liked to do for fun. Those are the biggest secrets, and those she gets to keep."

Samantha looked down at the delicate face below her, now half covered by the afternoon shadows. Her uncle's words made some sense to her, but she wasn't sure if she agreed completely. Nothing could take away from the sadness of death. Not even the passage of centuries.

She tried to refocus on the task at hand.

"So, Clare thinks she's Incan?" she asked. "Then what is she doing *here*?"

Jay seemed relieved by the shift in conversation.

"Good question! The Inca seemed to have really valued ancient sites—maybe kind of like we do. Spanish chroniclers even talk about how the Inca visited Chavín to worship. Buried their dead here too, I guess. Someone must have jammed her in there from an opening."

Samantha winced at the word "jammed," but her mind drifted elsewhere. Had this girl seen Chavín when she was alive? Was it a ruin then too? Did she live near here? Play near here? Questions seemed to echo from the hole at her feet.

She looked again at the girl, noticing how carefully she had been wrapped, her arms and legs tucked up in a protective ball, her shiny hair beautifully braided.

"Uncle Jay?" she asked softly. "Do you think someone loved her, at least?"

Jay didn't answer for a moment but finally nodded.

"Sure, Sam. I think that's safe to say."

●●◉●●

In a way, the archaeologists themselves seemed to love the Incan girl. For the next few hours, the three professors were incredibly gentle, even tender, with her body. She was not manhandled, ripped apart by scientific instruments, nor even taken out of her grave. Instead, they examined her where she lay, moving her only slightly for measurements and photographs.

They were happy to comply with the request of the mayor: the girl would be left as she had been found and the unit closed. Meanwhile, Clare told a still-somber Samantha, a new unit would be dug adjacent to the first so that the newly discovered gallery could be explored.

In the early evening, as the sun sank toward the Cordillera and the sky glowed orange, a long procession of people climbed over the wall separating the West Field from the road, descending down a second ladder placed there to ease the crossing. First came Chavín's mustachioed mayor in a fine blue suit with the Peruvian flag pin clipped to his lapel. He was followed by a train of the village's few elite. Then came Adam, the muscles in his neck taut and his face revealing some simmering scorn. Clare had invited the señora from the Hostal Jato, and she and Osvaldo helped the elderly woman over the pair of ladders to the safety of level ground. Several of the site's guards brought up the rear, their shotguns swinging from the braided straps across their shoulders.

As the group gathered solemnly around the unit, Samantha caught sight of two other figures peering over the West Field fence from the ladder on the other side. Chimay and Dijota were studying the proceedings with focused attention. Evan shouted a greeting, and Osvaldo and Jay marched toward the fence to shoo away the teenagers.

This was Chavín's second funeral of the day, and the

small assembly seemed reflective in their silence. In a formal voice, the mayor now stepped forward to address them. His precise Spanish was easy for Samantha to understand.

"We are here with friends and visitors to bury this ancient daughter of Peru."

As the guards paced in the background, their hands resting on their guns, a villager produced a small bottle from a pocket of his coat, unscrewed its cap, and tipped a single swallow of clear liquid into his mouth. To Samantha's surprise, he then took a step toward the unit and poured a small amount onto the mummy bundle below. He crossed himself and then handed the bottle to the man beside him, who followed his example exactly.

Adam was next, and after he took a deep swig and splashed a perfunctory splatter into the hole, he passed the bottle to Jay under Samantha's nose. She caught the sharp and conflicting scents of alcohol and licorice, and watched as Jay, Osvaldo, Clare, and the rest of the assembly each took their turn.

As the mayor added some final words, Samantha's mind cleared. The ceremony, despite its unfamiliarity, seemed fitting. Of course, it was nothing like any funeral she had ever heard of. It was also, she realized, probably not at all similar to an Incan ceremony, and she wondered if any part of it would have been familiar to the girl whose body had again been put to rest. But perhaps it didn't matter. It had been done with respect by people who loved Chavín, many of whom would live their lives out in this valley. To Samantha, it felt right.

By the time the village residents had left the West Field, disappearing over the ladder in reverential silence, the valley was bathed in the deep blue of the brief Andean twilight. Jay, Clare, and Osvaldo decided it would be safer to replace the giant ashlar stone in full daylight the next morning, given the potential danger of the job.

Samantha helped Osvaldo cover the unit with a plastic tarp, pull it taut, and pin it down with several large stones. They left the site to the guards, who promised that nothing would be disturbed during the night.

Everyone thought that that would be enough.

●●◉●●

Coming over the wall the next morning, Samantha saw the tarp first, fluttering among the boulders lining the Wacheqsa River. The blue plastic had been ripped asunder. She scrambled behind the others to the unit, finding it jagged and jumbled.

Someone had come in the night, and now the girl's mummy was gone. Samantha, who had first disturbed her, felt entirely to blame.

Pillager of the Past II

...on that it had caught Evan, but seeing him get chased was still pretty good

The dog

Temple map

Spanish → English

• Como quieras - as you wish
• Disculpen - sorry (if you're talking to more than one person)
• Puedo traducer - I can translate

Levels
• Stonehenge, UK
• Great Wall, China
• Inca Trail, Peru
• Akrotiri, Greece

Human skull!!

CCOLLANAN
PACHACAMAC RICUY
AUCCACUNAC YAWARNIY
HICHASCANCUTA

Pesos Perdidos
Lanzon
Laberintos galleries

...ro's house. His grandparents look like ghosts. And the sword doesn't help...

NORTH

So glad I don't have to work in La Banda! But there's something wrong about the galleries, too, I don't like

Loco Loco Loco
Loco Loco Loco
Loco Loco Loco
Lo... ...Loco

pig

159

CHAPTER 9

If Samantha was to blame for the Incan girl's disappearance, no one else seemed to realize it. In fact, over the next two days, no one seemed to notice her at all. Racked with guilt, she buried herself in her notebook as the professors conferred among themselves or met with city officials—the hostal's parrots screaming, "*Corre, corre, corre,*" above their heads.

As each discussion came to the same tense end, it became clear that responsibility for the looting was falling not on Samantha, but on her uncle.

"There have never been these problems before," said the mayor, his curt Spanish clear enough for Samantha to understand. And when the mayor excused himself, Jay's two colleagues were more specific in their concerns.

"There *is* a pattern here." Osvaldo said, as Samantha looked on. "And I do not think I need to tell you what it is."

"Please." Jay said coldly. "Do."

"*Como quieras.*" Osvaldo said, leaning over the table.

"The only two looted units have been Adam's. This is a very strange coincidence, ¿no? The only lootings in all these years?"

Jay threw up his hands.

"Before we start making wild accusations, can we first discuss the obvious? We're working in the middle of one of the poorest valleys in one of the poorest regions in one of the poorest countries in the world. Around here, looting antiquities and selling them on the black market is the surest way to make a living. It's expected in conditions like these. Maybe even understandable. And nothing we find remains secret for long. All someone has to do is keep their ears open, then pay off a guard or two to look the other way. That, by far, is the most logical explanation."

Osvaldo slapped the tabletop with his hand.

"Not here, Jay. Not in this valley. The *chavinos* know what is at stake."

"Fine. If you say so. But Adam?"

The Peruvian professor did not respond, but Jay found some answer in Osvaldo's silence all the same.

"Ridiculous. Adam is my best student—the best of my entire career. Sure, he's a little rough around the edges, but his methodology is good, his instincts excellent. He has the makings of a terrific archaeologist. I'd more likely believe that the stories are true—that the Loco is back from the dead to get his revenge."

Sitting unseen in the tourists' corner of the dining room, Samantha shuddered.

The *Loco?*

Back from the dead?

Revenge?

These were the ingredients of any ghost story. And while Samantha had little patience for supernatural tales, she let the story play out in her head. Typically in tales like these, the dead returned to punish those who'd harmed them or to finish something that they had left undone in life.

So how had this Madman been wronged, whoever he was? What had he left unfinished?

If this was a tale told around a campfire, some thread would connect everything together—the site, the missing mummy, her uncle's scratched-out note, *el Loco*, little Alejandro's wide-eyed fear. But this was not some summer camp. There were no campers here, huddled and giggling in the firelight. Jay's statement had silenced his colleagues and sucked all the warmth from the room. For the first time, she knew there was at least some truth behind it.

She sensed Clare steeling herself, readying to steer the conversation back on topic.

"Gentlemen, please. We can talk about this for donkey's years and still not accomplish anything. All this speculation and investigation is for the *policía*. As for the three of us, all we can do is be vigilant and carry on with our work."

Jay and Osvaldo straightened, ready to move on.

"Now," Clare continued. "The immediate concern seems to be our research plan. The West Field is off limits, by order of the mayor. Evan and Samantha can be reassigned, of course, but am I right, Osvaldo, in assuming that you are uncomfortable with the idea of Adam working in the Temple Complex itself?"

The parrots screamed.

"Yes," Osvaldo nodded stiffly. "*Muy incómodo.*"

"What, then?" Jay asked, defeated. "He's my best student, and you just want me to send him home?"

For a long moment, the three archaeologists shifted uncomfortably in their seats.

"Uncle Jay?"

Samantha's voice took everyone by surprise. She walked timidly across the room to sit down beside Clare. She did not trust Adam—especially after his mysterious outburst at the soccer game—and there was little she wanted more than to have him sent home. But she also felt sorry for her uncle, shamed before his colleagues, his pride destroyed. He needed to be defended.

"I might know of a place. Somewhere else to excavate, I mean."

She flipped backward through her notebook until she came to the sketch she had made from high above the valley floor.

"I saw something." She pointed at her drawing, where the megaliths towered from among the horses and pigs on the opposite side of the Rio Mosna. "Here."

The archaeologists leaned in.

"From the main site you can't tell that these are there," she explained. "The trees block the view."

"Have you seen these before?" Jay asked, and both his colleagues shook their heads.

"But I do know the land," Osvaldo replied with apprehension. "We call the area on the other side of the river *La Banda*, and the part of La Banda opposite the Temple Complex belongs to the Ocllo family."

"Ocllo?"

"Landowners here for four hundred years." Clare explained. "Not exactly known for their friendliness toward outsiders. Or anyone else."

"And you don't think they could be convinced to let us excavate on their property?"

"I can try, Jay," Osvaldo said. "It is unlikely. But for you, *mi amigo*, I will make every effort."

The meeting broke up, the tension eased and all friendships restored. Clare whispered a silent "thank you" to Samantha as they rose from the table, and a moment later Jay picked her up off her feet in a jovial bear hug.

Over the evening meal, as Samantha described the La Banda megaliths in more detail, she noticed Adam sitting by himself, hunched and glowering over his plate. He looked up abruptly, catching her through his mirrored sunglasses in a steely glare.

I just saved you, she wanted to shout. You owe me.

Adam was first to drop his gaze.

•••••

It was time.

Osvaldo had, with great difficulty, made an arrangement with the Ocllo family, and work on their property was ready to begin. So, as the Peruvian professor led the rest of the archaeological team back to their units in the main Temple Complex, Clare and Jay readied for their meeting with the Ocllos across the river, poring again over Samantha's careful sketch.

But when the appointed hour arrived, Evan was nowhere to be found. Not wanting to sour relations with the landowners by being late, the professors needed to leave without him.

"Catch up with us when your brother comes back, Sam." Jay called over his shoulder as he and Clare left the courtyard. "Adam knows the way across the river."

For several minutes, Samantha waited in silence, Adam pacing angrily some distance away. If he was aware of the cloud of suspicion that hovered over him, he didn't show it. In fact, he seemed emboldened, more arrogant than ever. He spat a glob of phlegm into the dust at his feet, and at that moment Samantha regretted coming to his rescue. Perhaps the other professors were right, and Jay was wrong to defend him.

When Evan did show up, bounding in from Chimay's video arcade, he was buoyant.

"Those games are *so old*!" he beamed. "I'm like a god in there!"

They set off. Though the Ocllo residence was to the south, opposite the main site, they made their way north-ward toward the easiest route across the Rio Mosna.

They walked to the sound of barking dogs. Over the

past few weeks, Samantha had come to realize that dogs had the run of the village. On any given day, they walked the streets with purpose, fought in bursts of enthusiastic fervor, and flopped down to sleep wherever they chose—even in the middle of the road. While each seemed to have an owner that left food and water at the door, few seemed to have much interest in humans. Still, Jay had warned his niece and nephew that these dogs should be avoided and that they could be dangerous if provoked or teased.

Still glowing from his victories in the video arcade, Evan seemed eager to test this theory. As they rounded a corner off the main street, a dog crossed in front of them. It was enormous, like a grown man on his hands and knees, and its coat was black and shiny through a layer of dust. It would have ignored them if Evan—giddy with mischief—hadn't decided to let out a low and hostile growl. While a dog back home would have recognized this sound as playful, the *perro chavino* did not. Instead, it wheeled in its tracks and charged.

There was almost no time to react. Swearing in quick gasps, Evan turned and sprinted back up the incline of the street. The dog ignored Adam and Samantha and went after Evan, snarling and growling like a bear. Adam muttered something low and ugly, and he and Samantha hurried to follow.

To Evan's luck, he found an open door. It was a women's clothing shop, selling the floral printed dresses, brimmed hats, and large swatches of patterned cloth that Samantha had become accustomed to seeing in the plaza and in the streets of the town. As she and Adam neared, she saw Evan veer and fake as if on a soccer field, and throw himself through the doorway. The massive beast skittered in the dust, righted itself, and charged in after him.

There was shouting, barking, and a loud plaintive wail— its origin uncertain until Adam and Samantha entered the store themselves. Evan had sought refuge behind the counter, and the dog now paced before it. The woman who owned the shop and her two customers were doubled over with laughter, much to Samantha's relief.

Adam gave the dog a sharp nudge with toe of his boot, and it retreated out the door without a sound.

"You done?" he asked Evan, his hoarse voice devoid of warmth.

"Yeah," Evan gasped. "If that thing is gone."

It was. But still Evan kept a wary eye open as they retraced their steps toward the river. With Adam cursing their tardiness, Samantha was unable to resist her urge, and whispered, "¡Corre, corre, corre!" in her brother's ear.

●●◉●●

Crossing the Mosna proved difficult, even at its narrowest point. With Adam leading the way, they picked a route across a line of slick and widely spaced boulders. Between the Mosna and the steep incline of the valley's eastern wall was just a narrow band of gently sloping land—La Banda:

its meaning now clear. They started up a path on the river's eastern bank until soon, through breaks in the eucalyptus tree, the Temple Complex came into sight across the river, looming grandly over the majestic sunken plaza.

They turned off the pathway to a wide, squat house where Jay and Clare stood waiting for them before the heavy wooden door.

"No answer," Jay shrugged.

"Let me!"

Evan grabbed the door's heavy knocker himself and slammed it against the wood as loudly as he could.

Suddenly, the door swung inward. But all that came through the opening was a dusky silence.

"¿Señor Ocllo?" Jay called, leaning into the opening. "¿Señora?"

There was no answer—just the cave-like silence of the ancient house, dim and musty on the brightest of days.

"¿Señor y Señora Ocllo?" Jay tried again, "Disculpen, estamos..."

"¡PIM! ¡PUM! ¡PAM!" a voice shouted, and everyone leapt backward.

Alejandro's grinning face came around the heavy door. Feeling a little foolish, everyone but Adam smiled too, and Jay offered his hand to Alejandro for an enthusiastic high five.

"You live here?" Samantha asked. Alejandro understood and nodded. "The Ocllos are his grandparents." Jay explained, as they followed the boy inside.

Their eyes adjusting to the dim interior, they saw

that rooms and hallways extended in every direction off the entry. There were few windows to speak of, and the atmosphere was stuffy as a tomb. The house was, however, spotlessly clean. The heavy wooden furniture shone from polish, and haunting photographs and oil paintings of the long dead hung from the walls in perfect alignment. Alejandro led them through the rooms slowly, proudly allowing them to take it all in.

"Parts of this house are three hundred years old. Maybe four." Clare explained, "The Ocllos were already here in this valley when the Spanish were putting down the last of the Inca rebellions in the jungles."

An enormous sword hung from the wall at the hallway's narrowest point, mounted on a thick wooden plaque. Jay paused before it, entranced by something scrawled down the length of the blade.

"Aha," he muttered. "So they *are* those Ocllos."

Samantha strained her neck to read what was written but was met with a strange sentence in a language that was neither English nor Spanish.

CCOLLANAN PACHACAMAC RICUY AUCCACUNAC YAHUARNIY HICHASCANCUTA

"It's Quechua, Sam."

"I thought you didn't speak Quechua."

"Speak it, no. But this is a line I could recite by heart: 'Mother Earth, remember forever how my enemies shed my blood.' The last words of an Inca hero before the ax fell. He was an Ocllo too. And this…" He rapped the sword with his knuckles. "Spanish. Toledo steel. Probably taken off some defeated conquistador."

They did not tarry any longer in the dark hallway, following Alejandro into the sitting room. From there, a heavy door led outside to the pasture where they hoped to excavate. Adam pushed through the others, impatient, but a low whispering stopped him in his tracks.

There, in the darkness stood the oldest surviving Ocllos, husband and wife. In the faint light, they looked exactly alike, bent low over a pair of canes, one in each gnarled hand. Samantha saw that both had a mane of snow-white hair, and—stifling a gasp—that their eyes shone as white and colorless as watery milk. The four canes flashed with a crusting of jewels.

"*Señor y Señora, disculpen,*" said Clare, apologetic. But Alejandro interrupted her.

"*No hablan español, señora.*"

"They don't speak Spanish. Just Quechua, then?" Jay asked.

"*Sí. Pero puedo traducir.*"

Alejandro translated Jay's words of thanks and greeting, but the Ocllos made no sign that they understood. They stood completely still, bent low on their canes, their colorless eyes unblinking. When Jay was finished, and when Alejandro had transformed the last of his words into song-like Quechua, the house returned to silence, and the archaeologists awaited the couple's response.

When it came, a low groan in the gloom, it was unclear which of the Ocllos was speaking.

"They have had some problems with outsiders in the past," Jay explained to his niece when Alejandro had finished the translation into Spanish. "Archaeologists, specifically, they distrust."

He gave his nephew a warning look.

"We will need to be on our best behavior."

Alejandro conveyed the archaeologists' understanding, and his grandparents retreated ghost-like into the shadows.

Giving Samantha a big thumbs-up, Alejandro swung the door wide, flooding the house with brilliant light. Blinded, they stepped carefully outside and, as their eyes readjusted, took in the scene before them.

A tall row of eucalyptus marked off the western edge of the property, shielding it from view from the site on the opposite bank of the river. A few thin horses grazed across the swath of land, and beyond them a pigsty, its inhabitants oinking joyfully in the mud. And there, on the far side of the plot, were the three massive megaliths that Samantha had spotted from the looted ruin high above the valley floor.

The Suttons strode with Clare and Adam toward the towering stones, coming into their lengthy shadows as they approached the sty. The smell of the pigs and their manure, tolerable a few feet away, grew thick and almost unbearable as they approached the wooden barrier. Evan's face twisted into a disgusted grimace.

"We're not digging here, are we?" he said, swatting at the large swarm of flies that had begun to circle his head.

"It may not be pretty, Evan," Clare answered, lifting her leg over and climbing into the sty, "but it's actually quite incredible."

Sending the cluster of piglets squealing, she made her way around their low plastic trough to where the megaliths were planted into the earth, looming thick and dark above the livestock. Adam separated himself from the group, examining the stones from the other side.

"Amazing," Clare said. "We have become so fixated on the Temple itself that we've neglected its wider context."

"Look at these." Jay knelt in the grass, plucking several objects from the muck beside the pen.

"Oh, great." said Evan. "More shards."

"*Sherds*," Samantha hissed.

"Loads of them," Jay said excitedly, "and not like any we've ever seen."

Samantha examined each in turn. Some were the same shiny black and mottled red of the West Field, but there were other types—deeply grooved brown pieces and "corrugated" ware, in which Samantha could see how the coils had been laid down and grooved by some ancient potter's thumbnail.

"So we're back to broken pottery?" Evan asked.

"What do you mean?"

"Well, in the West Field we had a gallery, a mummy… you know, interesting stuff."

His uncle frowned at him.

"Well, Evan, I guess you'll find out. I'm going to leave

you in Adam's capable hands. Clare has kindly offered to help you two get started."

"What? What about Samantha?" Evan asked, prying his foot from the sucking mud.

"I need your sister for something else."

Jay looked at her.

"That is, if she's ready."

Samantha hesitated. The onetime thrill of the Temple's galleries now sent a cold shiver from her soles to her scalp. There were looters on the other side of the river, and the grimacing features of the Lanzón haunted her still. But it was the shapeless threat of the fabled Madman that most unnerved her. If he had returned for purposes of revenge, she did not want to be there when he found it.

Still, she was eager to be away from Adam, who was now sharpening his trowel against a rail. Besides, the job in the galleries seemed important, something only she could do.

At last, she turned to her uncle and nodded.

"That's not fair!" her brother cried.

"Looks like you're stuck with me, Evan," Clare said shrugging. "Is that the worst thing in the world?"

●●◉●●

It took a while to cross the Mosna and make their way through town, and by the time Samantha and Jay arrived at the main site, the sun was beginning its downward arc. The mayor's security concerns had led to the closure of units in other parts of the site, and now students filled the

Circular Plaza, making rapid progress. The foundations of small buildings erected in more recent times had been recorded and cleared away, and the team had dug down to the plaza's original surface—an orderly pattern of yellow paving stones. Samantha spied Zoe and Marisol working together with practiced efficiency. Stuart stood at the nearby screen and flashed her his handsome smile, making her cheeks glow red.

But Jay would not linger. He was ready to get started and, with his niece trailing behind him, marched determinedly up the Circular Plaza's stairway to the entrance of Laberintos, and once again down its stairs and into the Temple's core.

There was no denying it. The foreboding that had hung over Samantha since the Incan girl's disappearance was much stronger in the dark of the Temple's interior. Strange things shone and twinkled at the edge of Samantha's vision as she followed her uncle through the passageways. Here and there, she sensed dull glimmers, impossible reflections in the utter darkness, like the watchful glares of coal-black eyes. Noises played their tricks on her too. Sounds that should have been on her left echoed oddly from her right.

All this disorientation wore at Samantha's nerves. She stayed just behind her uncle as they wended their way through the stone corridors, finding little comfort in the beam of his flashlight and jumping at each odd echo. The gnawing fear of the Madman had found its way back into her subconscious. Perhaps he was looking for some sort of sacrifice, a living girl to match the mummified one he had taken already.

Finally, they turned the final corner and their destination gaped darkly at their feet.

"What do you think, Sam? Still up for this?"

"I think so," she said, trying to sound brave. "I mean, yes. Yes I am."

On her uncle's instruction, she emptied her pockets and placed her trowel and notebook on the floor beside the opening, making herself as small as possible for her descent into the constricted space. Jay handed her a tape measure and then a head lamp, which he helped her to fasten tightly. Samantha twisted the bulb at her forehead into an "on" position so that a beam of light now followed every movement of her head.

"You're all set," Jay whispered. "Just tell me everything you see."

She knelt at the opening, debating for a moment the best way to proceed. Going headfirst would give her the best view of what lay before her but would require an awkward crawl backward when she was ready to exit. Still, to do the job well, it was the better option. She placed her hands into the shaft, took a deep breath, and inched inside.

The passageway consisted of a stairway of long, overlapping stone slabs, and she felt herself pitch forward as the downward slope increased. As she crept along, the slanted ceiling hung lower and lower, until she felt as if the entire mass of the Temple would collapse upon her. After a few meters, however, the ground leveled out, and some of her panic subsided.

"So?" Jay's voice could have come from any direction. "What have we got?"

Samantha cleared her throat and shouted her description aloud.

She was at a four-way intersection. A pair of tunnels ascended to her right and left, while her own continued straight ahead, obscured by the slope of the ceiling. The space widened where the passages met and she was able to rise into a sitting position. She brought out the tape measure and called out the various dimensions of the tiny gallery, the sound of her own voice rattling through her head.

"Wait, wait, Sam!" Jay cried. "Slower! I'm trying to write these down!"

It was small in here, she realized as she took the measurements, but not as small as it seemed from the outside. If they could handle the anxiety, even adults could fit through this passageway with relative ease. Someone as long and lanky as Adam or Chimay would have little difficulty. Even someone with her uncle's broad shoulders could make it through if they were willing to squeeze.

"Want me to measure the other tunnels?" she called.

"Please, Sam. If it looks like it's safe."

She studied each of the branches in turn. Those to her right and left climbed up and away at a gentle slope. When she flattened herself to the ground, her head lamp illuminated where each dead-ended in a wall of rubble and masonry.

But the tunnel ahead of her was different, plowing upward into the heart of the temple at a much steeper angle. The beam of her lamp was blocked by the passage's stepped ceiling, and the only way to find out where it led was to climb farther inside.

Her heart pounding, she moved forward up the incline, the cold of the stone against her hands causing her palms to ache. Ahead of her, her light played across the tightening walls.

Could the Madman find her here, she wondered, and whisk her away like he had the Incan girl? But she pushed the childish worry from her mind.

Finally, she came to the end. She could see from the way the masonry of the floor and ceiling disappeared behind it that the tunnel had once continued deeper into the Temple, but now it was blocked by some sort of debris.

Samantha was about to retreat back toward the intersection when something about the rubble before her caught her eye. Unlike the slate gray of the surrounding walls, the large objects that blocked her way were a yellowish-white and carried an oily shine. They were round in shape but seemed to be of a lighter material than stone. She reached out her hand and touched one.

It popped loose, rolling from its place in the pile and coming to rest between her knees. Samantha recoiled, bumping the back of her head into the ceiling and knocking her lamp askew.

The object staring blankly up at her was a human skull. And the yellowish globes stacked before her represented almost a dozen more.

There was a grating, clacking creak, and then the pile collapsed in an avalanche of bone. The passage was so confined that Samantha had no way to dodge them. Instead, she was propelled backward by the weight of the skulls, their upper ranks of teeth scratching at her forearms.

Samantha did not pause to turn around where the passageway met the others. She powered backward and upward toward the entrance as the skulls skipped and skittered into the junction, filling the chamber in a ghastly, clattering mass. And then she felt her uncle's powerful hands pulling her free, only to leave her gasping and shaken in the stillness of Laberintos.

●●●●●

They sat on the Temple's grassy roof as she recovered her nerves, and Jay tried delicately to make sense of what she had seen. He showed her the rough sketch of the tunnels he had made in his notebook, copied from her shouted measurements. Even in her rattled state, she was pleased by the precision of her uncle's drawing. Just as she had observed, the passageways came together in the shape of a "+." Samantha's voice had echoed terribly from inside, Jay added, and perhaps the passages had performed as some sort of ancient sound system. But whatever their original purpose, at some point in the past, they had come to be used as a burial place for the dead.

"Like how it was for the Incan girl," he explained gently and she shuddered, the Madman again invading her subconscious.

But as much as Samantha tried to share her uncle's viewpoint, she couldn't see things his way. The girl in the West Field had been laid to rest by loving hands, not decapitated and stacked brick-like in an anonymous heap.

Jay had already moved on, treating his niece like some sort of conquering hero. He handed her his notebook and placed a pencil in her hand.

"You explored it, Sam, so you get to name it."

She raised the pencil and, after asking Jay for some help with the translation, wrote four words in a shaking script beside his careful drawing.

Pasos de los Perdidos

The Passages of the Lost.

re Chunk (?)

A couple of good things happened. First Zoe asked what I thought about Then Isabel took me to the So much fun! But it got me thinki about th site. If the galleries

Spanish → English

- ~~Waylin~~ Huelen - they stink
- ~~Serdes~~ Cerdos - pigs
- Nuevo - New
- ~~Yah vey~~ Llave - key
- Divertimos - Have fun
- trece - thirteen
- ~~Pete~~ Peligroso, No Pasar - Danger, do not cross
- Aterrorizar - terrorize

Alfajor - it's like a cookie

Bat

Ceiling caved in! And Jay just thought it was funny

Answer to Stuart's joke:

Hamlet!

Arcade

Office   Pillager?

Temple map

pasos perdidos

Lumion   Laber- imtos galleries   murcielagos   cuartos

CHAPTER 10

"*G*uete morge, *Süße*."

Samantha looked up from her notebook to find one of the European tourists—the old man—standing above her table in the dining room. She had been eager for the time alone, hoping to record her thoughts before the rest of the team filed in for lunch. But the man's smile was friendly behind his full white beard, and Samantha welcomed the interruption.

"*Chann ich...?*" he asked, pointing at the bench opposite. At first, Samantha thought he meant to engage her in some kind of conversation. But then she realized that she had accidentally selected the table where the elderly tourist usually sat with his daughter.

"Sorry," she said, and began to collect her things.

"*Nein, nein,*" the man replied, motioning for her to stay. "All is okay."

Sitting across from her, he took a frayed trail atlas from his knapsack and began to plan his next hike.

"Much…excitement, yes?" he asked, after a few moments had passed.

It took some effort for Samantha to understand his meaning.

"At the site? Yes. We've had a few big discoveries. Some bad things have happened too."

The old man cocked his snowy head.

"Discoveries?"

Hearing her word repeated made it sound ridiculously vague.

"I'll show you," she said, and spun her notebook around. "We're starting to explore these galleries, here. This one is called 'Laberintos gallery.' It's the only way to get to 'Perdidos,' which is here…"

A soft cry cut her explanation short.

"*Chrüz heilige cheib, Papa!*"

It was the other tourist—the daughter—standing like some awkward stork in the doorway. The father threw up his hands in mock desperation as the woman approached.

"*Bitte*, little girl," she asked. "Does he bother?"

"Not at all!" said Samantha, making sure to smile. The woman's patience with her father had clearly thinned over the course of the summer, and Samantha did not want to aggravate the situation.

But it was not enough for the old man's daughter. With a few harsh words, she ushered him out of the dining room just as the excavation team rushed in.

Some minutes later, lunch was in full swing, the parrots' "*¡Corre, corre, corre!*" piercing the noontime ruckus. Adam and Evan seemed almost ready to comply with the parrots' screamed commands. From the way they hung their heads over their lunch plates and slouched glumly in their seats, they seemed likely to slink from the room, out the hostal's gates, through the mountains, and far away from La Banda and all the misery it contained.

It itched just to look at them. Though the pigs were penned inside the other side of the small corral in which Adam and Evan worked, an army of fleas was somehow making the journey through the mud and muck to find refuge in Adam and Evan's hair and clothing. Scatters of red bumps rose from their arms and hands, across their necks, and even below their hairline. Both had scratched themselves raw, and each of their arms was pinpricked with scabs.

And they smelled, quite naturally, like a barnyard. Smears of muck stained their foreheads and clothes, attracting flies while keeping their fellow archaeologists at bay. The señora alone went near them, and only then to place their bowls of soup before them and cluck her tongue against her iridescent teeth.

"Well, that's fitting," Stuart whispered to his table mates. "The Gorilla Guerilla smells like a zoo."

"*Huelen como los cerdos*," Marisol added, pinching her nose. But Zoe shook her head.

"Evan looks so sad, though," she sighed. "Poor kid."

And despite everything, Samantha agreed.

Clare's evening updates had confirmed that work in La Banda was hot, slow, and sticky—made slower and stickier by a few centuries of accumulated pig manure. Nothing of interest had appeared in the unit save a piece of a rusty old shovel blade, the roots of a long-vanished Andean resin-bush, and a Peruvian *10 céntimos* coin dating to the year before. While Clare had somehow managed to avoid the worst of it, directing excavation from a fair distance away, Evan and Adam were disheveled and discouraged, and ate their meals without looking up from their plates.

"Want an *alfajor*?" Samantha asked, approaching her brother with the cookie held at arm's length. He looked at her blankly for a moment before snatching it away.

"I hope you realize this is all your fault." he grumbled, crumbs falling from the corners of his mouth and onto his muck-stained T-shirt. "I'm stuck out in flea-ridden La Banda digging through pig manure all because you had to go and make your stupid little discovery."

At this, Adam raised his head sharply, matching Evan's accusation with a look of livid hatred. It was clear that he, too, blamed Samantha for his misery. But there was something more in his eyes—as if Samantha had thwarted his plans or hindered some dark design. She felt herself slinking away, and left the two of them glaring and seething in their pungent stench.

Stuart winked at her as she returned to her seat, and she felt a blush lay fire across her cheeks.

"Samantha! While we're on the topic, a question for you: which of Shakespeare's plays do pigs like best?"

But Zoe did not give her time to respond with *Hamlet.*

She rose elegantly and ushered Samantha to the other side of the dining room, leaving Stuart with the difficult task of explaining his terrible joke to Marisol in Spanish.

"I wanted to show you something, Sam," Zoe said, opening the door to the field laboratory with a graceful sweep of her arm. "Something strange."

Samantha had seen the laboratory before at the end of the work day, but there was something different about it in the lunchtime hour. Light streamed through the frosted windows so that the lab seemed bright and fresh in comparison to the cramped coziness of the dining room. Inside, among instruments and arrays of laptop computers, the sheaves of paperwork and the bags of artifacts were sorted with methodical care, and Samantha marveled at how order could be brought to the seeming randomness of the work outside. This was where the real archaeology was done, she realized, where patterns and conclusions were plucked scientifically from the chaos.

Zoe withdrew a bag from the shelf and slid its contents into Samantha's open palm.

"We've been finding a bunch of these in the Circular Plaza," she said. "No one seems to know what to make of them. I'd love to get your opinion."

At first, the object seemed to Samantha like a smooth lump of charcoal. She turned it over carefully to examine it from every angle. While one side was rounded, the other was filed flat, and she noticed immediately how it gleamed dully, like pencil lead.

"What does Dr. Huaca think?"

"That it was some sort of jewelry or attached somehow to the outside of the Temple wall as decoration," Zoe said. "They are kind of pretty, the way they glitter like that."

These theories seemed possible, but the beginning of an idea had found its way into Samantha's mind. The object reminded her of something else—something modern, familiar, and commonplace. She wanted to be sure before she offered more than a random guess.

"Can I think about it?" she asked.

"Oh, of course! That's what the rest of us are doing—mulling it over. I know you've done a lot of reading on Peruvian archaeology, so I thought I'd ask your advice."

It was, Samantha thought, the nicest thing anyone had said to her all summer. As Zoe carefully placed the object in its bag, and as they returned together to the raucous dining room, Samantha felt like an equal part of the team.

●●●●●

The deep satisfaction stayed with her through the afternoon and into the evening. But by night it had turned into something else, and Samantha lay restlessly atop her sheets, the light of the streetlamp shining too brightly across her pillow.

The talk with Zoe had altered her in some way. No longer could Samantha simply observe the goings-on around her—the constant analysis, the careful creation of theories and hypotheses. If she was to be an archaeologist here in Chavín, she needed to help in the difficult task of interpreting the discoveries.

Archaeology was, after all, a privilege—one cruelly withheld from the people who had lived in the valley all their lives. Her thoughts turned to Isabel and how excited she had been when she had joined them in the West Field. But the girl had work of her own to do—serious work. Not everyone could spend their days poking around in the mud.

"*Oye, Samantha.*"

There was a tap against her window. She pulled the curtain aside.

Isabel stood in the yellow glow of the streetlamp, readying to lob another pebble. But when she saw Samantha, she cast it aside, flashed her gap-toothed grin, and beckoned for Samantha to come down.

Samantha checked her watch—10:50—then glanced at her brother, out cold on the far side of the room. The misery of his day in La Banda had plunged him into a deep sleep, and there was no risk of waking him. Samantha pulled on her jeans and boots and slipped out of their room and down the stairs without a sound.

With the moon casting eerie shadows across the courtyard, Samantha slid open the bar that locked the hostal's gate and stepped into the quiet street, closing it slowly behind her so that it did not latch completely.

"*Entonces, ¡vámonos!*" said Isabel, and bounded off into the night, Samantha matching her stride for stride.

It was not long before they reached the ancient line of

barrier stones near the village's northern extreme. They gleamed dully in the moonlight, like animal teeth. The sign for the SALON DE VIDEOJUEGOS glowed too, with Chimay's handmade addition beneath it, claiming the Fuentes' family business as his own.

The girls came to a stop before the door, covered by a steel shutter. So this was what Isabel wanted to show her, Samantha realized with a thrill. The arcade, after hours. They would have the place to themselves.

She waited nervously for Isabel to unlock it, but the girl only kicked at the metal shutter.

"*Esto es nuevo*," she said. "*No tengo la llave.*"

Samantha tried to decipher the rapid Spanish—she didn't have the key?—but Isabel was already on the move again. They slipped between the enigmatic stones that marked the median of the street and into Isabel's home.

"But your cousin?" Samantha asked, trying not to sound too anxious.

Isabel dismissed her concerns at once.

"*Está en El Cóndor con Dijota.*"

They stepped inside the neatly kept house, lit by the light of the moon. The smooth dirt floor was covered in places with large rectangles of carpet, and Isabel pulled one back to expose a square of hammered steel. She slid this aside as well, and the girls lowered themselves into the opening beneath.

The cellar was lined with storage units, holding tools and broken video-game consoles. Between the shelves the walls glowed yellow in the soft electric light. They seemed familiar, somehow. Poking her head between two shattered televisions, Samantha was surprised to discover that the wall was made of enormous stone blocks, laid in place by some ancient builder before the Fuentes house was built above it.

Incredible. They were standing in another gallery, so far from the Temple itself. It ran from beneath the Fuentes' home, under the road and its ancient series of stones, to the cellar of the arcade on the opposite side. Samantha followed Isabel up a ladder at the gallery's far end and entered the *salon de videojuegos*.

She could see at once that the arcade wasn't anything like the ones at home. Other than a single pinball machine sitting in the room's far corner, none of the consoles that lined the walls would have been found in at an arcade in Davis, California. Instead, the machines here were all the kind that people could hook up at home, connected with tangles of wires to aging televisions on the tables that lined the room's four walls. They were all on: paused mid-game, or flashing demos and lists of highest scores. Isabel walked her past each one, making sure to point out the current favorite of the village's children—*Pillager of the Past II*—and those games which she herself had beaten.

"*Y ahora,*" she said with a sweep of her hand, "*nos divertimos.*"

It was hard to choose where to begin. Samantha selected a puzzle game, sliding falling blocks into place, while beside her, Isabel set to protecting the good villagers of FaereyRealme from the Daemon Meister's army of goblins. As they played, Samantha began to realize that language was not always the barrier it seemed. With only the bleeps and blurps of the video games to distract them, the girls seemed to be able to convey almost anything to each other in their own languages, using signs, gestures, and patient repetition. But in some ways, what Isabel told her as the hours went on seemed only to widen the gap between their worlds.

Poor, poor Isabel. Her summer had been a difficult one. First, her mother had fallen gravely ill, and it had been decided that she should travel to the south of the country to be among her family. Isabel's father had accompanied his wife, while Isabel stayed behind to care for the livestock and make what money she could by selling her tiny carvings at the site.

"*Pues, tengo trece años,*" Isabel explained when Samantha expressed her astonishment, as if being thirteen years old made the situation seem more reasonable or fair.

But Isabel could not handle all of the family's affairs on her own, and Chimay had been sent from Arequipa to look after the family arcade. As the paper sign in the window showed, the teenager had taken on the responsibility with brash pride, raising the prices of each game and pocketing the extra for himself. Isabel hinted that he also had other, darker dealings with Dijota, but Samantha did not want to press the issue.

And then Samantha remembered the anxious glance

Chimay had given Isabel on their way to the cliffside ruin and how he had kept an uneasy distance from her.

"Why is Chimay afraid of you?" she asked.

Isabel understood her at once.

"*Aja, mira esto,*" she said, pointing.

There was a desk near the arcade's front door, and in the faint light of the video monitors, Samantha could see an envelope. It was open, and a small stack of money peeked out—American bills—with a tally of the sum across the envelope's face.

The handwriting was familiar. Samantha knew it well from the unit and level forms of the West Field.

It was Adam's writing. There was no mistaking it. What business did he have with Chimay?

But that was not what Isabel was trying to show her. She was beckoning Samantha to the nearby window and the glow of the neon sign. With a flourish, Isabel ripped away the paper beneath it, where her cousin had added DE CHIMAY in an act of callous self-promotion.

Taking paper and pen from the desk, and ignoring the money completely, Isabel scrawled a sign of her own.

DEL LADRON

Of the thief.

She then pulled a wastebasket from the corner, uncrumpling her earlier editions for Samantha's viewing:

DEL HUACHAFO

DEL FAITE

DEL DURO

DEL TRAFICANTE

Of the slob. The bully. The cheapskate. The trafficker.

No wonder Chimay was afraid of her. The handwritten accusations, appearing each morning behind a seemingly locked door, would rattle anyone, especially if he had a guilty conscience or had committed some undiscovered crime. With Isabel's lifetime knowledge of the arcade and its secrets, it was only natural that Chimay would assume that his little cousin was somehow involved and that she had some power over him.

Isabel flashed Samantha a devious smile as she taped her newest creation to the windowpane.

"*Aterrorizar es confundir, Samantha. Y confundir es controlar.*"

An hour later, under the covers with a flashlight and a Spanish-English dictionary propped up on her knees, Samantha was finally able to decipher Isabel's words.

"To terrify is to confuse," the girl had said, with wisdom far beyond her years. "And to confuse is to control."

•• ● ••

The next morning, Samantha was back in the cool majesty of the Temple's interior. She was tired from her night's adventure but recovered from the horrors of Perdidos and thrilled by the promise of the day ahead.

Now they stood in a long gallery, bedecked on one wall with a string of bare electric bulbs. The wires were draped over a series of ancient stone pegs, protruding from the wall at regular intervals. Jay flipped a switch and a weak yellow light sputtered forth.

"This one's sometimes open to tourists," he explained apologetically.

"Where are we, Uncle Jay?"

"This," he announced, with characteristic flair, "is the *Cautivos* gallery."

"*Cautivos?*" Samantha asked, trying to come up with a similar-sounding word in English.

"Captives, Sam. Named by someone with an active imagination."

He lifted his hands above his head, placed his wrists beside two of the pegs, and pretended to hang from them like a prisoner in a comic strip.

Samantha smiled, and they moved farther down the hallway to a gap in the right-hand wall. A wooden sign had been wedged into the opening, screaming in large white letters: PELIGROSO, NO PASAR.

But Jay cast it aside before she could let the meaning sunk in.

"For tourists, kiddo," he said with a cavalier grin. "Not for us."

She stooped to peer through the opening, but the darkness of the inner chamber was impenetrable.

"What's in there?"

Her uncle's response was kind but firm.

"That's what you're going to tell me."

Samantha studied the doorway before her. It was clear

that it had once been large enough to allow a man of Jay's stature to squeeze through without much difficulty. But at some point in the last two thousand years, one end of the massive stone lintel had fallen from its place above the door so that it now cut diagonally across the opening. It would be a tight fit, even for a smallish, twelve-year-old girl.

The sign's meaning was now clear.

"You're sure it's safe?"

"I think so, Sam. But I can't honestly say for certain."

He must have sensed her anxiety because he continued in a gentler tone.

"But let's think about the odds. Over the last few decades—centuries, probably—that stone hasn't budged. Not through earthquakes or landslides, or from all the tourists who have tramped by it. The chances that you could dislodge it are small."

"Still," Jay added, "it's entirely up to you."

The urgency in his voice hinted otherwise.

She pounded the lintel with her fist. It seemed solid enough.

"Okay," she said at last. "I'll do it."

She slipped her head lamp into place, pulling her braids through the straps at the back and switching on the powerful beam. Now she could see a steep staircase inside, leading down into the darkness.

Dropping to her stomach, she reached her hands in first, gripped the edge of the uppermost step and pulled, pushing with her feet at the same time. Soon her head was through, and then her shoulders, and then—a grinding pain in her hips and a sickening panic in her stomach. She tried to squeeze back through the opening and into the dim electric light, but there was nothing to push against. She couldn't move.

"Uncle Jay?"

From somewhere above her, a pebble was dislodged, clattering against the stone walls and glancing stingily off her shoulder. She had a sudden, deep sense of dread—a frantic urge to retreat before the ancient ceiling gave way and crushed her.

"Hang on, Sam."

Samantha arched her back, giving a final kick with her feet. Nothing happened.

"I've got you," said her uncle. "Relax."

But when Jay's hands wrapped around her ankles, it was to push her forward, not to pull her back into the safety of the outer gallery. There was a tremendous pain in her back and hips, and a rising horror inside her chest. Then she was through—a crumpled ball at the top of the stairs.

She pulled herself shakily to her feet. She was fine, if a little scraped, but already she dreaded her eventual exit.

The fumes hit her almost immediately as she descended the narrow steps—a sharp chemical odor that seared her nostrils and brought tears to her eyes. They grew stronger as she made her way downward, and the head lamp's beam seemed to quiver as it passed through the thick vapor.

Soon, she was in what appeared to be a long, grand hallway at the foot of the stairs.

"Sam?"

She gave a last look backward and, through her watery vision, saw her uncle's face, framed by a halo of dim electric light.

"I'll be right here."

"Okay," Samantha managed, but she did not feel reassured.

She turned the head lamp to the right, and a chamber opened up, yawning darkly from the eastern wall. To her left, another chamber gaped gloomily, and shadows ahead of her showed that two more rooms came off this central corridor. The massive stones seemed to bow outward, straining under the weight of the centuries. She felt a quick wave of relief that Evan was not with her: he would have surely tested the stability of the masonry with a kick or a shove.

The floor was covered in a gritty gray substance, form-ing small hillocks in some places that Samantha had to sidestep. These, it was quickly apparent, were the source of the smell, and while many sat like mounds of dry sand, others gleamed wetly in the light of the beam. She did her best to keep the goo off her hiking boots.

When she came to the center of the long hallway, she stopped and opened her notebook. Her nose was running furiously now, the smell of the strange substance penetrat-ing everything. She found a dry spot to sit on the floor from where she could make her measurements, clearing the area as best she could with the edge of her foot. Again and again, she extended the taut yellow ribbon of her tape measure until it clacked against the chamber's walls, scribbling the numbers in her notebook.

"Sam?"

"All set!"

"Then come on back."

It had taken her several minutes, and by now, she had almost gotten used to the odor. As she stood, though, the smell broke through again with fury, and she decided to hasten her exit.

But halfway back to the foot of the stairs, she froze. Something above her had shifted. For the first time since she entered the gallery, Samantha looked up.

At first glance, the ceiling seemed to be draped with a blanket of dry, dead leaves, curled and blackened like the last of an autumn's foliage. As she passed the beam of her head lamp among the papery husks, a shiver seemed to go through them, making them sway as if stirred by the wind.

And then the ceiling collapsed on top of her.

She threw her hands up to cover her face, and immediately there was a warm and furious flapping along the length of her arms. Bats gripped at her hair and clothing. She swatted at them with her trowel, the beam of her lamp broken by hundreds of panicked rodents. The cloud grew thicker as they coursed in a churning mass for the opening to Cautivos, blocking her exit and the light it provided.

Coughing, she plunged through them toward the

staircase, dodging the mounds of their pungent guano. She leapt up the steps two at a time. Through the tiny opening, Jay was waiting for her, covering his own face with his hands as the bats flew for the open air outside.

"Grab my hands, Sam! I'll pull you through!"

She dove for the opening through the roiling frenzy, reaching frantically for her uncle. Her head went through easily, but to her horror her shoulders caught, crushing a pair of bats against the collapsed doorframe. She twisted away from their writhing bodies and was stuck again with hundreds of bats beating against her back and legs in their frantic struggle for an exit.

Jay tightened his grip on her wrists and heaved. There was a terrible moment when she felt her body stretch and crack, but at last she was wrenched free and on her feet. And then she was being pushed by her uncle through the stinking swarm to the gallery's entrance.

In a moment they were free, throwing themselves down on the Temple's grassy roof and sucking in deep breaths of the clean Andean air. Samantha examined her arms and legs, noting with relief that while she was a little scraped, she was unbitten and otherwise unharmed.

"*Murciélagos*," Jay announced.

"What?" Samantha asked, still breathless.

"A good name for it, don't you think? *Galería de los Murciélagos*: Gallery of the Bats!"

She was still in shock, unable to respond. But Jay took no notice of her distress, throwing back his head and roaring with infuriating laughter until tears streamed from his eyes.

•••••

Samantha was still trembling as they crossed to the other side of the structure, coming into sight of the Circular Plaza and the majority of the archaeological team.

They were not at work. Instead, the dozen archaeologists stood staring silently upward, transfixed. At first, Samantha thought they were looking at her, and again she quickly examined herself for signs of her misadventure. But then, Stuart and Marisol raised their fingers and pointed toward the sky behind her.

"*Mira.*"

"Look."

Wearily, she turned around. Bats were still streaming from the Temple behind them, a dark stain across the late-afternoon sky. But while some were winging their way in jagged lines from the direction of Cautivos' entrance, others coursed like smoke from some unknown exit on the Temple's western face—proving, yet again, that the Temple still held its greatest secrets fast.

A sharp cry brought everyone's attention around. From her vantage point, Samantha could see the main gate, and sudden rage pulled her from her stupor. It was Adam, chasing a wailing Alejandro into the site. Farther away, Clare could be seen, running up the road as fast as she could and shouting at Adam to stop it at once.

There were gasps when Adam and Alejandro came around the corner and into view of the crowd in the Circular Plaza. Jay's student wasn't touching Alejandro, but he was propelling him forward with a torrent of threats and cursing. The small boy's pleas served only to make Adam angrier.

Alejandro ran to them, hurrying to hide among the crowd. Adam must have pursued him all the way from his grandparents' house. The damp marks and dust on the boy's trouser legs showed how Adam had forced him across the ford of the Rio Mosna and then through the streets of the town. It must have been humiliating. It must have been terrifying.

"Professor Sutton, Professor Huaca," Adam spat, his sunglasses akimbo and his hat lopsided on his head. "I seem to have found our thief."

He tried to grab for the boy, screaming words in Spanish and English.

"*¡Demuéstreles!*" he shouted. "Show it to them now!"

But Alejandro shook his head, incensing Adam further. He pushed the boy's protectors aside and snatched him by the collar, sending the uppermost buttons flying. There was another gasp from the crowd as Adam pulled something free of the fabric and let it hang from its cord against Alejandro's chest. Samantha saw a metallic glint but was too far away to make out what it was.

Clare came running into the plaza. She threw herself between the boy and Adam, shoving hard against his wrestler's frame to clear a safe distance between them. Her face was flushed and furious.

"Don't touch him," she seethed, still out of breath. "You leave him alone."

Alejandro was crying now, sobbing and coughing in little gulping whimpers. Adam moved away, self-righteous and sneering, confident that his actions were just.

Alejandro looked embarrassed when he saw Samantha coming toward him and tried not to cry. But it was no use, and he buried his head in his arms.

"Are you okay?" she asked, but he was too upset to answer. Her eyes wandered to where the pendant dangled from a cord around his neck.

It was an artifact of some kind. And it was made of gold.

Osvaldo turned on Jay. With a finger pointed at Adam, he barked, "Get him out of here."

Jay reacted at once. He grabbed his student by the arm, shoving him through the crowd and out of the site just as Alejandro had been dragged in.

"He's the thief!" Adam shouted as they disappeared around the corner. "And he's friends with Samantha. That niece of yours must not be able to keep her mouth shut!"

Spanish → English

Alejandro's Pendant

- No te ~~prayoeupee~~ preocupes -
  Don't worry
- Todo está bien - Everything's okay
- No hice nada malo -
  I don't do anything wrong
- Regalo - present/gift
- Me lo dio - He gave it to me
- Calcinado - burnt?
- No teníamos la intención de ofenderse -
  We didn't mean to upset you

cuy - guinea pig.

Temple map

escalinata
pesos pecados
columnas - vigas gali
listecos
canchas
Laberintos galleries
murcielagos
Lanzón

So gross. She practically pulled off it's head, and then she used her thumbs to break open the rib cage and pull out all the guts.

Ofrendas gallery

Almost all the ceramics are broken, but it's stranger than that. It's as if someone took all the broken pie and

was going to Kill Jay.
And Evan still doesn't know what happened

CHAPTER 11

On Osvaldo's orders, the workday came to a sudden end. The students disbanded, casting confused glances at the small boy and his glinting ornament.

"*No te preocupes, amiguito,*" Osvaldo soothed him. "*Todo está bien.*"

Samantha stared at the object—a diamond-shaped medallion of flattened gold incised with a web of fine designs. It was clearly from Chavín—the patterns of jumbled eyes and teeth and beaks matched the shapes on other Chavín artifacts and even those on the Lanzón itself. But such an artifact must have been very rare. No one had found anything like it all summer.

"It happened so quickly," said Clare. "Adam saw it shining between Alejandro's buttons and just lunged."

They continued to comfort Alejandro, crouching around him in a protective circle, and at last he brought his hands away from his eyes.

"We should ask him where he found it, I suppose," Clare offered hesitantly.

Her colleague nodded, and framed the question as slowly and as gently as he could. Alejandro listened, sniffling and wiping his eye on his sleeve.

"*¡No soy ladrón!*" he spluttered when Osvaldo had finished. "*¡No hice nada malo!*"

But the professor's soothing voice again consoled him, assuring him that no one thought that he was a thief or that he had done anything wrong. The question was only where he had gotten the pendant. It was very important that he told them.

"*Era un regalo,*" the boy finally muttered, sliding the pendant back inside his shirt.

"A gift?" Clare asked. "From whom?"

But Alejandro was done talking. His distress had morphed into wounded defiance.

"It's just as well," Osvaldo said. "It could have been in his family for generations. I think we should just leave the poor boy alone."

They turned to leave.

"I'll wait with him," Samantha spoke up. "Just until he feels better."

••●••

They sat in silence as Alejandro plucked at the grass around his shoes, his eyes fixed sullenly on the ground.

"Alejandro," Samantha began, determined to cheer him up. "Do you want to see something?"

After a moment he nodded, and she helped him upright so that he could follow her across the Circular Plaza and up the grand staircase on its opposite side. Her plan was a simple one, but she was confident that it would work. Alejandro just needed a chance to prove his bravery. Then he'd feel better, for sure.

"*El Lanzón*," she announced when they reached the door to the gallery.

"*¿Aquí?*" he asked, unable to believe that the model for his tiny carvings was so close at hand.

She nodded vigorously and he stepped forward, pausing when he saw that she was not going with him. Samantha smiled and gave him her head lamp. It was his to keep, she did her best to sign. She could just get another from the lab.

"I'll wait for you," she said, pointing at her feet. "I'll be right here."

Alejandro nodded again, took a deep breath, and disappeared inside.

When he emerged a few minutes later, only his tattered shirt collar gave any hint of his earlier misfortune. Her idea had worked. He was himself again.

"*¡El Lanzón!*" he said, grinning. "*¡Wow!*"

Samantha grinned, and the two broke into laughter.

"Your pendant," she said, pointing at his chest. "Can I see?"

Alejandro's face grew solemn, but he slipped it from around his neck and handed it to her. She spent some minutes admiring it, running her fingertips over its beautiful designs and marveling at its unexpected heft.

"Who gave it to you?" she asked, and right away she regretted it. Even Clare and Osvaldo had said that Alejandro should be left alone.

"*Es un secreto*," he said at last.

"It's okay," she said. "You don't have to tell me anything."

Again Alejandro hesitated. When he finally spoke, his voice was just a whisper.

"*El Loco me lo dio.*"

She understood immediately.

The Madman had given it to him.

Two contradictory certainties clashed in her mind. There was no such thing as ghosts. She was sure of it. But still, Alejandro's every word rang true.

It could not be, and yet it had to be.

And for the first time, she knew that the Madman was real.

•••●••

The burden of Alejandro's secret weighed on Samantha for several days. As she and her uncle mapped gallery after gallery, images of the Madman flashed in her mind. She feared that he would come grasping for her around each shadowy corner to make his revenge complete.

Somehow, this fear had attached itself to her guilt over the theft of the Incan girl's mummy, and the two churned in her subconscious. Her creeping anxiety refused to leave her as days turned to weeks, and her nervousness returned each morning as she plunged into the darkness anew.

Of course, she would still get excited as the Temple Complex's chambers and tunnels revealed wonder after wonder. There were the stately columns and beams of the *Columnas-Vigas* gallery, the graceful double staircase of *Escalinata*, the spacious and complicated *Líticos*—though its namesake stone artifacts had been excavated, cataloged, and removed by other archaeologists long, long ago.

What were the galleries for? she continued to ask herself. How could their complicated twists and turns have been negotiated in darkness?

They were strange in other ways too. Jay would make a game of ducking into one of the Temple's shadowy entrances, leaving Samantha standing outside to guess where he would next emerge. And when he did reappear in the daylight, it was always a little more quickly and at a slightly greater distance than Samantha expected, as if the Temple's strange dominion reached through space and time.

But as the excitement from these experiments ebbed, the uneasiness would return, and Samantha would be plagued with nightmares. As she slept, she would find herself on the majestic stone staircase above the Circular Plaza—alone and unable to speak or move. Deafened by the buzzing of unseen flies, she would watch with muted horror as a shadowy form materialized across the Rio Mosna. It would vanish for a moment, only to appear again and again, closer and closer, moving toward her across the site at an impossible speed—first in the Plaza Mayor, then the upper terrace, then finally just below her at the foot of the stairs. Fixing her with coal-black eyes, it would open its jaws, releasing its tongue to slither snake-like up the steps. Only when it had curled around Samantha's waist would she wake to shiver in the dark until dawn.

She attempted to bury her anxiety in the pages of books. Sitting in the hostal's courtyard in the early evening, soothed by the aroma of the señora's rosebushes, she would try to focus on whatever volume lay open across her knees. And for a while, her fear would melt away and the specter of the Madman would fade from her thoughts.

This evening, the book that diverted her attention was one of Clare's own: a massive compendium on the art of Chavín, published two years before. Poring over the dense paragraphs, Samantha marveled at the professor's writing. She still could not believe she knew the woman described on the book's back cover as "someone who has earned her own place in Chavín's pantheon of mighty and enigmatic gods."

Samantha could hear her friend's voice in the book's lengthy sentences—authoritative, confident, but with a quiet humor, as well. She could tell why her uncle liked Clare so much.

When Samantha looked up from Clare's discussion of Amazonian animal iconography in Chavín carvings, she realized she was not alone. She was sharing the courtyard with one of the European tourists. The middle-aged woman sat at the bench just inside the hostal's main gate, surrounded by the backpacks, provisions, and hiking poles needed for another journey into the high country.

As Samantha watched, the woman's father came down the stairs to join her, and she rose to kiss him where his snow-white sideburns met his wispy beard.

Samantha's thoughts turned to her own parents. Raymond and Phoebe Sutton would not fare well in the Andes. Samantha knew both of her parents as people who preferred to control their surroundings. In their view, there was no point to travel unless it was a part of some business venture—a position evident in the box of cosmetics now collecting dust under Samantha's bed. A quick glance at the synced calendars on their laptop computers would show that among their client meetings and scheduled conference calls, specific time slots were allocated even for such basic activities as "coffee," "shower," and "dinner at home."

No, she concluded. Her parents wouldn't last two days.

Distracted, Samantha could not engage with the book again, and she was relieved by the friendly "*Hola*" that interrupted her. Isabel had entered the courtyard and was giving her a boisterous wave. Samantha set down her book and ran over to greet her.

Dangling from Isabel's hand was a cage, flat and wide, its four sides meshed with chicken wire. Within, half a dozen little bodies quivering in a furry huddle.

Guinea pigs, she realized, adorable and cuddly. Just like the ones in the pet shops back home.

"*Cuy*," Isabel explained, "*para la señora*."

Samantha peered closer. Perhaps the señora had tired of the obnoxious parrots at last, and would finally move them away from the dining room and out of earshot while the guinea pigs would take their place.

As Samantha tickled one of the animals' soft fur through a gap in the wire, Isabel raised her fingers to her lips and made a nibbling sound. Samantha nodded. She had played with guinea pigs before. She was not worried about getting bitten.

Samantha followed Isabel into the dining room and then into the adjacent kitchen, where a large, flat pan was spluttering oil on the old, blackened stove. The señora was waiting, and as they entered, she scolded Isabel for her tardiness. What was the rush, Samantha wondered? Dinnertime was approaching, but surely, the archaeologists could put up with one more meal without the new pets to entertain them.

Irritably, the señora placed the cage on the high wooden table beside the stove and lifted one rodent through the lid. It whimpered tiny cries of "*cuy, cuy, cuy, cuy*" as the señora inspected it.

"*Bueno*," she said to Isabel, satisfied at last, and placed a small stack of coins in the young girl's open palm.

Then the señora tightened her grip on the rodent's squirming body, grasped its head with her other hand, and twisted, as if she were wringing out a towel. There was a loud pop, and the guinea pig went limp in her hand. Samantha stared, open-mouthed, as the old woman used a knife to split the animal's belly from chin to tail, dug her thumbs into the opening, and pried it open like a grapefruit. With practiced technique, she gutted it, then slid a knife beneath the skin, removing it in a single piece, and placed the butterflied body in the sizzling pan.

Despite the delicious aroma that immediately wafted toward her, Samantha felt a wave of nausea. She was relieved when the señora shooed them from the kitchen, another live guinea pig wriggling in her grasp.

When the steaming bowl of cuy stew was placed before her that evening, and as the other archaeologists were heartily digging into their dinners, Samantha couldn't even lift her spoon. From her comrades' excited voices it was clear that they didn't know or didn't care that they were eating animals that were kept as beloved pets back home. She saw Stuart picking a tiny bone from between his teeth and Evan raising his bowl to his lips to empty it of its remaining broth.

Beside her, Jay had piled his own spoon high with the flavorful meat.

"Not hungry, Sam?" he asked, chewing happily.

Samantha raised her spoon to her lips and sipped some of the broth. But that was all she could manage. When she looked up, her uncle was shaking his head and smiling.

"Sam," he scolded. "Dig in! Tomorrow is going to be a big day for you, and you'll need your strength. Besides," he said, leaning in, "you've been eating cuy all summer."

●●◉●●

"This will be your claim to fame, Sam. I can just feel it."

Crouched low, Samantha smiled at her uncle's

pronouncement but kept her head lamp trained on the strokes of her trowel.

They were in a new gallery now, hidden in the rise of earth just to the north of the Circular Plaza. Two students had found it earlier in the week when the floor of their unit collapsed, sending them tumbling into a low, dark corridor below. No organized excavation of the gallery's floor had ever taken place, but the students' descriptions of the long chamber—with its scatter of potsherds and bone fragments—made it too tempting to pass up. Bruised and unnerved, the students were more than happy to hand the excavation duties over to Jay and his niece.

Entrance to the gallery was made through what had been the floor of the unit above. It was another unpleasant squeeze. Beyond the opening, a long corridor extended, just tall enough for Samantha to stand.

But Samantha found that it was not a simple hallway. A series of cells opened up to the left, one after the other after the other, until she had counted nine in her head. The matted glint of potsherds flashed dully from many of their floors.

As she troweled the soft soil of her unit, a cold wind seemed to emanate from the far end of the gallery. There was a square ventilation hole there, leading somewhere into the unknowable. The frigid air seemed to rush from the hole in human gasps, and she could see her own breath by the light of her head lamp.

Osvaldo was here too, keeping a cool distance. His visits

were far more supervisory than they were social. Whatever had broken in their friendship after the theft of the Incan girl's mummy remained unfixed, and Adam's man-handling of Alejandro had worsened the situation. Now the Peruvian professor crouched by the entrance, examining artifacts in the stream of outside light.

"*Hueso calcinado*," he announced, passing the artifact to his colleague.

Jay nodded, turning it over in its hand.

"Burned bone," he agreed, sliding the artifact into a bag, "and it's human."

The tension between the two professors was still palpable. It made Samantha wish that she was working under Clare's supervision on the Ocllo property, despite the fleas, the pigs, and their putrid manure. But the prospect of digging alongside Adam again, under the colorless gaze of Alejandro's sinister grandparents, pushed the thought roughly from her mind.

The soil inside the gallery was soft and damp, protected from the heat of the Andean sun that baked the soil outside into almost impenetrable concrete. Her trowel cut so easily into the dirt that she had to slow herself and made each stroke just a small flick of her wrist.

Minutes after Osvaldo left them, amazing ceramics began to emerge—shiny or black or featuring splashes of cinnabar red. At first, they bagged and tagged each one, but as more and more seemed to emerge in regular groups, Jay decided that each cluster needed to be mapped in some detail.

"This is amazing, Sam," he said. "Something is definitely going on here."

Just as she began to examine her uncle's sketch, there was a loud squawk from Jay's satchel. He threw it open and pulled free the walkie-talkie.

Samantha knew that the excavation team had three of these radios, one for each of the professors. She also knew that they were for emergency use only, and her pulse quickened as she strained to make sense of the radio's noises. The thick stone walls made it hard to get a signal.

"Hello?" Jay called, hurrying for the exit. "Hello? What did you say?"

There was a screechy reply, becoming gradually comprehensible as Jay reached the opening. It was Clare's voice, coming through in panicked bits and pieces.

"…situation here…very, *very* angry…"

Samantha could see the silhouette of her uncle, raising the radio to his lips.

"Wait, Clare. I can't hear you."

The response was clearer this time, and immediate.

"…come quickly, Jay," Clare's voice crackled through the speaker. "Come at once."

He pulled himself from the gallery, turning only to shout: "Sam! Stay put!"

Then all was silent again, the commotion swallowed by the gallery's depth and darkness.

●●●●●

At first, she followed her uncle's request, but the hush of the gallery slowly intensified her dread. Was someone hurt in La Banda? Had something happened to her brother? Had something happened to her brother?

Before she knew it, Samantha found herself scurrying outside. She rushed past the team in the Circular Plaza, ignoring their shouted questions of concern, and flew out the main gate. As she hastened down the road, Jay was nowhere in sight, and she knew that there was no way that she could catch up with him. And yet she tried, sprinting into the town, through the Plaza de Armas, and the alleys beyond, and across the angry torrent of the Rio Mosna—the stepping-stones rising just above the raging water. A near misstep brought her foot down in the river, and the water filled her boot like icy fire.

But there was no time to waste. Soon she was running again, charging through La Banda to the Ocllos' residence and the pigsties beyond.

From the riverbank, the monoliths completely blocked whatever emergency was unfolding behind them, and it was only when she ran around them that she saw what was happening.

It was a lot to take in.

The first thing she noticed was the state of the unit. Clare, Adam, and Evan had carved a tidy rectangle from the muck of the pigsty, its profiles beautifully smooth despite the piles of manure that loomed nearby.

But this precision had been violently defiled. On

the other side of the sty's rough-hewn fence, the pig trough had been overturned. As she looked more closely, Samantha realized that the trough had covered a deep recess, and she recognized the masonry of yet another gallery—here where it would never be expected, several hundred yards away and across the seething Rio Mosna from the Temple itself.

Slowly, Samantha began to take in the other people present. Adam, his face a fiery red, bristled beside the upturned trough, while Evan cowered in the unit, terrified. Alejandro watched in horror from several steps away, while Clare and Jay were speaking in frantic Spanish to a pair of people who seemed eager to do them harm.

These were Señor and Señora Ocllo. As the old woman clenched her two ornamental canes, raising them threateningly above her head, her aged husband gripped the sword of his ancestors. And he seemed more than capable of using it.

"Stay back, Samantha." Jay cautioned.

Clare was now speaking to the old man in a hushed, soothing tone.

"*Tranquilese, señor. No teníamos la intención de ofenderse.*"

But Señor Ocllo showed no sign of calming down. The raised sword flashed its graven motto of revenge.

"Evan," Samantha whispered across the yard. "What's going on?"

"What's it look like?" her brother hissed from the cover of his unit. "He just went crazy!"

"But what happened?"

"I don't know! Clare told Adam he was doing something wrong, and Adam got mad and kicked the pig trough over. And just as we see that there's some sort of chamber underneath it, all of a sudden *he* comes after us with that sword!"

Jay had taken a careful step toward Señor Ocllo, but the old man's grip on the hilt remained steady, poised to bring the blade down on the archaeologists in a sharp, deadly sweep.

"It seems that I've discovered an unfortunate family secret," Adam spat. "Looks like the Ocllos have been sitting on their own little gallery. I bet they've been stealing things out of it for years."

Clare continued her calming mantra, but Adam was having none of it.

"You're wasting your time, Professor. The old man only speaks Quechua."

But then Señor Ocllo seemed to fix his pure white eyes on Samantha and spoke in high-pitched, halting Spanish:

"*Él ha vuelto. Él viene.*"

"Who has returned? Who is coming?" Jay asked, his hands still up to protect his face.

The old man spoke again, almost whispering through his cracked lips, and as Samantha translated the words in her mind, a terrible understanding rippled down her spine.

"*El Loco,*" the old man hissed in Spanish. "*Está aquí!*" He's here!

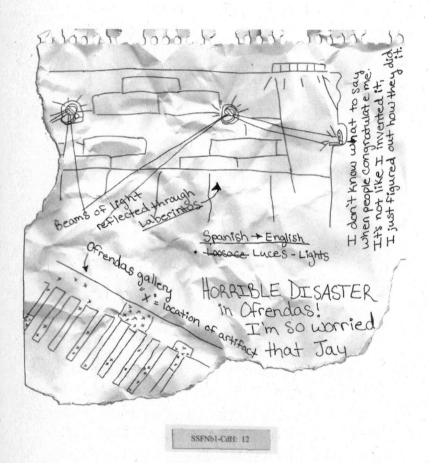

SSFNb1-CdH: 12

CHAPTER 12

Evan and Samantha were not invited to the emergency meeting at the hostal that evening, but none of the students were either. The three professors had secluded themselves in the lab. Rumors coursed among the dinner tables, Evan hastening their spread with his own embellishments in English and Spanish.

"That old Ocllo guy went *crazy*! *¡Completamente loco!* I swear he was trying to *kill* me and Adam! Good thing I'm so quick on my feet, because otherwise, he would've cut me in *half*."

But Samantha knew, or thought she knew, that this was not what had happened. She recalled the desperation in the old man's chalk-white eyes and heard again his high-pitched wail—his frantic pronouncement that the Madman had returned, and that he was coming for them.

Had he had been trying to warn them? Perhaps they owed him their lives.

Samantha picked up her fork, surprised to see that her

hand still trembled. The Madman story was strong in the Ocllo family, and the old man's intensity spoke of some terrible firsthand knowledge. It was as if he himself had witnessed the menace the Loco represented, and he alone grasped the danger of his ghost.

Samantha sighed, finished what she could of her cuy and rice, and retreated numbly to her room. Some minutes later, there was a knock on her door, and Samantha was relieved to see Clare in the hallway outside. She tried to keep a brave face as she motioned the professor in.

"I'm so sorry you saw that happen," Clare said, sitting down next to Samantha on her bed. "Unfortunately, I think Adam is right. Señor Ocllo is a sick old man."

Samantha looked up her, studying her remorseful eyes.

"Don't worry, Sam," Clare continued, placing a reassuring hand upon her shoulder. "You're safe, and your brother is too. We're closing the unit down and moving all work back to this side of the river. We won't let anything like that happen again."

Samantha was quiet for a moment. Part of her wanted to disclose everything she knew about the Madman, about Alejandro and his mysterious secret. But she couldn't bring herself to tell the professor. Clare might have no patience for the tall tales of a little kid. And besides, Samantha thought, remembering both Jay's hushed conversation at the soccer game and the professors' clandestine embrace, she wasn't the only one with secrets.

"What about Adam?" she asked, breaking the silence at last.

Clare exhaled slowly and gave her a sad smile.

"Jay is going to have to deliver some bad news to him tonight, I'm afraid. With everything that happened with your West Field unit earlier in the summer, Osvaldo is still not going to let Adam work at the main site. Your uncle says that he's just going to need to find some other way to occupy his time."

This was, Samantha thought, one of Jay's most terrible ideas to date.

●●◉●●

Over the next several days, the valley's troubles and terrors dissolved somewhat as greater and greater wonders were revealed. Every morning, after greeting a happy Isabel and a quieter Alejandro as they readied their tiny replicas for sale outside the site's main gate, Samantha and her uncle would descend into the quiet darkness of the new gallery beside the Circular Plaza.

Working by the light of kerosene lamps, they scraped slowly at the chamber's soft floor with gentle strokes of their trowels. The vapor of their breath was visible in the lamplight as it met with the cold air flowing in periodic drafts from the small opening in the gallery's eastern end. They would emerge into the searing sunlight and commotion of the Circular Plaza long enough to screen for any fleck or sherd they had missed, then retreat into the stillness of the Temple's interior.

Each day in the gallery brought a new surprise. In Samantha's unit, dug into the third cell off the chamber's main artery, she revealed potsherd after potsherd, until it was clear that some ancient hand had stacked them here, with careful devotion, in tidy little piles. Some were of the plain, gray type that had been most common in the West Field, but others were gloriously painted, slathered in vibrant cinnabar or incised with patterns or pictures of fanged and winged beasts. Jay let out a hoot when Samantha encountered her first intact vessel some inches down, just at the opening of the chamber. It was a jug, the color of fresh cream, with heavy lines of red across its body.

Jay was making discoveries of his own. Two bones emerged from the damp soil of the main corridor, just outside the light of the entryway. Each had a pointed end and another that had been flattened and widened, like a spatula.

Soon, the floor of her unit was a bristling carpet of ceramics—including complete vessels as well as the small stacks of carefully arranged potsherds.

"Look at how much of it there is!" Jay said, raising the lamp over the trove. "And the pottery types—some are from hundreds of miles away. They're like gifts, Sam. Like offerings to Chavín."

The observation rang true, and Samantha printed *Galería de las Ofrendas* over the diagram in her notebook.

The work was so exhilarating and provided such a satisfying refuge from the anxieties of the project that Samantha began to dread the daily break for lunch. She still liked the camaraderie of the dining room, of course—especially now that Adam was almost always absent—but she was too antsy to enjoy the company of others, too eager to return to whatever pot or bone tool that she had left poking upward from the gallery's floor. And after the theft of the Incan girl, there was always the risk that their finds would go missing if she were gone for too long, no matter how vigilant the site's guards promised they would be.

Lunchtime also meant coming into contact with her brother. With the Ocllo unit closed, Evan Sutton had nothing to do, and he made no effort to hide his frustration.

At first, Jay had tried to place him in the lab, sketching and classifying potsherds. That assignment lasted less than two days.

"Are you kidding me with this?" Evan had cried, catching sight of his uncle as the team assembled for the noontime meal.

"Settle down, Ev," said Jay.

"Oh, I'm pretty much as *settled* as I can be! Sorting broken stuff all day, drawing pictures of trash. Forget it! It's boring. And *they*," he indicated the other lab workers, "are boring too."

"Hey, hey, hey. Cool it."

"Why don't you just have the Archaeo Kid do this," Evan went on. "She's the one who likes the boring stuff."

In a way, he was right. Samantha knew that she would enjoy working in the lab. Fitting the excavated pottery into a sequence, establishing a timeline, seeing traces of fingerprints from thousands of years ago—it all seemed appealing to her. But her work in the gallery was more exciting. And, though the students were all still so kind to her, she knew from their envious glances that her work was truly special. Besides, according to Jay, because of the tight spaces that undoubtedly lay ahead, it was still a job that only she could do. She couldn't trade it with anyone, even if she had wanted to.

"Look, Evan. I'll find you something else to do, but you need to be patient. It might take a couple days. Read a book or something until I figure it out."

But if Evan spent any of the next few days reading, Samantha couldn't figure out when. He was far too busy exerting his dominance at the arcade or, to his sister's embarrassment, flirting with the village's many pretty girls in the Plaza de Armas. Evan needed reassignment, and Samantha was eager for it to happen soon.

So it was with mixed feelings that she heard the news.

"This is going to be a lot of work, kiddo," Jay said. "Documenting all this? Entering everything on the forms? We're going to need some help."

She nodded. But her hope that their assistance would come in the form of Zoe or—even better—Stuart was short-lived.

"I guess it's your brother's lucky day, Sam. Why don't you go find him?"

•••••

Samantha made her way back to the hostal at a deliberate pace. She crossed the bridge noting that, like the Mosna, the Wacheqsa was ferocious now, frothing up and over its banks.

When she reached the hostal, Evan was nowhere to be found.

"*¿Tu hermano? No está aquí,*" said the señora, stoking the fire under the hot-water heater in the courtyard.

"*¿Aquí? No,*" said Marisol in the lab, adding in a relieved whisper: "*Gracias a diós.*"

She thanked them and left the hostal. She knew exactly where she would find him. She trudged through town until she reached the ancient barrier and then stepped past the glowing neon sign and into the video arcade.

A crowd of young kids and teenagers had grouped around one of the televisions, and she knew that Evan was among them.

"*Cincuenta centimes,*" a nasal voice said harshly in her ear.

Chimay had removed himself from the spectators. A quick scan of the room confirmed that Isabel was not here to help her.

"What?"

"Mo-ney," he said, wrapping his lips around each syllable.

"You heard the man, Archaeo Kid," Evan shouted from the other side of the room. "Pay up."

Samantha fished five brass coins from her pocket and placed them in Chimay's waiting hand. She then squeezed though the assembled throng to where her brother sat, pounding away at a grimy controller.

"Hey, Samantha, remember this?"

On the screen, an earlier, cruder version of the Pillager was using some ancient spear to whack her way through a frenzy of giant bats, somewhere along the Great Wall of China.

"Now *this* is archaeology," Evan said. "Don't you wish this kind of stuff happened at Chavín?"

Samantha shook her head.

"Happens to me all the time."

Suddenly, the remaining bats on the screen coalesced into an enormous black dragon, and when the Pillager finished it off with a stab to the secret weak spot on its tail, there were astonished gasps from Evan's young fans. Alejandro spotted Samantha and gave her an excited thumbs-up.

"No one here has ever gotten this far before," Evan explained, bemused. "Look at them. They're in total awe."

But Samantha was unwilling to let her brother bask in his glory.

"Uncle Jay wants you up at the site."

"Now?"

She nodded.

"But the Inca Trail level is next. Come on, Samantha. I've got to show them Peru!"

She pried the controller from Evan's grip and placed it in Alejando's waiting hands.

"Him?" Evan sneered, as she pulled him through the crowd. "He's not even going to make it past Pachacuti!"

He was right: Alejandro's turn lasted a matter of

seconds. As the Pillager materialized on a cliffside pathway, a condor swooped for her, grasped her in its talons, and hurled her writhing from the precipice.

●●◉●●

Two days later found Samantha crouching low, ignoring the dull aching of her knees. Embedded in the soil before her was a large stone bowl, its circumference lined with the head, fins, and tail of a realistic stone fish.

In its small way, this was a momentous find. The cell in which Samantha now worked, the second from the entrance, had already produced several fish bones, which Evan had begrudgingly plucked from the screen outside and placed in the labeled bags. In the lab, Clare had used her ample zooarchaeological skills to identify them as the bones of *Sciaena deliciosa*—the lorna fish of the Peruvian coast. The stone bowl seemed to represent a lorna as well. Samantha worked carefully—using a pair of wooden chopsticks so that she wouldn't scratch the bowl with her trowel's sharp point.

Samantha glanced to the far end of the corridor where her uncle was delicately clearing the soil from a small cluster of burned human bones, including a forearm and a scattering of teeth. She preferred her current task, she thought to herself.

Suddenly, a beam of light tore through the darkness and she was blinded. Disoriented, she threw up her hands to protect her face, scraping her knuckles against the gallery's coarse walls. It took a moment for the dizziness to clear, but even then the passageway felt much darker, and she could barely see the stone bowl protruding near her feet.

"Evan!" she shouted angrily, guessing the likely cause of her discomfort.

"Bull's-eye!" he called back. He was sticking his head down into the gallery's entrance, his smile upside down. "Check out what I just found!"

In his hand, Evan clutched a polished chunk of graphite, much like the one Zoe had shown Samantha in the lab. She examined its flattened surface, gleaming with muted brilliance in the glow of her head lamp. The more she looked at the shiny lump, the more an idea took shape.

"I'll be right back," she shouted to her uncle, and bolted from the gallery and past her brother before they had time to respond.

She returned to the site within ten minutes, clutching the box beneath her arm. It had been just where she left it earlier in the summer, gathering dust beneath her bed.

"Evan, follow me!"

But it took more than that to get her brother to move.

"I've got an idea," she tried again. "Come on!"

Leaving their uncle at his work, they ran up and across the Temple's grassy roof to the entrance of Laberintos, then down its twisting stairs.

It felt strange to be in this gallery again. It seemed like ages since she had followed her uncle inside, squeezed into the tiny opening in the gallery floor, and fled the clacking avalanche of skulls. But now her heart pounded with a different kind of discovery. She had, as her uncle would say, a hypothesis.

"Hold this."

She shoved the box into her brother's arms and plucked out one of the ruined compacts her parents had mailed to her earlier in the summer. The name of the makeup, Quito Cutie, flashed in gilt letters on the plastic case. She flipped it open and raised it above her head to set it— just so—in one of the small, square ventilation holes that dotted the wall.

As they hurried back toward the entrance, Samantha placed Bogota Beauty and Chiapas Champagne in the similar shafts along their route, lining them up at precise angles until each had an open compact inside it, its mirror glinting through the shadows.

"Now stay here," she said, her voice quivering a little. She bounded up the stairway to the Temple's roof, found the notch she remembered near the top, and placed Color de Caracas inside. With trembling hands, she pried the compact open until it caught the rays of the noonday sun and conveyed them downward into the gallery's mouth.

"Samantha!"

So her hypothesis had been right. Evan's cry alone told her that much.

"Samantha! Come quick!"

When she ducked back inside, it was like entering another world. Brilliant shafts sliced through the darkness, bouncing from one mirror to the next to the next. The fiery beams carried with them the full power of the sun and swirled with the dust of centuries.

Samantha and her brother stood open-mouthed and silent. But only for a moment. Soon, they were jumping up and down, erupting in wild cries of delight.

Samantha had solved an ancient riddle. She had wrestled the light of the day indoors. For the first time in centuries, the Temple was illuminated, all the way to its shadowy core.

"Wow, Samantha! Wow!" was all that Evan could muster. He threw his arms around his sister, and they hugged for the first time in months.

••◉••

News of Samantha's discovery spread quickly. Members of the team were eager to share how the Temple's innermost chambers had been illuminated by an ingenious series of graphite mirrors, and how Professor Sutton's niece had figured it all out.

And everyone agreed that the find was a cause for celebration. As darkness fell, a large group made its way deep into Laberintos in single file. Osvaldo had invited all but a few of the site's guards in what seemed like an effort to break the summer's tension.

"Is that a good idea?" Samantha asked her uncle. "Don't they need to be protecting the site?"

But Jay only leaned back his head and laughed.

"Oh, Sam. That's not your problem. This is all for you! At least try to have some fun!"

And now the guards were leading the way though the twisting passages. Musical instruments were handed down the line when the footing was sure and the height of the massive stone ceiling allowed for them to be passed overhead. Samantha felt the bulk of a guitar case thrust into her arms and handed it forward to Clare. A second guitar followed quickly, and then a large set of panpipes, which Samantha held until Clare was down the steep interior staircase, ready to receive it and pass it along.

When they came to the widest part of the gallery, the guards arranged themselves in a row with all flashlights trained on them so they could tune their guitars. The rest of the group sat cross-legged and excited, pressed together by the closeness of the room.

"*¡Apaguen las luces!*" someone cried, and the flashlights were turned off, one by one.

There were some whispered directions among the guard-musicians, and the hushed sound of "*uno, dos, tres.*" Then the music began. First came the beautiful, wavering note of the panpipe—just as much wind as tone. As one guitar and then the other joined behind it, strummed in a marching rhythm, Samantha noticed that something weird was happening with the sound. The music was muted, dampened by the earthen floor, but seemed to emanate equally from every wall. Had she not seen the musicians a moment before, she would never be able to guess in which direction they stood. It was almost as if the sound was being generated from inside her mind, and she felt her head begin to whirl, disoriented.

This feeling intensified as the music grew in speed and volume. Was the floor leaning forward or pitching slowly to one side? Only a barely perceptible breeze gave away the direction of Laberintos' opening. But were the instruments moving around the chamber? Was the panpipe somehow behind her?

Under different circumstances, the experience would have been deeply unsettling. And only the quiet beauty of the music was able to temper the odd effect.

The first song came to an end and people began to clap, but the ricocheted sound of the applause so surprised the group that it quickly turned to laughter. Then the second song began: two guitars in a tight and intricate harmony, punctuated in parts by a rattle from the maracas. And again Samantha's head swam, and she planted both hands on the ground.

Beside her, her brother began to fidget, knocking his knee against hers.

"Evan, be careful," she murmured and was embarrassed to hear her words reverberate around the chamber. Evan's only response was a gurgle that Samantha knew all too well. The sounds of the concert had clearly gotten to his stomach. He was going to vomit.

Quickly, Samantha sprang up, pulling Evan to his feet by the hood of his favorite soccer sweatshirt. Luckily, they were the two closest to the chamber's entrance, and she was able to pull him away without disturbing the others. Steadying herself against the wall with her free hand, she led her brother through the maze of corridors, trailing the hint of a breeze back to the gallery's entrance and into the star-bright evening.

It was not a moment too soon. By the blue light of the moon she could make out her brother, bent double and emptying his stomach onto a patch of grass.

"Are you okay?" she asked, but he raised a feeble hand to silence her.

Eventually, he wiped his teary eyes with the back of his hand, then pointed at the puddle at his feet.

"Hey, it's my Inca Kola from earlier. Want some?"

"Be quiet, Evan."

"No, *you* be quiet!"

"Shhh, Evan," she hissed again, with an urgency that silenced her brother. "*Listen.*"

They stood very still, their senses primed and taut. There were faint noises in the starlit vastness before them.

Human noises.

There was someone out there.

Samantha's mind spun as she tried to make a checklist of all the people who might be inside the site this late at night. She had assumed that the entire excavation team had been at the concert as well, but had everyone been accounted for?

Or was it the two guards who were still on duty, engaged

in some hushed conversation? But they would never have roamed the site as a pair, leaving the gate unmanned.

More noises, and Evan lowered himself slowly to the ground beside her. He must have heard it too—the trace of a voice and the grass-muffled sound of approaching footsteps. She sank down beside her brother.

"Samantha, what *is* that?" Evan voiced almost silently, just beside her ear. But then his breaths turned short and sharp, and Samantha felt her pulse behind her eyes.

Shadows loomed about ten feet away, blocking the stars in human silhouettes. The figures were silent now, but the night sky behind them was bright enough to see one make a signal with an outstretched hand.

Were there two of them? Three? Whoever was in front of her, she realized, was listening with the same intensity, frozen in place.

Had they been spotted? Had her brother's voice made their presence known?

The raspy whispering began again, but Samantha couldn't make out the words—or even what language was being spoken. In the light of the southern constellations, a wisp of vapor could be seen rising from the mouth of the speaker. The first voice was too low to hear clearly, but the response was louder—a sequence of words that Samantha still couldn't understand.

And then the shadows began to move toward them, growing as they came, blocking out more and more of the starry sky. Samantha pressed herself as flat as she could against the ground and cradled her head with her arms. The dewy grass was cold against her face. All her senses were on fire, ready to flee, or fight if she had to.

Then nothing.

They waited, shivering in the night chill of the valley. And when she finally risked another look, the shadows had vanished.

All had grown silent.

Beside her Evan began to mouth a countdown from one hundred. But Samantha was on her feet at eighty-two and chasing the strands of music back into the gallery.

"Stop! Please, everyone!" she shouted. "There's someone outside!"

The joyful melody came to a ragged end, and the audience members rustled for their flashlights, training them on Samantha as Evan burst into the chamber beside her.

"Sam! What are you talking about?" asked Jay. "Who are you talking about?"

"I don't know, but not anyone who is supposed to be there. Hurry! We have to find them!"

While the guards raced from the Temple with their guns drawn and spread quickly across the site, the archaeologists' behavior was less uniform. Some raced to check their units. Others hung back, too frightened to move. The three professors caucused at the entrance of Laberintos, and Samantha and Evan stood with them, adrenaline high.

"Is anyone missing?" Clare asked.

"Where's Adam?" asked Osvaldo, after a pause.

Jay and Samantha turned to look at each other with the same horrible realization.

"Evan, Sam, come with me."

All three Suttons bounded across the Temple's roof, down the stone staircase, and across the Circular Plaza by the light of the moon. Jay twisted on his head lamp as they neared the Ofrendas gallery, and they dropped one by one into its opening, landing hard.

They took in the destruction all together. The gallery's floor was pitted and hacked away, stripped completely of its artifacts. Gone was the lorna-fish bowl. Gone were the intricate pots, the bones, the careful stacks of offerings. Gone were hours of Samantha's careful effort and hundreds of years of miraculous preservation.

"Find Adam," Jay rasped, in a whisper raw and trembling. "Find him now!"

CHAPTER 13

They're coming," Jay hissed, pressing a flashlight into his nephew's hand. "Hurry! Go!"

Samantha and Evan ran for the gate, stumbling across the rough terrain, propelled by the force of their uncle's order. Everything depended on Adam's innocence. Not only was the future of the excavation at stake, but so was their uncle's entire career.

They raced down the road toward town, almost losing control as they accelerated downhill. A power outage had extinguished the town's few streetlights, making the blackness of the night complete. While Evan's flashlight produced a faint beam, his pounding legs and shaky hands jostled it uselessly across the landscape. Their way was lit only by whatever candlelight escaped from the windows that they passed.

They reached the Hostal Jato, ducking first into the dining room and then the lab. Adam was nowhere to be found. They ran next to his room, pounding on his door and rattling the locked doorknob. Nothing.

"*El Cóndor?*" Evan wheezed.

"I guess."

They headed again into the darkness, moving as fast as they could. Samantha let her brother take the lead, trailing him as he navigated a series of sharp turns through a complex of alleyways that she had never known existed. They splashed through some invisible puddle and heard the angry barking of an unseen dog. Finally, they reached a squat cinder block building, its windows taped over with black plastic bags. Its flimsy door thumped with the vibrations of loud music, powered by a generator inside.

Samantha had never been to El Cóndor, and the disco was not at all what she had expected. This was not the dismal saloon of a cowboy Western. In fact, the interior was sparklingly clean, and the disco ball and colored lamps that hung from its ceiling lit the place warmly.

A deejay station had been set up in one corner, and as the Suttons burst in, Dijota looked up in surprise from his turntables. But El Cóndor's only two customers remained at their stools at the bar, too deep in conversation to note the new arrivals.

Their glasses were full—they had not been there long—and Samantha could just make out their words over the heavy drumbeat of Dijota's selection.

"*Amigo,*" Chimay was saying. "*Es un buen precio.*"

"I don't care about the price," Adam growled back from behind his mirrored sunglasses. "I just need it to be soon."

"Adam!" Evan cried, and only now did the conversation

at the bar come to an end. Adam and Chimay exchanged a hasty look.

"What do you want?"

"Ofrendas. The Ofrendas gallery has been looted!"

Adam slammed his sunglasses down on the empty bar and stepped forward, bringing a handkerchief up to wipe his nose.

"When?"

"Just now! We saw the looters, I think, Samantha and me. Jay wants you back at the site. Hurry, we have to—"

Suddenly, Adam lunged for him, shoving Samantha aside.

"Did you see who it was?" Adam spat.

"Let go of me!"

"Did you see anything? Hear anything?"

"It was too dark! And I couldn't understand anything they were saying—it wasn't Spanish. And it definitely wasn't English either."

"Who was it?" Adam barked again.

"I told you. I don't know!"

Adam spun to face Samantha.

"What about you?"

There was something animal about how he gripped her arm. When she tried to wrestle free, she felt his grasp close even tighter, just above her elbow. It would be enough to give her bruises.

"What did you see?" Adam hissed again through gritted teeth.

She was about to spit an answer back in his face when

her gaze came to rest on his eyes. Two dark pits stared back at her, as black as obsidian, as deep and distressing as the night outside. From his nose flowed two ropes of mucus. It was as horrible as one of Chavín's monstrous tenon heads, and Samantha wanted to look away.

And then Evan was beside her, prying at Adam's fingers. "Stop it! Let her go!"

Adam cast Samantha aside, retrieved his sunglasses, and moved quickly for the door.

"We'll finish this later," he muttered in Chimay's general direction, and lurched angrily into the night.

●●◉●●

When the trio neared the entrance of the looted chamber, all eyes turned toward Adam. A generator and a pair of powerful lamps had been hastily arranged in the Circular Plaza, and the students stood around the pool of light as the site's guards scoured the site's periphery.

"Well?"

Adam asked it as a challenge.

"*¿Entonces?*" he said, repeating himself in Spanish.

Stuart's livid voice was the first to call out from the darkness.

"You've got some nerve, boyo."

"*¡Ladrón!*" cried Marisol.

"Thief," a British student jeered, in echo.

"Oh. I'm the thief? I'm the looter?" Adam shot back, holding his handkerchief over his nose. "I get it. I don't come to your little concert, so it *must* be me."

There was an angry chorus of shouts and murmurs, and the crowd pressed forward. But Adam was unfazed. He rolled up his sleeves and balled his fists, ready for all comers.

The arrival of the mayor put an end to the impending riot. Clare and Osvaldo, who had awakened him with the news, now flanked him as he strode into the courtyard, a finely tailored overcoat flung over his pajamas.

He scanned the faces that he passed with a quiet rage. He seemed to be searching for someone—a fact confirmed when he saw Jay emerge from Ofrendas. Without a word, he walked toward the American archaeologist.

"*Señor alcalde*," Jay began, but the mayor held up a hand to silence him. There would be no discussion here. A decision had already been made. And as Jay bowed his head, the mayor issued his terrible decree.

••◉••

No matter what the rest of the team was saying, Samantha knew that the mayor's proclamation was fair.

All excavation at Chavín de Huántar was to cease immediately.

The students were understandably upset. Marisol had burst into tears immediately and had not stopped crying for two full days. Stuart, too, was devastated, and Samantha's own heart broke for him when he explained his situation to her. He needed the summer's excavation to complete his degree back in England, and without it, the university's officials might not let him graduate.

But Jay's despair was the deepest of all. Not only were the Peruvian and British students giving him a wide berth, but his own pupils were growing distant—fearful of the taint of his company.

Samantha and her brother both tried to cheer him up at mealtimes, telling jokes and keeping the squabbling to a minimum. But Clare alone seemed capable of raising his spirits. Osvaldo barely acknowledged Jay at all.

At an emergency meeting in the dining room the following day, Osvaldo and Clare announced that the team would have the weekend off to regroup. With most of the team exploring the valley—some taking overnight buses all the way to the coast—Jay spent both days struggling to convince his colleagues that his basic work in the galleries should continue.

"It's just putting points on a map," Samantha heard him say over a tense and awkward lunch. "We wouldn't be digging. There would be no risk of looting."

"No, Jay," said Osvaldo, frowning into his soup. "The mayor's decision was very clear. Yours is a distinction he might not have the patience to make."

"Jay," Clare said, more gently but with equal conviction. "We need to let things settle down for a bit. Just wait a week. Maybe two. I'm hopeful that when security at that site gets under control, we'll be allowed to continue with our work."

But Jay would not let the matter rest.

"A week?" he said. "Two? Then we might as well go home. The summer's almost over, after all."

His colleagues wouldn't budge.

"Come on," Jay went on. "Let me salvage what's left of the field season. Even if I have to stay in the galleries all night and guard the entrances myself."

In the end, Osvaldo relented first.

"I do not think that will be necessary, Jay. But listen closely," he said, enunciating every word. "*No. Digging.*"

From her vantage point on the other side of the dining room, Samantha could see her uncle rest his hand on Clare's knee for a few seconds before the British professor brushed him away.

"No digging," Clare echoed, her finger raised in emphasis.

Jay leaned back on the bench.

"Fine, fine, fine, fine, fine. At least not until this has all settled down."

●●◉●●

Try as she might, Samantha could not beat back her anxiety the next morning as they made their way to the site with her uncle. She sucked in the dusty air—fragrant with the familiar scents of manure, eucalyptus, and exhaust. It was lovely, pleasant, calming, but it was not enough to push away the thought of the danger that surrounded her. Somewhere in the valley were thieves—dangerous, desperate people who might have seen her that night, and who might be waiting to do her harm. And there was still the lingering specter of the Madman, lending a different, supernatural terror.

The site's gate was now heavily guarded. Jay held up his hand as they entered, demonstrating in an exaggerated manner that he held no tools with which to dig. But the guards just stared at him coldly.

Samantha followed him in silence to the Temple's northern face. For the first time, she noticed a small ledge halfway up the slope of the structure's northern side and a low, dark opening almost entirely hidden by a curtain of tall weeds.

"Here we are," Jay said, and set his satchel down beside the entrance. "I came up this morning to take a look, and this one's a classic. Twists, turns, everything that you could ask for. It's not well explored, but it's already got a name…"

He let the silence linger for dramatic effect.

"*La Galería del Loco*, Sam. The Gallery of the Madman."

Samantha took a hurried step backward, catching herself just in time to avoid a tumble down the Temple's sloping flank.

"*The* Madman?" she gasped.

"Just a rumor, Samantha. Remember?"

His voice was the same as when he had told her about the Madman on their flight to Peru. It wasn't angry, but it was not exactly patient.

She chose her next words carefully.

"I…I've heard more about the Loco from the kids in town. Some of them seem really afraid."

Jay smiled, relenting.

"Well, Sam, allow me to separate fact from myth. That is, after all, part of what I do for a living."

He sat down behind the waving stalks of grass. Samantha sat too, casting an uneasy glance into the dark opening that seemed to emit an occasional frigid breeze. It was as if it were breathing.

"A long time ago, Sam—well, maybe not very long at all, by Chavín's standards—a stranger came to visit the site. He was from somewhere far away, and his behavior seemed odd to everyone he met. This was well before any real archaeology had been done here, so the locals weren't used to people poking around. As time went on, the stranger's interest grew stronger, becoming more like an obsession. He moved all of his stuff into the site itself—into this very gallery, they say—and set up camp."

Now Samantha couldn't even bring herself to look inside the gallery's mouth. So this had been the Madman's home?

"He must have had someone helping him, though, because he never came into town for food and supplies. The only time people would encounter him was near the site itself. And his behavior became very odd. His eyes were huge and black, and he raved wildly about strange hallucinations he had been having. And then, one day, he disappeared into the Temple, never to be seen again."

Samantha shuddered. But her uncle hadn't finished.

"But this is where all the mystery and spookiness comes in. Two months after the Madman was last seen, the village was going about its business. All of a sudden, an enormous wave of mud and stone and trees came crashing down over the western edge of the valley. It was a massive landslide: the *Cataclismo* that we've talked about before. The whole southern end of the valley got covered, wiping out the roads, killing livestock, burying a few of the more isolated houses, knocking out the bridge over the Wacheqsa, and coming very close to demolishing the southern edge of the town.

"It was pandemonium, total chaos. Still, one of the first things the villagers did when the dust settled was to organize rescue parties. One group came to the site, specifically to see if they could save the Madman. But when they got here, everything was buried, covered in mud and fallen trees, all the way down to the edge of the Mosna. He had to have been killed immediately or died somewhere inside, unable to get out."

"And did they ever find his body?" Samantha asked in a quivering whisper, not sure if she wanted to hear the answer.

"Never. When the first archaeologists came here a decade later and cleared out all the mud that had covered over the gallery doors, there was no sign of him."

"And what about the stories I've heard? About the ghost? About how he's still here haunting the place?"

Jay lobbed a pebble at a llama that had wandered toward them over the Temple's grassy roof.

"I admit it, the whole thing makes for a perfect ghost story—a lunatic, a tragedy, a missing body. I'm sure kids will be telling that one for years to come. If someone was helping him, they have kept their secret well. But come on, Sam. It's just a story. No one over the age of eight believes it."

She thought of Alejandro before correcting him.

"No one over the age of *ten*, I think."

"Fair enough, kiddo," he chuckled. "Anyway, I need your help on this one. What do you say? Can we get started?"

But he turned too quickly for her to answer, and there was nothing she could do but follow him inside.

•••●••

From the moment they entered, she didn't like it. There was something different about the Loco gallery, separate, even, from the dreadful story that went with it. It felt claustrophobic, like a trap. The faint, cool breeze that coursed from some hidden opening should have felt nice after the heat of the sun outside, but it was damp, musty, and carried a repellent smell.

Staying close to her uncle, Samantha switched on her head lamp to see a long corridor extending far beyond the range of their lights. Chambers and tunnels opened to the left and right, promising a complicated network of rooms. No wonder the Madman had chosen this gallery for his hiding place, Samantha thought. And no wonder his bones had never been found.

"Look at this!"

Ahead of her, Jay reached for a cleft in the masonry wall.

"Hungry?" he asked with a grin, and held something up so she could see it: an old can of corned beef, its label rendered grimy and almost unreadable.

She tried to smile but remembered Alejandro's terrified eyes as he told her of the Madman. She remembered his grandfather, Señor Ocllo, clutching their ancestral sword and raving about the Loco's return.

Soon, they came to a wide wooden plank lying across the gallery's floor, worn and bowed at its center where it sagged into an unseen cavity below. Jay found its edge with his fingers and heaved it aside, revealing the top of a staircase. It descended steeply downward, deep into the terrifying heart of ancient Chavín. But the low slope of the staircase's ceiling made it impossible to determine just how deep it went.

The only way to see what lay below would for someone small to squeeze inside.

"It's a tight fit in there, kiddo," he said, handing her his head lamp. "I was only able to get down two or three steps."

"I can do it," Samantha said, fighting back every instinct that she had. "Really."

Two steps down and it was obvious that this hole was the source of the upper Loco gallery's frigid air. It came swirling up at her in cold, clammy gusts, chilling her through her clothes.

She shouldn't be here, Samantha thought. This was no place for the living or the sane.

Another step down and she noticed the walls. While the gallery above—and every other gallery she had seen—were lined with bare stone, the staircase's had been slathered with plaster by some ancient hand, and traces of reddish paint could be seen in the beam of her light.

To reach the next step, she needed to lean back slightly, squeezing between the staircase and the low ceiling above it. The stones hung inches above her chin, and once again, she had the feeling that the entire Temple dangled above her.

"Keep going, Sam. It can't go on too much farther."

Samantha squeezed downward once again. At last her foot found even ground. She had reached the end of the staircase.

She pulled herself free of the constricted stairway and cast a glance back and upward, seeing her uncle's determined face in her yellow lamplight.

"You're doing great, Sam. Just tell me what you see."

But just as she turned, and just as her mouth opened to describe whatever lay before her, the beam of her head lamp landed on a living face.

Two dead black eyes shone back at her, like pools of ink. Monstrous lips were pulled back in a toothy grimace, fierce and ancient.

The face seared itself into her vision, full of ancient fury for violating the sanctity of the gallery that bore its name. And then her lamp was knocked from her head to skitter—extinguished—into the total blackness.

She cried out, scrambling for the steps and clawing her way upward as fast as she could. The knees of her pants shredded against the coarse stone and the flesh of her elbows tore as she pulled herself higher. She hit her head badly on the tight ceiling.

At last, she shot into the upper Loco gallery like a wounded animal.

"Sam! Sam! Stop!"

But she charged past her uncle, hurtling toward the gallery's outer door and bursting from the Temple into a hard-driving rain.

A storm had descended on the valley. Black clouds were pouring over the cliffs like liquid smoke, unleashing torrents of rain and crackling booms of lightning. She slipped in the wet grass, sliding down the slope. But in a moment she was on her feet again and running—past the outstretched hands of the guards at the gate, down the streaming road, and through a herd of rain-slick cattle. Wiping the wet hair from her eyes, she ran harder—slipping again and almost falling on the bridge over the angry Wacheqsa River. And then she ran harder still—past the shop-keepers and stall owners as they raced to pull tarpaulins over their wares.

Gasping in terrified sobs, she charged across the Plaza de Armas, through the hostal's courtyard and dining room and into the lab, throwing herself, soaking, into her brother's startled embrace.

•• ● ••

Samantha lay in her bed in the darkness, listening to h brother's even breathing and the remnants of the storm it beat against her window.

She had told no one what had happened to her, even Jay. He had chased after her through the rain, arr at the hostal only a few minutes behind her, but she re to open the door. When he knocked again and again, hour after hour, she gave him the same vague assurances.

"I'm okay. Really."

"But what happened in there, Sam? Tell me."

"I'm fine, Uncle Jay. Please."

Under the covers with her flashlight, she had tried to map the gallery from memory, as if reducing it to a sketch on the page would erase the horror concealed inside. But each straight line she attempted went curvy, each corner went crooked and awry. She ripped out page after page until she finally got it right.

Evan had come back to the room after dinner, and she had to let him in. But even with her brother to distract her with the news of the day, she could not forget the face she had seen in the Loco gallery, and she saw it again every time she closed her eyes.

Was it all just a strange invention of her mind? Was her _n just playing tricks on her, muddled by the summer's _ting anxiety and the terror she had felt when she had _ which gallery—whose gallery—she was in?

There was someone in there. She was sure of it.

ost sure.

he time she fell asleep, she wasn't sure at all.

shook her awake the following morning and

her to get dressed and meet him outside.

shook her head.

o work in the lab for the next few days,

Jay fixed her with a quizzical look but seeing the fear in her eyes, he smiled.

"I can respect that, kiddo. Clare's going to head up work in the lab, now that her units are closing down. I think it would be great if you two got to know each other better."

Relieved, Samantha settled back into bed. But then she heard more whispering from across the room, the creak of Evan's bedsprings and his muffled grunts as he wrenched on his boots. Through half-closed eyelids, she watched jealously as her brother shut the door behind him and went to take her place.

●●●●●

In the laboratory, Samantha had little opportunity to regret her decision. Even though the room was full of students, their units all closed, there was still simply too much to do. And when her brother and uncle returned that evening, smiling and joking and relating their adventures, she felt only a tiny twinge of envy.

Each day, as the team bustled about—taking photos, weighing finds, recording them on the fleet of laptop computers—Clare made sure that Samantha had plenty of her own work to keep her occupied. The artifacts she gave her to analyze were pleasantly familiar. Samantha recognized the finds from the West Field and the few she had collected from Ofrendas before the looters had struck. It had been amazing to find these bits of evidence in the units, to see them emerge from the soil at her feet. But here in the lab they took on a new importance, and processing them brought a gratifying structure to the confusion in her mind.

Samantha was so engrossed in her work that she tended to stay when the clock struck five and the students left the lab. To her delight, Clare stayed with her one evening, teaching her in a kind but professorial voice about faunal analysis, lithics, and dating techniques.

But Clare's tone changed when she opened one of the bags from Samantha's work in the West Field and slid the familiar torso and feet of the ceramic action figure into the palm of her hand.

"Oh, Sam. How I wish I could speak to the person who owned this." She closed Samantha's fingers around the fragile artifact. "Doesn't it make you feel so…so human?"

Samantha smiled, knowing exactly what she meant.

"That's the feeling I can never get enough of," Clare continued. "Not since I was a little girl, when my mother and father would take me to the museum in Salisbury. There was one artifact on display there…a chess piece found under Ivy Street not far from my home. I remember thinking—a person used this. Not because they had to, or because they thought we would find it one day, but just to bring some amusement or comfort to their lives. It just makes me feel like we're all the same: all people, no matter where we live. Or when."

The sentiment could have been Samantha's own, and she wished, more than anything, that Clare Barrows would become her aunt.

•• ● ••

It was midmorning, some days later, when they called for her.

The students were working in the lab when the sudden squawk of Clare's radio brought everything to a standstill. Everyone looked nervously at the radio, but it was only Jay cheerfully requesting that his niece bring some drinking water to the site for him and Evan to share.

She grabbed a bottle from her cache upstairs and trudged to the site. She felt a little resentful of the errand, but after days in the stale air of the lab, it did feel wonderful to be outside. The town seemed friendly again. The tension of the last few weeks seemed to have vanished.

But not one of the guards offered so much as a nod, and their hands remained fixed on the barrels of their guns. Samantha gave them a friendly "*Buenos días*" anyway.

She found her uncle in the Circular Plaza.

"Thanks, Sam," he said, smiling. He seemed like his old self. "Now come over here. Your brother wants to show you something."

She followed him, clambering up onto the raised area that made up the southern half of the plaza's circumference. They were directly opposite Ofrendas now, and she looked down to see the entrance of another gallery lying open beneath her feet. She tucked the water bottle under her arm and lowered herself in, and a welcome wave of excitement eroded some of her unease.

But only for a moment.

Because at the far end of the chamber she could make out her brother by the light of his head lamp. He was digging. Just as the mayor had expressly forbidden.

"You have got to see this, Samantha," Evan said from where he crouched, picking at some protrusion in the gallery's floor. "You're not going to believe what we've found."

<u>Spanish → English</u>

- trompetas - trumpets
- 'joven - youngster
- tu tambien - you, too
- Me estás tomando el pelo? -
  Are you pulling my hair?
  (kind of like "are you
  pulling my leg?"...
  It means "are you
  kidding me?")

Even if he does have permission,
I think it's a terrible idea.

Conch trumpet

Sound comes out

water goes in

Monumental stairs

So amazing. Everyone
is excited about it
(not Osvaldo, but

_oth of our discoveries.
But he's coming all the way from
Lima to see what Evan and Jay fou
_'m nervous something bad will happen soon.

El las quiere

El loco quiere las trompetas

Chapter 14

Shaking with rage, Samantha felt the air around her go cold and clammy as she neared a ventilation shaft at the gallery's end. At her brother's feet was a shiny object, which Samantha first took for the crown of a human skull. But the shape was wrong, and as Evan's light flickered across it, she struggled to make out what it was.

Even in her anger, what she saw amazed her. It was a large seashell: a *strombus* or a conch. Her brother was using a wooden chopstick to clean the shell's surface, revealing a web of beautifully carved lines. An image of some sort of animal had begun to emerge—a jaguar, perhaps, or some kind of dog.

"And here's another one."

Evan reached behind him and picked up a second shell, placing it gingerly into his sister's hands. It glowed as it passed through the beam of Evan's head lamp, its carvings illuminated in striking relief. She turned it over and over in her hands. The engravings were beautiful, masterfully done. She was surprised by how little it weighed until she realized that the central spire of the shell had been removed, the core left empty and resonant.

"It gets even better, Samantha. Let me have it back for a second."

She did so, and watched as he raised the shell's hollowed tip to his lips and blew. The chamber filled with a high, quavering note.

"It's a trumpet," she said, slowly.

"No, Archaeo Kid. It's a whole trumpet *section*."

She followed the beam of his head lamp to another patch of white in the gallery's floor. Behind it, she saw another, and then another, extending back toward the entrance in a uniform line.

They were things of such beauty that Samantha could not take her eyes from them. As pieces of art, their natural wonder had only been enhanced by the ancient artisan. But as archaeological evidence, they were exhilarating. Here they were, seashells, among the world's most rugged mountains and a hundred miles from the coast. What an amazing job it must have been to get them all the way up here. What unimaginable power must have commanded the effort.

But as amazing as the trumpets were, her uncle and brother had broken the rules by excavating them. Samantha could have no part in this. She made for the exit, her head hung low.

"Hold on, Sam," Jay cried, chasing after her. "Let me explain!"

"What are you doing?" she cried, wheeling on him. "Don't you know what could happen to you if anyone finds out?"

She realized that tears were forming in her eyes, but she was far too angry to wipe them away.

"Everyone's counting on you, Uncle Jay! Everyone trusts you to follow the rules!"

"Here," he said, stuffing a crisply folded piece of paper in her hand. "Read this."

But Samantha did not stop, marching from the gallery, across the Circular Plaza, and up the stone staircase. She sat heavily on the uppermost step, slamming the water bottle down beside her and began to cry in earnest.

"Open the paper, Sam. Please. It'll explain everything."

Jay had followed as far as the foot of the stairs and stood looking up at her with a pleading look on his face.

She unfolded the page and tearily reviewed its contents.

It was a letter from the mayor. The words were in Spanish, of course, but from what she could make out, it appeared that her uncle had, in fact, been granted permission to dig.

"We had a long talk, Sam, the mayor and I," Jay called up in a gentle voice. "I told him that I needed to show him that I was trustworthy—that my word was good. And he was willing to give me one last chance."

She set the paper aside.

"Do the other professors know about this?"

"No. Well. Not *both* of them. I agreed to keep this work

a secret among the few people I trusted most. The guards have been ordered to leave us alone. That," he pointed at the letter, "is just in case anyone gives us trouble."

"And why did you have to tell me?" she asked, wiping her eyes across her forearm.

"I trust you, kiddo." He paused for a moment and then gave a smile of devilish charm. "And we could really use your help."

She weighed his words, not warming to his tone. The trumpets were the find of the summer. That was certain. But even with the mayor's permission, it didn't feel right. Jay had hidden his activities from his colleagues, and the weight of his secret project was not a burden that she wanted to bear.

She unscrewed the water bottle and took a long sip, then set it down beside her. But her placement of it was awkward and it tumbled heavily on its side. She watched, numbly, as the water glugged from the overturned bottle, pooling beside her on the stair and dribbling into the small hole cut into the step beside her hand.

And then, somewhere below her, there was a noise. As the water pushed its way through the centuries of accumulated debris, a gurgle began to echo from each of the stairway's small holes.

It began like a throaty gurgle, as if the Temple was clearing its throat. But the volume grew as the water coursed through the hidden canal that ran below the length of the stairway, becoming a murmur, then a growl, then the rumble of distant thunder.

Samantha rose to her feet, locking eyes with her uncle as the volume grew and grew. Soon, it was an all-out roar. Evan pulled himself from the gallery's entrance, befuddled. The noise crackled off the mountainsides, adding to its intensity. It grew louder still, impossibly so, building to the point where all three Suttons almost had to cover their ears. It was the sound of joyous applause—a simultaneous ovation of a million concert halls filled with a million people each.

"Samantha," Jay shouted, barely audible over the clamor. "What did you do?"

"It was water!" she managed. "Just water!"

But that water had triggered some sort of ancient device.

Now the sound hammered back and forth between the valley walls, attracting villagers from their homes, storefronts, and classrooms to stand in silent shock in the streets and plazas.

Jay and Samantha merely stared at each other, stunned and silenced, their minds racing to explain how such a small amount of water could unleash the fury of ancient gods. But then came the realization that the entire valley would soon be descending on them and that their forbidden unit in the Galería de las Caracolas—the Gallery of the Shells—would soon be known to the world.

●●◉●●

As Osvaldo led the group of confused archaeologists and townspeople into the site, the roar of the water duct still crackled in the distant reaches of the valley—ripples of thunder on the clearest of afternoons. But while the rest of the crowd fanned out to look for the source of the sound, Osvaldo made his way straight for the Circular Plaza. His face contorted in rage when he saw Evan, covered in the dust of their covert excavation, and he pushed his way through the Suttons and into Caracolas.

When he emerged some minutes later, he seemed, at first, a different man.

"Jay," he said, "I offer my heartiest congratulations."

Jay grinned and shook his colleague's offered hand with relieved gusto. But his smile faded as Osvaldo refused to release his grip. He was shorter than Jay but of a much stronger build, and there was little the American professor could do as Osvaldo pulled him close, leaned forward, and whispered harshly in his ear.

"And may the world forgive you for what you have done."

At last Osvaldo let go. Jay fumbled in his pocket and produced the mayor's letter. Osvaldo snatched the page and scanned its neatly typed lines, a contemptuous smirk spreading across his lips.

"Of course. I should have guessed."

He returned the letter, crushing it into Jay's chest.

"It is always this way, ¿*no?* I have worked in this valley for a decade. And all that time, I have given it the respect that it deserves. I have protected it. I have shielded it with my sweat and my body and my blood. But all for nothing. Just so you can bring down this destruction upon us.

"But are you punished for it? Are you penalized for your *arrogancia descuidada*? No. Not *el charlie*, not the *recién llegado*, the recent arrival. You are rewarded. All because of your foreign education and your foreign credentials and your foreign connections. It is to be expected. It is the way it has always been."

Jay was about to speak, but Osvaldo continued, his voice tightening to a hiss.

"You had better do what you can to protect what you have found in there. Should something happen to them, it will take more than a mayor *de poca monta* to save you."

Osvaldo's angry gaze shifted to where Samantha and Evan stood gaping some feet away. Caught in the wild intensity of the professor's glare, Samantha felt herself shrinking behind her brother. Osvaldo was a man unhinged. A buried stratum of rage had torn through the surface. In that moment, there was no telling what he would do to rid the valley of his American colleague, or what he had already done.

But at once it was as if Osvaldo had awakened from a fit of delirium. The rage drained from his face, replaced with hollow shame. He stood for a moment, his lips parting as if to say something, but he was broken and humiliated by his outburst, and he could not find his voice. He dropped his gaze when Samantha's eyes found his and stammered a hasty apology.

"Samantha, Evan...I...I am sorry. *Discúlpenme. Discúlpenme.*"

He turned awkwardly and stumbled away, leaving the Suttons in silence.

•••••

The praise Samantha received over the course of the afternoon did nothing to lift her spirits. Over and over Stuart and Zoe filled small water bottles from the nearby Wacheqsa, pouring them one after another into the aperture at the top of the grand staircase. And each time, after the dizzying roar had subsided, the archaeologists and townspeople answered it with an ovation of their own.

Samantha politely accepted the wholehearted cries of congratulations she received. But nothing could shake the unease caused by Osvaldo's outburst. His voice had been that of a stranger, not the man she had come to know as her friend.

Evan's discovery was attracting enormous attention, as well. Twenty *Strombus* trumpets were now exposed on the floor of Caracolas—all intact, all engraved, each a work of humbling beauty and skill. Four of Chavín's guards had been hastily assigned to the gallery's entrance, and fascinated villagers were led inside one at a time to view the objects where they lay.

"Is this a good idea?" Jay asked, "Advertising our finds at a time like this?"

"An outrageous question," said Osvaldo, too angry to meet his colleague's gaze. "This is their valley, their site, their past. These people were here before you ever came to Chavín, and they will be here *después*."

For their part, the townspeople entered the gallery in reverential silence, emerging moments later with expressions of solemn awe. Chimay and Dijota were among them, and they bombarded Evan with questions. But Evan's uncharacteristic shyness and his reluctance to take credit for the discovery revealed to Samantha that her brother's mind was as troubled as her own.

With Clare taking the lead, the professors approached the mayor. He had stationed himself at the entrance of Caracolas, monitoring the comings and goings of curious visitors.

"I will take all the appropriate precautions," he said in his near-perfect English. "The protection of the site is my solemn duty. But, I am sorry, a thing of this magnitude must be publicized. Our village relies on such discoveries and on the tourists that they bring."

"Of course, *señor*," said Clare. "And we are happy… obligated to share the discovery with the village. But given the…the security situation…we would ask that you give us more time to arrange the appropriate protection for greater publicity."

The mayor straightened his tie, then smoothed the lapels of his tailored suit.

"It will be arranged, Doctor Barrows, but not by you. All summer, you have taken, taken, taken. It is now time for Chavín to ask for something in return."

And so two long-distance calls were placed from the mayor's office by day's end, each looping their way from pole to pole through the town, up the valley, over peaks and passes, and down the Andes' sweeping apron to the sprawling capital on the edge of the sea.

The first reached the offices of the national television network, and the reaction was immediate. Reporters were reassigned, deadlines rearranged, and broadcasts rewritten to accommodate the promised sensation.

The second call was transferred from Huaraz to Lima, and then from ministry to ministry up the chain of command. At last, the phone was picked up in La Casa de Pizarro and directed to the country's most powerful man.

News of the discovery had reached the president of Peru.

In Chavín, the mayor replaced his phone in the receiver and turned to face the small crowd of archaeologists gathered in his office. He wiped his brow with a silk handkerchief and cleared his throat.

"*El Presidente de la República*—the President of Peru—has declared the trumpets a national treasure. His Excellency will be in Chavín in two days to inspect the objects himself."

●●●●●

It was early evening when large clouds of dust appeared up valley. From where she stood with the rest of the team on the Temple's roof, Samantha could just make out the troop carriers as they moved heavily along the valley floor until they were close enough that she could see the shouldered guns bristling from beneath the canvas roofs.

The site now had the protection that it needed. The mayor had been true to his word.

The soldiers dismounted, standing in tight formation inside the site's main gate as their commander met briefly with Chavín's own somewhat-anxious security force. Later, as the sun dropped behind the curtain of the western cliff-face, the commandos dispersed with practiced precision around the site, impressing the assembled crowd with their ordered expertise.

"This will be a circus." Jay said, as he, his niece and nephew, and everyone else were escorted out so that the site could be locked down for the night.

"All because of my discovery?"

The arrival of the soldiers had revived Evan's spirits, and Samantha was actually relieved to see that some of his boastfulness had returned.

"You bet. These trumpets of yours are going to get a lot of attention. But it's more than that. Peru has a special place in its heart for Chavín de Huántar. In a way, it's where the country began."

As the gate clanged shut behind them, and as two dozen commandos took their positions along the site's perimeter, Samantha felt some of her tension evaporate. Nobody would be brazen enough to challenge the site's security now.

One would have to be insane.

•• ● ••

The next morning, the archaeological team again climbed to the Temple's roof. A line of news vans had been spotted, streaming into the valley along the same route the soldiers had used the day before.

Samantha fixed her eyes on the long dusty column, counting more than twenty vehicles racing toward them at a frantic speed. When she finished her count, she was startled to see that Osvaldo was standing just beside her.

"The paparazzi!" he said with a conciliatory grin, and Samantha mustered a timid smile in response.

Over the next several hours, Isabel did a healthy business beside the gate, selling off many of her carved replicas as the site filled with newspeople of every type. Alejandro was not with her.

The print journalists came from Peruvian and foreign newspapers, and all were polite, professional, and prepared. Samantha was impressed when she overheard the informed questions they posed to the three professors, how they verified that they had understood each response, and how their follow-up questions showed knowledge built over careers of responsible research.

The television reporters were a different breed. They swarmed around the site, cameras rolling, testing the limits of the security staff. The cameramen shoved and pushed as their on-screen counterparts jockeyed for the best views of the gallery's entrance, and tensions began to rise. A cadre of four commandos lost their cool when a news team clambered up the fragile walls above Caracolas. Their angry shouts brought the entire site to a standstill, and they ordered the crew off the monument with their guns drawn.

But if the television crews demanded scandal and intrigue, the archaeology students were happy to oblige. With two cameras rolling, Marisol spoke at length about all they had found that summer, and when a third camera approached, she started over with added embellishment. Samantha saw the handsome Stuart grant an interview without having been asked, approaching a television cameraman and gesturing for him to begin recording. Even Zoe, normally the model of grace and refinement, was eager to be on camera, and Samantha cringed when she heard her describe Chavín as a "real-life Temple of Doom."

One student, however, was nowhere to be seen.

"Where's Adam?" Samantha asked her uncle.

"Lying low at the hostal. He was very interested in the trumpets, and I'm sure he's excited to see them when the chaos dies down. But I think all this…" Jay waved at the assembled mass. "Well, it's just not really his thing."

Samantha looked away from the frenzy, scanning the peace and quiet of La Banda across the river. The terrible incident with Señor Ocllo seemed so long ago now, and the hazy menace of the Madman had been replaced by tangible physical threats.

A movement caught her eye. It was Alejandro, gesturing furtively in her direction from the other side of the Mosna. Telling her uncle she'd be right back, she ran down the terraces and across the great plaza to the river's edge. She gave a friendly *hola* as she approached, but on the opposite shore, the small boy's face was tight and drawn.

Alejandro cupped his hands over his mouth and began to whisper in hurried Spanish. She was directly across from him now but still could not hear him over the rush of the water. Samantha removed her notebook from around her neck and tossed it to him.

Alejandro snatched it from its landing place and immediately flipped it open, finding an empty place to write. His feeble return throw barely cleared the water's edge. She turned through the pages until she could find the little boy's scrawled handwriting:

el las quiere

Samantha's Spanish had improved enough to understand these three simple words, but still she did not immediately grasp what Alejandro was telling her.

"Who wants what?" she called across the river. "I don't understand!"

For a second time, Alejandro motioned for the notebook, and Samantha winced this time as he fumbled the catch, almost dropping it into the churning water at his feet. He looked left and right as if to make sure he was not being watched, scribbled something new, and again flung the notebook across the rapids.

el Loco quiere las trompetas

Samantha felt the all-too-familiar wave of fear go through

her, but she fought it off. It didn't matter who wanted the trumpets—the Madman or anyone else. No one would be getting into Caracolas tonight. Not with half the Peruvian army here.

"Samantha?"

It was Clare, calling for her from the center of the Plaza Mayor. "Sorry to interrupt, but you've been requested."

When Samantha turned to leave, Alejandro hung his head, alone with the gravest of secrets.

••◉••

Clare escorted Samantha through the throngs of camera-people around the entrance of Caracolas, sending them jostling again for the best position.

Samantha had never been on television before and was anxious that she'd say something wrong, or misremember some important date or fact. But it was an archaeologist's duty to educate the public and she would have to do her best. Besides, after hearing snatches of the other archae-ologists' accounts—which dwelled too heavily on bats and skulls—she wanted to set the record straight.

Evan was eager for camera time as well. They were made to sit together inside Caracolas, positioned on either side of the line of shells. Before long, their cheeks were sore from smiling for the cameras and their voices hoarse from answering questions shouted at them from the cordoned area just inside the gallery's entrance.

"*Joven, ¿eres arqueologo?*"

"*Sí.*" Evan snorted back. "What does it look like? Of course I'm an archaeologist…next question, please!"

"*Y señorita, ¿tu también?*"

The question was obviously posed to Samantha, but her brother was eager to field it on her behalf.

"*Ella es mi assistanta.* No, that's not the word…"

"*¿Ayudante?*" someone offered.

"Right. Yeah, she's my *ayudante.*"

Samantha glared at him. She was not his assistant or his helper, and she was about to clarify the point when another question rang out.

"How about a little digging?"

The American-accented English caught Samantha off guard.

"Come on, guys. Dig something up," the reporter suggested. "Maybe pretend to find one of the trumpets?"

Evan shrugged and, as the American camerawoman heaved the heavy camera to her shoulder in anticipation, he heaped some loose soil on one of the shells, only to whisk it clean with a brush when the camera's "record" light glowed red, and turn it over and over in his hands in pretended concentration. Over the next hour, as Samantha withdrew embarrassed into the shadows, her brother made the identical discovery, again and again, until each news agency had captured its own version on film.

●●◌●●

They returned to the hostal at sundown. Samantha was too exhausted to face the excitement of the crowded dining room and too tired to care when Evan pushed by her to run up the stairs and claim the first shower. She trudged across the twilit courtyard and collapsed onto a bench, cradling her head in her hands. She just wanted a few moments by herself.

But then someone loomed above her, blocking out the light of the moon.

"I hear you did well today, Samantha Sutton." Adam said, his voice dripping with contempt. "You should have your own TV show."

"What do you want?" she asked, her voice quavering much more than she would have liked.

"I just wanted your take on how things are going. Are you pleased about what you and your brother have brought to Chavín? I mean, it's exactly what we need right now: all these people getting in the way, publicizing our finds when we can't even protect what we've found already. Pretty soon, every looter in the world will be descending on this valley. Chavín will be stripped clean. And it will all be because of you."

To punctuate his scorn, he turned his head ever so slightly and spat, his phlegm landing inches from her shoe.

"It isn't my fault. I didn't ask the reporters to come."

He stared at her for a moment, the reflection of the evening's first stars in his sunglasses.

"Dr. Sutton made a mistake bringing you here," he

declared. "I'm sure that even he realizes that now. You're in pretty serious danger. Your brother is too. I bet your uncle would like nothing better than to send you both home."

With a snort, he turned to slink across the courtyard and into the street where Chimay and Dijota were waiting, leaving Samantha alone.

●●◉●●

It appeared that the president would be late.

Surely, one of the hundreds of people crowded onto the hillsides above the road would have spotted the motorcade by now if it had been on schedule. No telltale trail of dust had yet appeared in the southern end of the valley, but still they waited, their excitement only growing as the hour approached.

And then a distant thumping shifted all attention to the sky. The three helicopters appeared in a close V, skimming the western cliffs on their descent into the valley. Within the site, the commandos snapped to attention. They held their rigid posture as the helicopters settled in the center of the Plaza Mayor, sending out great blasts of heat and dust.

Samantha waited with the rest of the archaeological team near the mouth of Caracolas, straining her neck to get a look at the approaching dignitaries. Several men and women emerged from each aircraft, ducking beneath the still-whirling blades.

Marisol bent to Samantha's height and pointed.

"*Eso es él.*"

"The president?" Samantha asked. "Which one?"

"*¡Sí! El hombre con el traje azul.*"

Samantha watched as an elderly gentleman in a dark blue suit was greeted by the mayor and led up the terraces to the Circular Plaza, where a select group stood waiting.

On the mayor's cue, Clare, Osvaldo, and Jay stepped forward, and the president shook each of their hands in turn. But from then on, only Jay was to be part of the proceedings. While Clare beamed, Osvaldo slipped resentfully into the crowd.

As the news cameras rolled, and with Jay beside him, the mayor addressed his honored guest. It was the biggest moment of his political life. Viewers from Huaraz to Cuzco to Lima itself would be watching, and who knew what the future might hold. Making the most of it, he handled the occasion with the dignity and polish of a much more powerful official.

"*Señor Presidente*," he began, and Samantha could just understand the Spanish that followed. "Welcome. It is a great honor to present to you the esteemed Doctor Sutton, who has discovered what will long be considered a treasure of Peru. Now, if you will permit me, we will accompany Dr. Sutton into the gallery itself."

An officer stepped forward from among the squad of commandos and offered the president his arm for support. But the president waved him away and lowered himself gingerly into the opening of Caracolas, marring his suit with a long gray line of dust. The mayor and Jay followed, and the crowd fell silent.

Then from the entrance of the gallery came a dumb-founded cry. At first, Samantha and the rest of those assembled took the noise as a reaction of awe. But when the president emerged, reeling into the full light of day, his face told a different story.

"*¿Me estás tomando el pelo?*" he barked at the mayor. "*Una humillación. Una infamia.*"

And at once Samantha knew that the trumpets were gone. Around her, the same realization rippled through the crowd in a wave of gasps.

"*Señor Presidente,*" the mayor was saying. "*Todas precauciones...*"

But a soldier put himself between the mayor and the head of state, and pressed him back among the stricken professors.

The scene erupted into chaos. As commandos rushed this way and that, and as the crowd dispersed in confusion, Samantha's attention was fixed on something in the middle distance. She did not look at the president as he was ushered quickly to his helicopter, nor at the scurrying television crews, nor at Clare as she fought to keep the students under control.

Instead, Samantha's eyes were fixed on Osvaldo and her uncle. They had separated themselves from the rest of the group and now stood engaged in a furious argument, their words drowned out completely by the roar of the helicopters.

Samantha had never seen her uncle like this before. His finger jabbed at Osvaldo's chest, harder and harder, and angry sprays of spittle accompanied each spoken barb.

Osvaldo seemed to be drawing himself in, contracting all his anger into the ball of his fist. And then, as Samantha watched in horror, Jay gave Osvaldo a hard shove, and Osvaldo planted his feet, reared back, and knocked Jay off his feet with a terrible blow.

Samantha bolted forward, but a commando immediately caught her around the waist and flung her backward into the scrambling mob. She was then ushered roughly from the site with the rest of the crowd.

Newspaper reporters all seem really smart, but the people from the TV stations seem really, really

Loco gall

Jay's planning on waiting in the dark for the thief to come down the stairs.

Jay

Stairs

Spanish → Englis
• Es la verdad? -
  I s that the truth?
• Alégate de nosotros /
  déjanos en paz? -
  leave us alone or go
                   away
• Solo - only/alone

hit him so hard in the face.

Soldiers, and Jay says they will make sure everything is secure.

SSFNb1-CdH: 15

279

CHAPTER 15

There was a curfew that night. The bewildered students were happy to remain within the walls of the hostal while the fearsome commandos outside scoured the area in search of the looters. Bands of local policemen also roamed the streets, interrogating the poor citizens unlucky enough to have been included on the hastily compiled suspect list.

From the hostal's office, Samantha tried each of her parents' many phones, letting each go to the message before hanging up and trying the next. They were probably still at the office in some sort of meeting. But she tried the home phone just in case, slamming down the receiver when she reached the jarring sound of her own voice, asking her to leave her name and number.

She shuffled to the dining room and sat down to write in her notebook, doing all she could to distract herself.

"Do you mind if I sit?"

Samantha made room for Clare at the table.

"A sad day," the professor said.

Samantha nodded but did not respond.

Clare moved close and covered Samantha's hand with her own.

"Sam, you are the most resourceful girl I have ever met. You are a great help to our team here, one of the best archaeologists we have."

Samantha felt somewhat buoyed by the gentle words, but then she realized that Clare was preparing to say something difficult.

"I'm just not sure if you should stay here any longer. The valley has become very dangerous. I'm worried that we won't be able to keep you safe. You or your brother."

Samantha was too startled to answer. As the hurt took hold in the silence that followed, she could not blink away the tears that were pooling in her eyes, nor force back the lump as it rose in her throat.

"I won't make this decision for you, Samantha. It's up to you. Well, up to you and your uncle. But I want you to think about it. Can you promise me you'll do that?"

Cooking sounds clanged from the kitchen as the señora readied the evening meal, but Samantha could barely hear them, lost in feelings of her own. She just didn't understand this place. Even as she had tried to grow comfortable with it, even as she was learning to live with its language, its foreign tastes and smells, all its troubles and inconveniences, it had turned on her. And if this was what it was to be an archaeologist—fighting with your colleagues, negotiating with angry politicians, losing your finds to looters, putting yourself in danger—than maybe she *was* too young. Or maybe she wasn't meant to be an archaeologist at all.

But it was Jay, not her, who had the biggest stake in how the ongoing catastrophe would unfold.

"Clare?" she said, wiping away her tears. "I wanted to ask you something too. It's about my uncle."

"Ah," Clare smiled, turning a little red. "And what, exactly, do you want to ask me?"

But Samantha's question was a serious one.

"I just wanted to know…is he…is he a good archaeologist?"

Clare's reply was full of tenderness.

"Yes, Samantha. Jay Sutton is an excellent archaeologist."

"But, I mean, why is this happening? Is all of this his fault?"

Clare sighed.

"No, Samantha. It's all very confusing. But one thing I am sure of is that your uncle is beyond reproach. His colleagues respect him. He is worshipped by his students. No. I can promise you that your uncle is not to blame."

"But Osvaldo seems to think…"

"Osvaldo is frustrated, like we all are. He takes this all personally. He's from this region, as you know, and there is tremendous pressure on him to see that the excavation is conducted carefully, respectfully, and without incident. He may be irritated with your uncle, but if anything it's Jay's students that he distrusts. One of them, specifically."

Samantha thought about Adam and his menacing

conduct all summer: his attempt to sneak the bird bone from the West Field, his odd behavior at the soccer game, and the money-stuffed envelope at the arcade—his handwriting across its face.

"Yes," Clare continued, "Adam is certainly Osvaldo's prime suspect. And it's worse than you might know, now that things have gone missing from here, as well."

"From the lab?" Samantha asked, alarmed.

"An odd selection of artifacts: that mortar and pestle they found in the Circular Plaza, some pots, your lovely bird bone, I'm afraid. We haven't yet alerted the police to our suspicions, but Osvaldo and I think it may be time."

Samantha sighed.

"I don't know why Jay sticks up for Adam so much."

"Well, that's your uncle for you. He has always done all he can to help those who can't seem to help themselves. I'm sad to say that it's a quality that has made him more enemies than it has friends."

"Have you known him for a long time?"

"We were at graduate school together in England. Hasn't he ever told you that? You would have been a baby then. I was getting my PhD when he was getting his Master's. That meant that I taught him in some of his classes."

"Really?"

"He was such a bright student. A little headstrong, as I'm sure you can imagine. He absolutely refused to focus on any particular period or region, bouncing around the globe doing his fieldwork—two weeks here, a month there.

But he was so dedicated. So intelligent. An expert on everything he pursued."

Samantha detected an amount of pride in the professor's kind smile.

"Anyway, when I heard he had been working in Peru for the past few years, I knew that I wanted him up here. I introduced him to Osvaldo at a conference in Lima last year, and Jay made a very positive impression."

But then Clare's smile faded.

"It's sad, really," she said. "I was hoping that this summer would be the beginning of something truly wonderful."

There was something more than professional regret in her voice. Samantha knew love when she heard it.

●●◉●●

She skipped dinner, sitting instead in the hostal's courtyard and watching the clouds roll in to cover the moon. She had not seen Osvaldo or her uncle for hours. Students came and went from the dining room in singles and pairs. Distrust prevailed. All sense of camaraderie was lost.

"Sam?"

Samantha looked up at her uncle and wiped away the hair from where it had stuck to her tears. In the faint light, she could see that the left side of his face was hideously swollen. He managed a sideways smile.

"We make a pretty sad-looking team, don't we?"

"Uncle Jay," she sniffed. "Your eye looks really bad."

"It's nothing. Remember what I looked like when I

came back from Laos? After that kid monk tried to rob me at the Plain of Jars? Now *that* was something!"

He sat down beside her.

"Do you have any idea what happened?"

Jay shook his head.

"With the trumpets? No. But Osvaldo didn't seem to take kindly to my suspicions."

"What did you say to him? That it was an inside job?"

"It's the only thing that makes sense. Those soldiers were everywhere last night. I heard that there were four posted just outside the gallery, working shifts."

"And you think someone was able to bribe them?"

"I don't know. Possibly. It's a tough life in this country, Sam. People are poor. And if you figure that each of those trumpets could fetch thousands of dollars on the black market, it's not too big a stretch to think that even the most dutiful soldier would look the other way for a share of the profits."

Samantha was quiet for a moment, thinking.

"Couldn't it be one of the students?"

"Maybe. Who knows? The evidence certainly points to someone with a detailed knowledge of our operations. Osvaldo and I happen to agree on that point. But while I suggested it might be one of his students, he made it pretty clear that he thinks it's one of mine."

He pointed to the swelling around his eye and laughed—a full-throated, jovial guffaw.

Something within Samantha snapped. How could he

be laughing at a time like this? The site's most precious artifacts were missing, and he was laughing? Dangerous criminals might be lurking nearby, and he was laughing? He was laughing when his friendship with Osvaldo had been destroyed, his reputation ruined, and his career threatened to teeter off the edge? The situation was serious, gravely so, but if she had learned one thing this summer, it was that her uncle couldn't be serious about anything for very long.

Suddenly, Samantha felt desperately alone. Her uncle, she realized then, was not a parent. What if something had happened to Evan or to her? Would that be a laughing matter too?

It felt like the decision had been made for her. She sat for a minute, weighing the awful words in silence, but when she spoke at last, her voice was clear and resolute.

"Uncle Jay," she said, "I want to go home."

His smile faded at once.

"Did Osvaldo say something to you?"

She hesitated.

"No. But Clare did."

Just then Adam emerged from his room and strode past them toward the front gate and the street beyond.

"The curfew!" Jay called after him. "Where are you going?"

"El Cóndor, Dr. Sutton," his student replied without turning around. "Don't wait up."

He slammed the door behind him so hard that it

jumped on its hinges, then swung slowly outward once again so that Samantha could see his figure fade into the dusk. A moment later, two other figures emerged from the shadows of the Plaza de Armas to follow him. From their shapes, Samantha could see that they were army commandos, their automatics slung from their necks and their army caps silhouetted in the dim blue light.

"Samantha," Jay said at last. "I don't want you to leave. You or your brother. Not yet. We need to find the actual thief."

Samantha shook her head. Enough was enough.

"We? Come on, Uncle Jay. Shouldn't that be up to the police?"

"No, Samantha. My reputation is on the line. I need to fix this before I'm kicked out of here for good. I have a plan, but I need someone's help. And you and your brother are all I have left."

The reluctant look on Samantha's face was her only response.

"Sam. Please."

If Jay needed her, she knew she had no choice. And with her last ounce of confidence in her uncle, Samantha listened to his idea.

●●◉●●

"I have a big secret."

It was morning, and as a pair of dogs tussled in the center of the Plaza de Armas, Samantha felt almost queasy as she began the great lie. But it must not have shown, for Isabel and Alejandro stared at her with open earnestness.

"¿*Pues?*" Isabel was impatient. "¿*Cuál secreto?*"

There was no stopping now. If Jay's plan was to work, the rumor needed to spread as widely as possible. Evan had been dispatched to El Cóndor to plant the seed with Dijota and Chimay, and Jay himself set to telling his adult contacts, but—he had said—nothing would spread the tale more quickly than the excited chatter of Chavín's children.

Samantha paused. Even with everything at stake, she hated doing it. Lying had never come naturally to her, and Alejandro and Isabel were her friends.

"There is a tomb at the site," she explained in uneasy Spanish. "A big one, full of pottery, shell trumpets, and gold. We just found it yesterday when we were mapping the galleries."

As Isabel and Alejandro listened, mouths agape, she went on to describe the pretend find, trying to remember all the details her uncle had invented. She explained that it had all been situated in a hidden room at the bottom of a stairwell, deep within the Temple's mass, its narrow entrance covered with a large wooden board.

"It's in the Galería del Loco," Samantha whispered, and watched the color drain from Alejandro's cheeks.

Loco, Jay had determined, would be the perfect spot. The thief, if he got inside, would squeeze down the stone steps and become instantly trapped. A hidden sentry could easily hold him there until police arrived. Now, the bait needed to be amply spread, and Samantha hoped that her reluctant lie would have its intended results.

She braced herself for her finale.

"But you can't tell anyone, okay?"

Alejandro raised a hand, as if to swear to secrecy, but Isabel fixed her with a questioning look.

"*¿Es la verdad?*" she asked.

And Samantha nodded.

"Yes," she managed, "it's true."

There was a noise from in front of the hostal, the opening of a car door. As her friends chatted excitedly, Samantha watched her uncle reach into the passenger's side of the excavation van and open the glove compartment.

At first, she could not see what he had retrieved. But as he came around the side of the van into full view, the glint of gun metal flashed above his belt.

The plan was now set. And it was deadly serious.

●●◉●●

That evening, Jay trudged up to the site and slipped quietly into Loco, the eyes of the security force barely registering his entrance. They left him alone, even after the sun went down, and did not even bother to retrieve him when the guards changed shifts at midnight. It made no difference. He was just one man, easily monitored, and carried no tools with which to dig. Any effort he made to take material out of the site would be noticed immediately.

Samantha went to check on him in the morning,

doubtful that his first attempt to catch the thief had been successful. He was red-eyed and miserable from his all-night vigil, but he gave her a thin smile as he accepted the packet of bread, jam, and coffee that the señora had prepared for him.

"Nothing?" Samantha asked, as gently as she could.

"Believe me," he said, as he chomped on his breakfast. "You wouldn't have had to ask."

He was just being sarcastic, but there was a nastier edge to his voice.

"Sorry, Sam. I guess I'm a little tired."

"Need anything else?"

Without even looking at her, he shook his head no, and she trudged back to the hostal with her feelings hurt, leaving Jay for a second day and night.

••●●••

The team members were anxious and short-tempered. Their summer of work was winding to a close, and they bickered bitterly with one another when they weren't longing out loud for their coming departure.

"Have you seen your uncle?" Clare asked her privately, over dinner. "I've been looking around for him all day, and he seems to have vanished!"

Samantha didn't know what to say.

"He's busy," she managed. "But I'm sure he'll be around tomorrow."

Clare fixed her with a quizzical look.

"Sam. Please tell me he's not doing anything crazy."

"He's okay. And don't worry. He's going to fix all this."

The professor shook her head, dismayed.

"Oh, Samantha. That is not what I wanted to hear. Not at all."

The next morning, Samantha hurried to the site again, passing through the gate and to the entrance of Loco under the policemen's steely stares.

It was clear as soon as she saw him that Jay had had another sleepless night. There was a desperate irritability about him, and several seconds went by before he even acknowledged her presence. He reached for the coffee and packet of food without a word.

"Anything?"

"What does it look like?" he snapped, then softened his voice. "No. Nothing yet."

She studied him as he sipped his coffee. His movements were erratic, his muscles tense. He caught her gaze for a moment, and she had to look away. Something in her uncle was changing, and it was terrifying to behold.

"Do you want to take a break, Uncle Jay? I'm sure it would be okay, at least for a couple hours."

He sat in silence, his eyes staring straight ahead.

"No, Sam. I need to do this. Please just leave me alone."

Samantha spent the rest of the afternoon trying to read, but her worry kept her from focusing. For a moment, she even considered joining her brother at the arcade, but the idea of running into Chimay put her off the idea. Adam had somehow shaken off the commandos who had been assigned to follow him, and the police had interrogated Chimay about where Adam might be hiding. Samantha worried that the Peruvian teenager would focus his anger on her. In fact, as keeper of her uncle's secret, she dreaded an encounter with anyone and only left her room to eat.

And so she flinched when Osvaldo took her by the arm as she entered the hostal's dining room that evening, leading her without a word toward the lab as the students looked up anxiously from their plates of cuy and eggs.

"Samantha, *pulguita*," he said, as the door closed behind them. "It is very important that you tell me what your uncle is doing. I am the director of this excavation, and it is my duty to be aware of everything that happens on the site."

She looked at her feet.

Osvaldo's voice was soft but stern.

"*Ahora.* There are rumors that he has made a discovery of some kind—a tomb, they say. It is within my power, of course, to go to the site and see for myself what he is doing. But, in all honesty, I worry what will happen if your uncle and I have another disagreement. And so, for your uncle's sake, and for my own, I hope that you will give me the information that I need. What, *exactamente*, is he doing?"

She was quiet, squirming in his gaze.

"I…I'm not supposed to tell you."

Osvaldo frowned. Samantha could feel the tears as they pooled in her eyes and tumbled down her cheeks.

"I'm sorry," she cried. "I really am. But I promised I wouldn't say anything."

Osvaldo knelt to face her, placing a kind hand on her shoulder.

"I will never forgive your uncle for putting you in this position," he said, smiling sadly. "Samantha Sutton, you are like no one I have ever met. But you are also just a child, and this is wrong. Very, very wrong."

Though she did nothing to tell him so, Samantha agreed with him completely.

"Perhaps I can ask you some questions, and you can just answer yes or no?"

She nodded through her tears.

"*Entonces.* Is there some new discovery at the site? Something that needs my attention, so that I can assure it is properly protected?"

"No," she voiced, very quietly.

"And is your uncle continuing to excavate, despite my warnings and in spite of the mayor's specific instructions?"

"No. He isn't digging."

Osvaldo studied her for a moment.

"*Bueno.* Thank you, my dear."

When he led her again into the dining room, the conversation of the students came to a sudden stop. All eyes were on Samantha as she walked through the room to take her seat beside her brother.

●●◉●●

The third day of her uncle's vigil, Samantha rose just after dawn. As she came down into the courtyard, the European tourists were just returning, looking invigorated by their early-morning trek. But she was too lost in thought to acknowledge the old man's gentle greeting or to answer his strained questions about her work.

And then, a welcome feeling of relief. Beside the flag-pole in the Plaza de Armas, Alejandro and Isabel sat in quiet conversation.

The children's rapid Spanish halted suddenly as they noticed her approach, and the looks on their faces stopped Samantha's "*buenos días*" in her throat. Alejandro's eyes were wide and wet, and Isabel's face was a mask of paralyzed terror.

"*¡Aléjate de nosotros!*" Isabel wailed. "*Por favor, Samantha, ¡déjanos en paz!*"

Samantha took a step back, feeling as if she'd been punched in the stomach. What had she done? Isabel's outburst, asking her to stay away from them, made no sense. Why were they afraid of her? Did they suddenly suspect her in all the thefts?

"It wasn't me!" she cried. "Please, you have to believe me! It was Adam! Osvaldo knows it. Adam is the thief. I have nothing to do with it!

Behind her, Samantha heard the clank of chain on metal

and turned to see the mayor frozen in the midst of his daily duty, hoisting the Peruvian flag into the sky. As the red and white banner unfurled above them, she realized that he was staring at her intently. He had heard her every word.

"No, Samantha," Alejandro whispered fearfully. "*Tú no, ni Adam tampoco. El Loco, Samantha. Solo el Loco.*"

•• ● ••

Later that morning, Samantha did not want to go to the site alone. The hostility of Isabel and Alejandro had knocked her off balance, and she worried what the mayor would do with the information she had so carelessly provided. Her uncle's dark mood the day before had also rattled her, and she was nervous to bring him breakfast by herself.

"Come on, Evan. Please?"

"Not now, Archaeo Kid. I've got to get over to the arcade to practice. Tomorrow everyone's coming to see me beat *Pillager II*. Chimay is selling tickets. I've just got the final boss left—Otzi the Iceman, remember? I have to warm up."

"But Uncle Jay is really different lately, Evan. Can you please come with me? Then you can go straight to the arcade."

Evan pushed past her, making his way for the door.

"No, Samantha! And maybe you shouldn't go either. If Uncle Jay has to come back into town for his breakfast, maybe he'll forget about this whole stupid plan. Besides, the summer's pretty much over. It's almost time to go home."

And so Samantha approached the Loco gallery alone,

worried to see what Jay's third sleepless night had done to him. As she stooped to enter the gallery, she heard the heavy breathing of deep slumber and was relieved to find her uncle asleep around the corner of the entryway. She touched his arm to wake him.

Immediately, the peace was broken. Jay started, thrashing his legs and clutching at the air, seemingly as mad as the gallery's namesake. And then, to Samantha's horror, she saw him lunge toward the cleft of the wall.

"It's me, Uncle Jay!" she shouted, before he could retrieve the gun from its hiding spot.

Jay gave a soft cry and fell back, holding his head in his hands for several moments before finally turning to face her. Tears streamed from his eyes, dripping through the whiskers on his unshaven face.

"Oh, Sam. Oh, Sam."

"It's okay," she said, her voice trembling.

"Oh, Sam," he said again, "I am so sorry."

She let him hug her, her own arms pressed to her sides.

"How long have I been out?" he slurred, still a little disoriented.

"I don't know. I just got here."

He nudged the gun back to its place with the toe of his boot and Samantha took a step away.

"It's not loaded, Sam. Probably hasn't been in ten years."

"Oh," she muttered. "I guess I assumed it was."

Again, Jay's face took on a wild seriousness.

"And so will our looter. As soon as he makes his way in

there," Jay motioned to where the staircase descended into the Temple's uncharted depths, "I'll hold him at gunpoint and shout like crazy until the guards come."

Samantha saw a broken man before her. His career was in tatters and his confidence destroyed. The plan had been a failure. From the look of shame on his face, it was clear that he knew it too.

"I thought someone may have sneaked by me into the gallery last night, Sam. I heard voices inside. But I think it was just one of those really strange dreams. You know the kind where you think you're awake? "

They were silent and still for a very long time, until at last Jay pulled himself to his feet. Stooped and limping, he followed his niece into the late-morning sunshine, holding a shaky hand over his eyes.

Neither of them spoke a word as they were patted down by the guards and ambled slowly into the town, eventually leaving the main road for the maze of alleys and side streets.

All seemed well in Chavín. Shopkeepers splashed pails of water outside their storefronts to tamp down the dust, exchanging pleasantries with their neighbors. A cluster of children broke and came together again, laughing and singing in their game. Life would continue when the archaeologists left, just as it had in this valley for thousands of years before.

As Samantha walked beside her uncle, she realized that in his silence was his surrender. It was all over now, and he was beginning to accept with grim finality that the damage they had brought to the site could never be repaired.

"Uncle Jay," Samantha said. "It's not safe for me here. You know I have to go home."

There was a silent moment before he answered.

"Okay, Sam. We'll leave in the morning."

A sort of calm had come over him, and with every step, the madness of the gallery and the summer's disasters seemed to leach from his system like poison.

"How's your brother?"

Samantha was quick to embrace the change in mood.

"Annoying. He's more interested in that stupid video game than he is in anything else. Stupid Otzi the Iceman. He throws exploding mammoth tusk spears and shoots ice beams from his tattoos."

Jay's laugh, though hoarse and guttural, came as a welcome relief.

"I'm starving, kiddo. Wanna grab a bite to eat?"

They came to stop at El Ficho, the upscale restaurant where Samantha would come to pick up the expedition's mail. They sat down across a small table, gave their orders for pizza, and shared a quiet chuckle as the sound of a microwave whirred from the nearby kitchen.

"Let's talk, Sam."

"What about?"

"Anything. Anything but Chavín."

And so, as the beautiful waitress delivered their pizzas, Samantha asked Jay about his earliest forays into archaeology. He told her how he and her father had done their own amateur archaeology in their backyard one summer—marking out units with dental floss, fighting over the shovel, and threatening the foundation of their childhood home with their crooked trenches.

The experience had ended Raymond Sutton's interest in archaeology forever. Besides being dangerous, there was no stability in the profession, no future in any career that left so much up to chance. But Jay, the younger brother, had been hooked.

When the señorita approached, glancing shyly at Jay as she set down a plate of *alfajores*, his narrative changed direction. Love had always eluded him, he said. While Samantha's father had always planned to marry a woman he met in business school and had done just that, Jay's love life, like his career, had relied heavily on coincidence and fate, and had so far yielded nothing.

The resignation on her uncle's face made Samantha want to throw her arms around him. She knew that Jay was thinking about Professor Clare Barrows and that the summer's calamities had taken their toll on that possibility, as well.

"Your dad's is the best path in the end, Samantha," Jay said, his smile sad as the light outside tinged golden. "Maybe if I were more like Ray I wouldn't have gotten into this mess. And I'm happy to see that you're just like him. Reasonable. Cautious. You're not like me. Not like me at all."

There was a time when such a statement would have wounded her, but now Samantha took comfort in its truth.

It was then that Marisol burst into the restaurant, anguish on her face as well. "*¿Qué tal?*" Jay asked, placing some coins on the table to cover the bill. "*¿Todo está bien?*"

Marisol shook her head no. Everything was not fine. Something serious was happening at the Hostal Jato and Jay was needed there right away.

He leapt up, upsetting his chair and knocking the salt shaker from the table. They charged across the plaza, through the hostal's wooden doorway, and into the entire police force of Chavín.

find out
~~what this means~~

Get out
Capitalists

FUERAS CAPITALISTAS

VIVA LA REVOLUCION → Long live the people's revolution

Popular

Spanish → English
• Buscando - looking for

He looks horrible, but I'm more worried about what will happen to his job.

snuff tube for snorting the cactus powder

stirrup vessel

a carving showing someone holding a cactus + under the influence of San Pedro cactus.

a mortar + pestle for crushing San Pedro cactus into powder

I want to get out of here. It's too dangerous. I wish everyone else would too. I don't want anything bad to happen to them.

Tenon head showing a person unde the influence San Pedro ca

SSFNb1-CdH: 16

301

CHAPTER 16

Samantha and her uncle diverged as they entered the hostal. Jay sprinted through the dining room to safe-guard the lab, while she dashed madly up the steps to check on her room.

Two sets of hands grabbed her as she entered the upstairs hallway.

"Easy there, Sam," said Clare, from her right.

"*Tranquila, joven,*" came Osvaldo's muted baritone from her left.

Almost a dozen policemen were crammed into the passage at the top of the stairs, conducting a search of the guest rooms with authoritative efficiency. She could hear English, American, and Peruvian voices through the open doors, some raised in angry protestation.

Stuart burst from his room at the end of the hall, holding his computer with both hands.

"Well, you're not confiscating my laptop. Not while I'm breathing."

No one stopped him as he barreled through the crowded passageway, down the stairwell, and into courtyard, holding the computer tight against his chest.

Samantha wrenched free of Osvaldo and Clare and pushed herself into the room she shared with her brother. He was sitting on his bed, his head in his hands as two policemen ruffled through their belongings. One policeman, who Samantha recognized as a guitar player from the concert in the galleries, was examining Evan's collection of carved Lanzóns.

"You don't have to do it so roughly," her brother was pleading, his voice agitated and fast. "Have you no respect for art?"

The other officer had turned Samantha's suitcase over onto the floor and was poking each carefully folded item with his shoe. But his search was halfhearted, and he made no effort to stop her as she picked up each stack and placed it neat and upright on her bedspread.

"You okay, Evan?" she whispered.

"No, I'm not okay! I paid Isabel more than ten dollars for all these *lanzones*. They're commissioned artwork! Each one of them is one of a kind!"

Suddenly, the two policemen snapped to attention and the mayor entered the room. He nodded curtly at Samantha, then turned to face Evan where he sat.

"Where is Señor Quint?"

His tone was businesslike. He did not seem to care that he was talking to a boy of fourteen.

"You mean Adam?" Evan replied ruefully. "How should I know? He doesn't even let me hang out with him anymore. You should try Dijota and Chimay."

The mayor gave a commanding look to one of the guards, who immediately slipped out of the room, no doubt in search of the teenagers.

There was a commotion in the hallway, and then Jay entered the room and pushed himself between the mayor and the boy.

"Ah," said the mayor, "Doctor Sutton."

Jay looked at the scene before him, fuming.

"Can someone please explain why my nephew is being interrogated?"

The mayor extended his hands to calm Jay.

"Your nephew is...¿cómo se dice?...cooperating in our ongoing investigation. He is under no suspicion. Nor, I might add, is your formidable niece."

"But you just barge in here, searching our rooms, going through our belongings?"

"Doctor Sutton. As you know, the site of Chavín de Huántar is a symbol of the heritage of this village, a symbol of Ancash, a symbol of Peru, and indeed the heritage of all mankind. It is therefore my duty to all these entities to recover what has been stolen."

He gave Samantha a triumphant look.

"Your niece has been very helpful. Because of her and certain recent developments, we suspect the involvement of some of the members of your team."

"What developments?" Jay barked. "Show me."

"If you will allow me," the mayor answered, "I will be most happy to."

●●◉●●

Adam's door had been forced wide open. Articles of his clothing were flung across the doorstep and into the dirt outside, where some of them now marinated in a puddle in the flower bed. Samantha, Evan, and the three professors followed the mayor to the doorway, and the pair of armed guards flanking the entrance parted. Samantha could see the glint of more guns and more policemen inside.

"*Miren*," the mayor said, as everyone crowded into the room.

The reaction was delayed. Then Osvaldo issued a low dark oath and Clare pounded the doorframe with her hand. What they were seeing was impossible to believe.

Covering every surface of Adam's room were artifacts. His dresser absolutely glistened with plastic find bags. Samantha recognized the delicate bone tube that she had recovered from the Ofrendas gallery, sitting among several others just like it. And there were three intact stirrup vessels that Zoe had so proudly recovered, and the mortar and pestle that Marisol had so lovingly unearthed. Beside his bed was one of Chavín's tenon heads, its stone tubes of mucus curling from its nostrils like tusks. Above it all, taped crookedly above the bed stand, hung a rubbing of one of the carvings from the Circular Plaza—the monstrous individual clutching a spiky club. The room's bounty was laid out before him like an offering.

"So, as you see, Dr. Sutton, I am merely doing my job. The trumpets are as yet unaccounted for. The mummy also is not here. I am afraid that every member of the *proyecto* is a suspect until these objects are found."

Jay raised a hand to his brow and gave a long, guilty sigh.

"*Señor alcalde,* I'm afraid you've got things all wrong. This is not what it looks like."

"Jay? You knew about this?" asked Clare.

"No. No, not exactly," Jay spluttered. "Please. Just let me explain. Adam is not behind the looting. This…this is something else."

"We are listening," Osvaldo hissed.

Jay steeled himself for a moment, then let his secret come tumbling forth.

"What we're looking at, all of it, is part of Adam's research. I'm sure that when we compare what's in this room to our inventories, everything—everything—will be accounted for. He is not planning to sell these things or stupid enough to sneak anything with him out of the country. He is not a thief. A disobedient student, most definitely, but not a thief."

"Then why?" Clare asked, bewildered.

Jay turned to her.

"Adam's interest in the site is its psychoactive pharmacopeia."

"Hallucinogens? Drugs?"

"Narcotics, yes. It is his theory that the people of Chavín made ritual use of the San Pedro cactus."

"This is no great hypothesis. I have heard this theory before," Osvaldo interrupted.

"As have I," Clare said, her voice low and shaky. "So why all this secrecy?"

Jay held up his hands, begging their patience.

"Adam's approach was different. He came to me, his advisor, with a research proposal. It was his idea to engage in some…" he trailed off, glancing at his niece, "some *applied* archaeology. He wanted to evaluate, firsthand, the experience of someone on the site who was under the influence of one of these agents."

Around them, the police shifted impatiently.

"And you told him…"

"Well, of course I told him not to. San Pedro is a very dangerous substance, especially if you haven't been trained in its preparation. But he ignored me. Several weeks ago, when you two were in San Marcos, he approached me at the soccer game and told me that he'd located a source for some San Pedro."

"A source?" snorted the mayor. "The hillsides are full of it."

"Well, this source—these sources, I should say—were willing to teach him to prepare it in the traditional way: to show him how to boil it into a liquid to be drunk or grind it into a powder to be snorted. Again, I told him no. I was pretty emphatic, I might add. In fact, I told him that if he went forward with such a dangerous research plan, then he would need to find another advisor. I would not be responsible if something went wrong. But, from the looks of this, he seems to have moved forward all the same."

There was a long, awkward silence. Samantha's mind whirled.

San Pedro. It made sense, of course. Adam's hushed meetings with Chimay and Dijota, the envelope full of money, his occasional spurts of animal fury, his runny nose and the dull blackness of his dilated eyes: all effects of the drug the cactus contained.

"So, this all pertains to his research?" the mayor asked. "Everything is accounted for?"

"Yes, I'm positive."

"Show me."

Jay stepped around the guards to investigate the artifacts on the dresser and floor.

"These vessels?" he pointed at Zoe's discoveries, which Samantha now saw were lined with tiny markings. "Covered in San Pedro iconography. This mortar and pestle? Used to grind the cactus into snuff. These bone tubes and spatulas? Used as inhalers. The tenon head? A shamanic figure, mid-transformation. The mucus flowing from his nose is a side effect of San Pedro's inhaled form. And this," he pointed at the rubbing that overlooked it all, "a man—a priest—carrying a stalk of San Pedro cactus in his hand."

The mayor cleared his throat.

"And the trumpets? The mummy?"

"Not his doing. Adam Quint would not have been

interested in an Incan mummy, or the trumpets either. They are totally unrelated to his research."

The mayor kept his steely cool as he strode toward the doorway.

"We will need to confirm this story with his own testimony. And there are likely to be consequences, regardless."

"Of course, *señor alcade*. As you wish. If he returns to the hostal, I'll do my best to ensure that he complies with your instructions."

The mayor gave orders to the policemen, then turned on his heels to walk stiffly across the courtyard. His orders were repeated up the stairwell, and soon the entire police force was marching from the Hostal Jato in search of Adam Quint.

●●◉●●

It was hours before the furor died down, and Samantha spent the time huddled in her bed. Evan was in the dining room, sensing that his sister needed some time alone. Word had spread that she was the cause of the police raid. And it was true: the raid would never have happened if the mayor hadn't overheard her foolish outburst to Alejandro and Isabel outside in the plaza.

She had listened as the three professors railed at each other into the night. Most of the wrath was reserved for Jay. Samantha knew he deserved it. He had not been honest with his colleagues. They had invited him to work among them, and for all their trust and kindness, he had brought them

chaos and disgrace. Even if Adam were innocent of any looting, his behavior had been selfish, harmful, and deceitful.
And Jay had suspected it all along and had done nothing.

Tears still streamed from her eyes, and now, where she
could not be seen, she made no effort to stop them. The
San Pedro cactus revelation had seriously unnerved her,
adding a component to the site that she simply did not
understand. Over the summer, she had felt like she was
getting to know the people of ancient Chavín. She had
come to understand what they found beautiful and had
grown to love them through the small glimpses of their
lives. But drugs? She felt foolish and betrayed. She did not
know these people at all.

The rain that had been falling all night had started to
let up, and the fearsome gusts were losing some of their
strength. She wiped her nose and nestled into her pillow.
She could swear that she heard voices just outside her
window, under the dying whistles of the wind. She pulled
the blankets higher and held her breath, trying to separate
the human whispers from the sound.

"Are you being followed?"

It was her uncle. There was only one person he could
be speaking to.

"The police? I lost them hours ago."

Samantha raised herself to an elbow and, as carefully as
she could, moved the curtain aside, flooding the room with
the yellow glow of the streetlamp outside. Jay and Adam
were just below.

"So, Dr. Sutton, are you going to let me through? I'd really like to see what those morons did to my room."

There was a sudden movement and a string of angry cursing as Jay lunged at his student, grabbing him so that his shoulders slammed hard against the wall.

"Listen to me," Jay hissed. "The police won't stop until they find you. And if I say one word to them, I guarantee that you'll be spending the next several years in the Canto Grande prison."

"For what?" Adam spat. "For conducting legitimate scientific research?"

"You may see it that way. But the authorities are looking for someone to pay for all this negative publicity, and your little stunt makes you the obvious target."

Adam struggled free and took a step away from his advisor.

"But you know I didn't steal anything. It's all there. All of it."

He reached into his pocket and shoved a folded piece of paper into Jay's hand.

"Look at this. An inventory of all the artifacts I've borrowed. Each is accounted for. Every single one."

But Jay let the paper fall to the ground.

"Get out of here, Adam. Now, before it's light. Take the trail through the mountains to Olleros, get on the first bus to Lima, and go home before anyone thinks to alert the authorities in the capital."

Adam blanched.

"But all my work? My research? What about my PhD?"

"Forget it," Jay commanded. "Go. Now."

For a moment Adam stood his ground, seeming to contemplate some terrible act. And then, to Samantha's horror, he looked up, fixing her in his coal-black gaze before she could move away from the window.

"You've ruined me," he said, speaking just as much to Samantha as to Jay, "and I will remember it forever."

He slid his sunglasses over his dilated eyes, spat, and disappeared completely into the night.

•••●••

It was barely light the next morning when Jay came for her. She moved as quietly as she could, but when she scooted her suitcase into the hallway for her uncle to carry down to the van, Evan stirred in his bed.

"You're really leaving?" he asked from beneath the covers.

"Yeah."

He sat up sleepily, watching her tie her hiking boots.

"Bye, Archaeo Kid."

The sadness in his voice triggered an old, familiar feeling—rare in the past few years. So, on the way to the door, she gave her brother a hug. To her relief, he squeezed her back.

It was too early in the morning for any other good-byes. Clare and Osvaldo, Stuart and Zoe, Alejandro and Isabel—all would wake to find her gone. But maybe it was better this way.

She followed her uncle to the waiting van and climbed

into the front seat. As her uncle clambered in and found the ignition in the early morning light, she looked up to the window of her room. Evan had pulled back the curtains and was giving her a final, melancholy wave.

••●●••

Soon, driving through the scent of woodsmoke and the sound of barking dogs, they left Chavín in the shadows of the mountains, climbing to where dawn had broken some hours before. It was not the altitude that made her drowsy now, but the exhaustion of all that had happened over the past few days. She watched the changing scenery through the window from beneath heavy eyelids, lulled as her uncle hummed along to the songs of Frank Sinatra.

Her thoughts turned to what awaited her back at home. She would face a boring two weeks of summer back in Davis, California, before school began. And to her surprise, she felt completely resigned to this fate. No soldiers with guns were needed to protect her there—no angry dogs prowling the tree-lined streets, no sword-wielding old men waiting for her in the Yolo County Library, no Madman haunting the playgrounds and soccer fields she knew so well. Soon, she would be in the insulated comfort of California's Central Valley, reading by flashlight on the backyard patio as embers from her father's barbecue cast moving flecks of brilliance across a fixed and familiar sky.

Now, the dirt road climbed its narrow switchbacks,

each turn so steep that she could smell and hear the strain of the engine. With each bend, the view out her window alternated from the dizzying spectacle of the valley to the massive wall of cliff-face—patched with crudely painted advertisements in red and white. Some areas were scrawled with ugly graffiti, and she absently deciphered phrases like "*Fuerzas Capitalistas*" and "*Viva la Revolución Popular*" as they ground slowly up the road.

In some spots, hulking blackened shapes lay in the places where the road turned in on itself, constricting the route to a narrow channel. Samantha finally realized that these were the metal skeletons of buses, twisted and mangled from their falls off the cliffs above and charred by the explosions and fires of their impact.

It was with a start that Samantha noticed something was missing. The familiar weight against her chest was gone. In her frazzled state, and in her frantic hurry to pack and get away, she had left her notebook behind.

It was too late to go back for it. But maybe that was just as well.

"Oh, Sam," her uncle said, breaking the silence at last. "What was I thinking taking you here? You're such a smart kid and so grown up for your age that I sometimes forget how young you are."

She didn't answer, just turned away from the window and closed her eyes. When sleep came over her at last, she did not fight it, hoping to wake with the Andes far behind her.

But instead she woke in disorienting darkness. Only when she saw the small button of light far, far in the distance did she realize that they were in a mountain tunnel. But the van was not moving. Something was wrong.

"Uncle Jay?"

She could see him sitting bolt upright beside her, his window open. From the faint shimmer of his watch, she could tell that his hands were clamped to the steering wheel.

"Samantha, don't move."

Just past her uncle, through the open window, she caught sight of another metallic glint. As her eyes adjusted, she realized that it emanated from the polished barrel of an enormous gun. The van rocked a little as someone threw open the back hatch and then came around to slide open the door on the passenger's side.

"Don't turn around, Samantha. Just look straight ahead."

She heard rummaging behind her, and—beneath the sound of her own heartbeat—the rustle of her duffel being unzipped.

"Bandits?" she voiced, as softly as possible, wondering if Jay had replaced the pistol in its compartment by her knees.

"No," Jay whispered back. "A citizen patrol."

"You say that you are an archaeologist?" came the muffled Spanish of the person with the gun.

"*Sí*." Jay replied.

"And you work in Chavín?"

"*Sí.*"

The figure leaned in the open window, and Samantha knew she was being studied.

"And the artifacts. Where are they?"

"What?"

"The *concha* trumpets. You have them?"

The gun's barrel raised a couple of inches and her uncle sat up even straighter.

"No."

The gunman weighed Jay's answer in the darkness of the tunnel. And then there was a hissed order, and the side and rear doors were slammed shut. Samantha saw the glint of the gun swing to the side in a gesture for the van to move along. The jingle of the keys told her that her uncle's hands were shaking. But he managed to find the ignition, and in an instant they were on the move again, speeding toward the semi-circle of light and out into the brightness of day.

Samantha was bolt upright in her chair, gripping her seat belt hard.

"Idiots," Jay spat, before continuing his tirade in coarser terms. "They think that whoever stole the trumpets is going to just drive them out of the valley? Here, along the most obvious route? No. They know better. It's all just smoke and mirrors. Terrorizing people. Confusing them. Just a pathetic attempt to make it seem like they have everything in hand."

Something opened up in the recesses of Samantha's mind

and poured forth in a rush of memories. The Ocllo's pigsty. The blasts of cold air from Ofrendas' far wall. Alejandro's pendant. The story of the Loco and his disappearance.

And above all, Isabel's torment of her cousin Chimay via the hidden gallery and her statement in the arcade:

Aterrorizar es confundir. Confundir es controlar.

To terrify is to confuse, and to confuse is to control.

And at once, Samantha knew that there was no time to waste.

"Turn around, Uncle Jay. I need to go back."

•●●●●•

The sun was dipping toward the western cliffs by the time they parked in front of the hostal. Samantha sprang from the van, leaving her luggage behind. She needed to find her brother to see if her solution made sense.

She knew where he would be. Today was his day of Pillager glory—his battle with Otzi the Iceman—and he wouldn't lose the opportunity to impress his local fan club, no matter the chaos of the policemen's search.

"Samantha, what's going on?" Jay asked. "Where are you going?"

"I'll be right back."

She ran toward the arcade, stumbling along the uneven streets. But when she ducked inside, it was clear from the restless crowd that he was not there.

"Where is your brother?" Chimay cried in hoarse Spanish. The scattering of dismayed ticket holders still awaiting Evan's battle with Otzi added grumbles of their own. "He has to kill the *hombre de hielo*."

Samantha stepped outside, unsure of which way to turn or where to look. Where could he be?

A muffled whimpering turned her attention round. Just a few feet away, cowering against one of the ancient stones that lined the road, was Isabel. She was frantic, sobbing. A purple bruise marked her cheek, and her lip was bleeding where something had struck her across her mouth.

"Isabel?"

The girl could barely answer between her sobs.

"*Él está buscándote*," she wailed, grabbing Samantha's hand.

"Who? Who's looking for me? Evan?"

"*¡No!*" Isabel cried. "*¡El Loco!*"

Samantha felt the blood drain from her face, but Isabel would not let her tarry for long.

"*¡Corre, Samantha!*" she screamed. "*¡Corre, corre, corre!*"

And run Samantha did, sprinting once again across the Plaza de Armas and into the courtyard of the hostal. She rushed up the steps two at a time and came to a stop outside her room.

Why was the door slightly ajar?

With a cautious push it swung the rest of the way open, and she risked a quick glance inside.

Evan was not here either.

She slammed the door behind her, dragged her brother's suitcase against it as a feeble barricade, and sat on the edge of her bed, bewildered and afraid.

Where was Evan? Where had he gone, the one time in the summer that she needed his protection?

She lay down, curling into a ball. But she felt an uncharacteristic firmness as she laid her head on her pillow. Something had been placed beneath it. She slid her hand under and knew what it was at once.

Her notebook.

Seeing Evan's handwriting scrawled across its open page, her first response was anger. Not only had he run off when she needed him most, but he had gone and defaced her most prized possession.

Only then did she make out her brother's hurried writing.

"*Ayúdame*," it said, followed by its English translation: "Help me."

As she slipped the notebook over her neck, her puzzlement gave way to an icy calm. There was just one explanation for Evan's note, and it came to Samantha with terrible clarity.

Their trap in the Loco gallery had worked after all. Someone hungered for the tomb that wasn't there.

And now her brother's life was in peril somewhere in the labyrinth of lies.

AYUDAME

HELP ME

[Out of context]
SSFNb1-CdH: XVII

CHAPTER 17

Later, people would ask why she didn't go straight to the authorities when she left the safety of the hostal—why she didn't run north out of the Plaza de Armas to the police station, but to the south, charging back uphill to the Temple Complex in the dwindling light of day.

In truth she didn't think about it. The Madman had come for her at the hostal and for the notes he knew she hung around her neck. But Evan had secured them just in time and was taken in her place.

It was up to Samantha to save him.

She could not feel her feet as they pounded up the slope and across the bridge, which was crowded with the animal traffic of the late afternoon. Her burning lungs barely registered. If she was right—and she knew she was right—Evan was in the gravest danger. There was no time to waste.

But as the site came into view, she saw that the gate was shut, the heavy chain hastily attached. There were no guards to be seen. They had probably joined the rest of the force in searching the valley for Adam Quint—a search that, Samantha knew, was already too late.

There was a small amount of slack in the chain, and she was able to squeeze through the gate. She ran for the Temple, scrambling up the slope to the Loco gallery's black mouth. Only now did she realize that she didn't have her head lamp with her. She would have to rely completely on her knowledge of the gallery's layout. She would have to enter blind.

Light penetrated far enough to help her locate the wooden board on the gallery's floor. She cast it aside, revealing the space below. A cautious prodding with her toe located the first step and then the second. She crouched to a sitting position and, with her heart pounding in her ears, began her descent.

The staircase constricted immediately against the ceiling, pushing her flat and driving the edges of each step painfully against her spine. Even in her panic, she tried hard not to damage the fragile plaster that some ancient hand had slathered across the staircase's walls. This caution slowed her. But then her feet found even ground, and she squeezed herself the rest of the way into the dusty chamber.

All was black at the foot of the stairs. Not a single ray of sunlight pierced the darkness. The air felt heavy and carried an unpleasant chill, and Samantha realized that she was shivering.

This was where she had seen the Madman. It hadn't been

an illusion or a trick of her mind. And, if Samantha's hunch was right, somewhere up ahead, he waited for her still.

She raised a hand, confirming the height of the ceiling before taking a few cautious steps. She was in new territory, guiding herself forward with her outstretched fingers.

The ground was rough at her feet, as if freshly dug. And sure enough, as her fingers grazed the gallery's wall she bumped against the handle of a leaning shovel and caught it just before it fell. Someone had been digging here, lured by the Suttons' tales of a tomb and a treasure. Jay's plan had almost worked, and yet whoever it was had somehow evaded her uncle's determined vigil.

A new fear crossed Samantha's mind. Whoever had been here had come away with nothing, and now they were angry, more dangerous than ever.

The walls tightened, the gallery angling still downward and to the right. Something slapped against her cheek, emitting a ghastly squeal. A bat. She froze and pressed forward again only when she knew there were no others to follow.

She continued forward in the dark until ahead of her, barely perceptible at first, was a glimmer of light. As she neared it, the temperature of the gallery seemed to change, and the air grew lighter and less stagnant. She moved faster, her feet shuffling across the hard, uneven floor as she neared the source of the glow.

Soon, on her right, she came to where the dim light seeped through a slanted opening in the wall of the corridor. It was just large enough to enter, if one was willing to squeeze. Through it, she could look into another gallery, lit dimly by the remains of the daylight streaming through its doorway at the opposite end. She studied it long enough to see that Evan was not inside.

But just as she was about to move on, she froze and stared through the opening once more.

She knew this gallery.

In fact, she knew it very well.

It was Ofrendas, where she and her uncle had spent many happy days, sharing knowledge and telling jokes and retrieving the pottery of untold millennia. She remembered the unpleasant draft at the long corridor's far end and the small ventilation hole that seemed to be its source. She had been so focused on her work in the gallery's side chambers that she hadn't given it a second thought. It had never seemed big enough to fit through, though, and now she could see why. The opening slanted steeply upward as it entered Ofrendas. The final squeeze would hurt, but she saw that even an adult could manage it if he or she could withstand some momentary pain.

As the truth began to sink in, another faint glimmer caught her eye—ahead of her, farther down the corridor. Her heart grew heavy as she moved toward it, realizing what that second opening would bring. A single glance confirmed her suspicions. There, just on the other side of another, narrowing shaft, was the Galería de las Carcolas— the source of the trumpets—the very place where her magical summer had come to an end. She remembered how small the ventilation shaft had looked from the other side, how it seemed to dead end into a sloping wall.

But from this angle, the illusion was revealed.

Even as the entrance of Caracolas was guarded by the most elite corps of the Peruvian armed forces, a thief could travel freely throughout this gallery and the others, stealing artifacts without being seen.

Samantha felt so stupid. *El Loco* had made a fool out of her, her uncle, and everyone else. Her summer, the excavation, and her uncle's career may well have been ruined because of this one secret. The Madman had manipulated the ancient illusions of Chavín's priests in order to plunder its most sacred relics.

For several minutes, Samantha pressed on into darkness, the fear pushing back against her like a physical force. She stumbled, and when she reached to steady herself in the darkness, she felt an unexpected emptiness to her right. She tested it with a sweep of her hand. She had come to a fork in the gallery, and Evan's life depended on the route she was about to choose.

She struggled to orient herself. Ofrendas and Caracolas were well behind her by now, she thought, and if she had judged the turn of the tunnel correctly, she was now nearing the Central Plaza itself. That would mean that the new passageway, branching at a steep angle off to her right, led back in the direction of the Temple Complex. Perhaps it went as far as the modern road or passed under it, crossing into the West Field.

Samantha gasped. So this was how they had stolen the Incan girl. And now Samantha's anger began to overcome her fear.

Filled with rage, she charged forward but quickly realized her mistake when the floor came to an end below her feet. Her hands found the walls of the corridor just in time, saving her from a deadly fall down the undetected staircase. The panic subsiding in her chest and her throat, she took the stairs one at a time until she reached level ground.

The gallery straightened now, running for several yards without a turn. Above, she sensed that the stone ceiling was tall and grand, as it was far beyond the reach of her fingers. As she quickened her pace, she perceived a slight tilt downward, and she knew she was descending deeper and deeper beneath the earth.

And then a curtain of stone blocked her way, and she came upon it so suddenly that it scraped the palms of her outstretched hands. Here, the roof of the passage must have collapsed—ten years before or maybe a thousand. Only a faint draft of damp air against her shins told her that the way had not been blocked completely. If she wanted to go farther, she would need to crawl: forced to her knees at the mercy of the Temple's whims.

And so she kneeled, tracing the collapsed roof lintels with her hands to where they met the floor. The passageway was so small that she needed to lie flat on the ground, pushing hard with her feet and pulling herself forward across the soil on her stomach.

Samantha crawled on and on, and in some places the passage became so narrow that the back of her head pressed against the ancient masonry above, and her shoulders strained and scraped against the walls. Now she could not turn around even if she wanted to. The darkness was so thick and the silence so powerful that it felt like she was floating in space. The only noises were the intermittent scrapes of her boots on stone and the sound of her own breathing.

Suddenly she stopped crawling. Through the silence ahead of her, she could hear the murmur of voices. Evan was somewhere in the passage before her, and he was not alone.

There was no way to gauge how far away they were. Samantha knew by now that Chavín's galleries distorted the sounds within them. Something nearby might seem distant, and something far away might seem to generate from within one's own mind. The whispers she could make out in the darkness seemed to come at her from all sides. It was enough to drive a person mad.

She inched ahead once more, feeling the ceiling angle up and away. Here she could pull herself forward and stand, if she wanted to. But the approaching sounds of human voices made her anxious, and against all her instincts, she wriggled backward into the tight space.

They would be upon her soon.

She gritted her teeth, trying her best to hold off her fear by focusing on the facts at hand. Somewhere up ahead lay another way in, somewhere secret, somewhere outside the site itself. She twisted a braided pigtail around her finger.

The voices were clearer now. Or at least Evan's was, and he sounded as if he was only a few feet away.

"Ouch! Can you stop it? You just made me hit my head again!"

There was no response, just a low murmur as other voices conferred.

"Would you stop pushing me?"

Samantha knew her brother well enough to recognize his terror, but he was keeping up a good fight.

"Let go!" Evan's voice sounded closer still. "Come on, I can't see anything."

There were whispers in a language that was neither Spanish nor English, and then a deep voice, almost hypnotically smooth, that seemed to radiate from the gallery's very walls.

"There is a remedy for that. Open your hand."

She could sense movement in the chamber.

"What is this?"

"It is a potion. It will help with the darkness."

Samantha knew, almost immediately, what the "potion" contained and fought the urge to yell out a warning to her brother. But Evan, too, had been paying attention.

"Nice try. I know it's that cactus drug. And I'm not drinking it."

When the voice came again, it was to issue a statement of fact.

"Oh yes. You will."

Samantha realized that Evan really had no choice in the

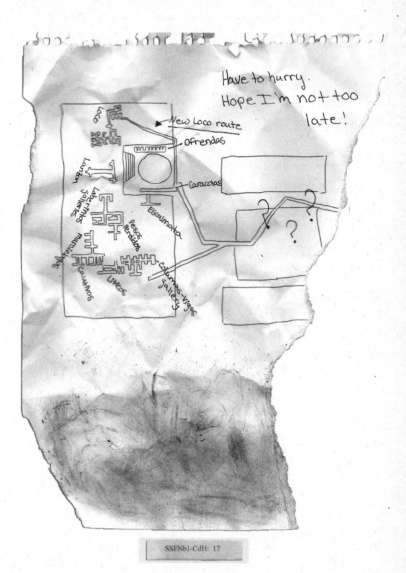

matter, and yet her brother impressed her with one last attempt. There were some exaggerated slurping noises, a couple of overly loud gulps, and a noisy, theatrical "ahhhh."

But Evan's ruse had not fooled anyone.

"You did not drink," the voice said, with plain intensity. "*I can see you.*"

The four words coursed over Samantha like the icy Rio Mosna. As she shrank backward, she heard Evan whimper in the dark. And then silence came as he at last relented and choked the substance down.

"Sit," the voice commanded. "We will continue when the potion takes hold."

There was a soft, damp slap as her brother slumped to the floor. His shoes squeaked with wetness too. Of course. He had been dragged across the Rio Mosna by his captors and into the gallery's other entrance inside the Ocllos' farm.

"Where are you taking me?" Evan asked, and Samantha strained to hear if the terrible narcotic had begun to take its effect.

"It is you who are leading us, *liebe bueb.* You will show us the tomb of gold that your uncle discovered."

Evan summoned the dregs of his remaining bravery.

"You can't be serious," he snorted.

There was a dangerous pause.

"I assure you. I am most sincere."

"Well, I can tell you now that there's nothing there." Evan sounded shaken. "It was just a rumor we started. It was supposed to be a trap."

Even flat on her face in the darkness, Samantha could feel a wild fury rising in the chamber before her.

"He's lying," snapped a woman's voice. "Look, it is written on his face."

"Patience, *töchtere*," was the man's response. "There are other questions to ask him, now that we are all alone. And no one unaccustomed to San Pedro's effects will have the ability to lie."

Samantha twitched uncomfortably, and the scuff of her boots against the ground sounded as loud and startling as a string of firecrackers. But now the sound was distorted in Samantha's favor and seemed to issue from the opposite side of the chamber. "*Si kömme!*" the woman hissed. "*D'polizei!*"

There was some rapid conversation in the unknown tongue, and then the Madman shifted again into English.

"We need to see if we are truly alone, *liebe bueb*. But should you decide to go exploring before our return, remember this: the passages are very confusing. I know them well, and should I have to retrieve you, there will be consequences."

"Zair vill be consequences," Evan muttered, mimicking the man's accent as he departed with his accomplice. But his bravado quickly slipped, and Samantha could hear as he began to cry.

She could reach out and touch him, he was so close, but Samantha fought the impulse. For all she knew, her brother's captors still stood watch, staring at him with their puzzling powers of sight. It was not a risk she could take.

Inexplicably, though, her brother beat her to it.

"Samantha?" Evan said, through his sniffles. "You came for me?"

She heard him struggle to his feet.

"Shhh. I'm rescuing you," she whispered, trying to sound brave. "But Evan, how can you see me?"

"I...I'm not sure. I can see everything, all of a sudden. It's like someone is turning up the dimmer on a light switch."

"It's the San Pedro." Samantha sighed. "You shouldn't have drunk that stuff."

"Well, what was I supposed to do? It's not like I had a choice."

He trailed off, taking in his surroundings as the drug coursed through him.

"Wow, Samantha. It's like their secret hideout or something. There's a ton of food, some tools, and oh my gosh...hold out your hands."

She pulled herself forward to where she could rise off the ground, and Evan placed something smooth and cool across her palms. She explored it with her fingers, feeling its intricate grooves.

"A shell trumpet! Are they all here?"

"One...six...twelve...I think so. Our pots too. And tons of other stuff. Stuff they must have found on their own."

"Evan?" Samantha began, biting her lip in the dark. "Is *she* here?"

"The mummy? The Incan girl? Yeah, Sam. She is."

He fell silent, and Samantha knew that something was wrong.

"I don't feel very well."

"What do you mean?"

"My stomach hurts," Evan managed. "My head feels really funny. And your voice sounds so weird."

The potion was taking its hold.

"We have to get you out of here, Evan. Here. Follow me!"

She pressed the trumpet back into his hands and pulled him by his shirt into the low opening

"But they're going to be back in any second!"

Noises somewhere ahead confirmed Evan's guess.

"Then we have to hurry. Come on! I know the way!"

She pulled down again, hard. Evan's movements were slow, and she had to yank him into the passageway. And soon, with Samantha in front, they were crawling as fast as they could manage, scraping their backs against the ceiling.

They had just reached the end of the cave-in when they heard the shouts behind them. They staggered to their feet, clutching at each other. Then Evan forced his way past Samantha, and she felt the cool surface of the trumpet brush against her forearm.

"Let me go first, Samantha. I can see!"

He grabbed her around the wrist with his free hand and charged ahead into the blackness. Somehow, Samantha managed to keep pace with her brother as they reached the staircase, flying up the steps two at a time.

New cries rang out behind them. Their pursuers had already left the collapsed section and were on their feet themselves, gaining rapidly and shouting with the anger and fury of primeval gods. They knew the galleries better than anyone alive, maybe even as well as the ancient priests who had used them for their rites.

At last, Samantha and Evan turned the corner. Far ahead of them was the aperture into Caracolas, still emitting the dwindling twilight of the distant sun. But as they reached it, Evan ground to a sudden halt.

"Ugh. What is that? It's killing my eyes!"

"Just a little sunlight," she hissed. "Keep going!"

"I can't! All those noises. Can't you hear them? Those awful popping sounds? And those colors. Don't you see?"

"No, Evan! It's just the stuff they made you drink. We have to keep moving!"

Her brother wrenched away from her, and she heard a splatter on the rock walls as he emptied the contents of his stomach.

"Come on!" she yelled, but her brother wouldn't budge. She took a look backward, weighing their options, and then squeezed past him, grabbing hold of his sweatshirt and dragging him down the corridor to the next faint light, the entrance to Ofrendas.

"Run, Evan! They're right behind us!"

And just as she said it, their pursuers rounded the corner behind them, their faces visible at last in the thin light. She recognized them at once. The summer's most dangerous mystery was solved. But it was tragically, uselessly too late.

They had been with them the whole time, sharing their mealtimes, listening to the gossip of each day in the field and the shared excitement over the more significant finds. Samantha had even shared her notes with them on occasion, so that when they set out in the mornings and evenings to loot the team's discoveries, they had known exactly where to look.

But seeing the once friendly faces of the two European tourists, now set in maniacal masks of fury, was still a shock. The old man's transformation was especially horrific. Gone was the impression of a genial Santa Claus. The face she saw now was the same demonic and twisted visage she had encountered in the Loco gallery some weeks before, the same one that had sent her scrambling from the Temple with a desire never to return.

The Loco gallery.

His gallery.

So this was the Madman, back to retrieve the riches he had discovered all those years ago, before the landslide had interrupted his plan and forced him to abandon his accumulated stash of looted artifacts. And from the way he reeled as he ran, Samantha realized that maybe he was insane, his mind addled by a lifetime of drinking the potent San Pedro or snorting its powdered form.

With desperate strength, Samantha forced Evan toward the shaft. She threw all her weight into his back, and at last, in a daze, he tucked the trumpet under his arm and climbed through to freedom.

Just in time. Because as Samantha clambered through behind her brother, a hand grabbed wildly at her feet.

Reeling around, Samantha was face to face with the frenzied grimace of the Loco, framed with its wild ring of white hair. His hand was cut and bruised from where he had slapped Isabel across the mouth. His pitch-black eyes darted left and right, and Samantha kicked out hard, driving away his grasping fingers.

Scrambling to her feet, she dragged her brother through Ofrendas and into the cool evening air of the outside. Evan held the trumpet up to cover his face, blinded even in the faintness of the twilight. It was then that Samantha caught the first glimpse of her brother's eyes, their usual blue surrendered entirely to the blackness of his widening pupils.

In the sheltered quiet of the Circular Plaza, it was easy to think that they had left the nightmare behind them, deep underground, and for a moment Samantha thought they may have escaped. But the only guards she could see were far away along the riverside—still on their hopeless search for Adam Quint.

Angry shouts from the opening of Ofrendas confirmed that their pursuers were now squeezing their way through the gallery themselves. And then they emerged slowly, like stalking jaguars. Samantha reached for her ailing brother and dragged him in his stupor toward the Circular Plaza's grand staircase. He collapsed heavily on the bottom step, the shell trumpet upon his lap.

"¡Socorro!" Samantha cried. "Someone help us! Please!"

But the Madman and his daughter knew that Samantha

was no match for them on her own and that her girlish voice could not be heard by the guards over the rush of the river. They also knew that the boy had been rendered fully incapacitated by the drug, and that it would not leave his system for hours.

They could be methodical in the steps they would need to take to protect their stolen secrets. They could take their time.

But suddenly, something held the Madman back. He cocked his head, seeming to look for the source of a noise that only he could hear. The woman noticed too, and twisted her stork-like body around.

It was Alejandro, emerging cautiously from Caracolas gallery, the head lamp Samantha had given him weeks before askew across his forehead. His clothes were dusty from the underground passage and streaked with the pig manure that obscured the gallery's secret entrance in his grandparents' yard. But it was the object in his hand that most attracted the group's attention: the sword of his ancestors, taller than the boy who held it, its fearsome motto reflecting some of the glint of the purpling sky.

"You have brought that a long way," the Madman said gently in Spanish simple enough for Samantha to understand. "I hope your grandfather does not find it missing."

Alejandro raised the blade, and the Madman inched forward.

"Give me the sword, Alejito. I have more gifts for you, if you behave."

The small boy hesitated. But before the words had even left the air, the Madman charged at him, racing across the plaza in a few short steps. To Samantha's surprise, Alejandro stood his ground. He was unwilling to live with the same regret as his grandfather, who had let the Madman come and go freely through his pig pasture all those decades ago.

Since it had been pried from the hand of a vanquished conquistador, the Ocllo's sword had not lost its sharpness. The small boy's awkward swing drew a crimson line across the Madman's shirt. The old man howled and reared back, clutching at his side.

It was now the woman's turn to act. With a terrible shriek, she darted not at Alejandro but across the plaza to Evan, wrapping a lanky arm around his listless body and dragging him up the staircase. The Madman dodged Alejandro's second swing and scuttled after her. Together they disappeared into the Lanzón chamber with their captive.

"Let's go!" Samantha cried, and indicated a metal pail that sat forgotten against the plaza's curving wall. It had been left some weeks before, when the team had been forced to abandon their excavations, and now spilled over with rainwater from the recent storms.

Alejandro laid down the sword and lifted the bucket. He could see that she had a plan, born of her knowledge of Chavín.

They moved up the staircase cautiously, veering off to

the left when they reached the ledge that would lead them to the Lanzón gallery. But when Alejandro moved to its entrance, Samantha held out a hand to stop him.

"Wait," she said, and pointed at the head lamp on Alejandro's forehead and then at the small ventilator that pierced the Temple's outer wall.

One of her parents' sample makeup mirrors still sat wedged inside it, the name Chavín Cherry embossed across its lid. It was an artifact of one of the summer's most exciting discoveries—one of her own—and now she needed it desperately.

When she was sure Alejandro understood her meaning, she took the dripping pail from him, made her way quickly back to the staircase, and climbed to the topmost step.

But before they could act, a strange sound issued from somewhere below her. It was a long, clear note at first, breaking gradually into a discordant warble. Evan was playing the shell trumpet, stupefying his captors with the weird acoustics inside.

"Now!" Samantha shouted, and emptied the bucket into the hole, just as Alejandro twisted the head lamp on and focused its beam on its target.

Howls of pain and terror echoed from the Temple as the blinding light flooded in, but the cries were gradually drowned out as the roar of the water chamber subsumed them. The sound went on and on, filling the site, the village, and the entire valley with its resounding thunder.

A quick glance toward the riverside confirmed that the

guards were running toward them, racing across the plaza and up the steps, their shouts inaudible above the din. Somehow, the sound of the trumpet could still be heard, its terrible call rising out of the ground.

Below her, Alejandro had lost none of his focus, sending forth into the Lanzón gallery a fiery spear of light. Samantha poured very, very slowly, manipulating the Temple's power to its full effect.

Suddenly, Evan stumbled from the gallery, the trumpet pressed absently to his lips. He stared up at her with his dilated eyes.

"The Lanzón!" Evan cried in his delirium. "We're bringing it to life!"

She did not stop pouring the water when the guards reached the Temple. She did not stop when the Madman and his daughter were removed from its depths, raving and clutching at their ears. Only when the last of the water gurgled into the hole did she stop, when the ancient thunder had swelled to its maximum volume, when the Circular Plaza had filled with police, when Clare and Osvaldo had surrounded her fallen brother, and when she felt her uncle's reassuring arms around her, lifting her into his comforting embrace.

You've Heard His Story, Now Be Part of

HISTORY

Peruvian cults, curses, and how he barely survived

Adam Quint

anford University's very own

dventurer Archaeologist

Saturday, September 25
Memorial Auditorium

Main Quad
Building 50

njured really bad. I hope he doesn't blame me for that too.

Jay says not to worry, because he's been invited to go do some work in ___ this winter. I think he wants me ___ ut I don't think ___

CHAPTER 18

With its red-tiled roofs, thick sandstone arches, and hordes of cheerful students playing Frisbee among the spindly palm trees, Jay's university was nothing like Chavín. Yet as Jay pulled his pickup to a stop in the shadow of the massive bell tower, and as Evan unbuckled his seat belt and swung open the truck's dented door, Samantha felt that familiar Andean dread.

The visit was all Samantha's idea. For his part, Jay had been reluctant to pick them up from their house in Davis and drive them out of the valley and across San Francisco Bay. Two weeks back from Peru, and he was eager for his nephew and niece to return to their normal lives. It was a luxury he could not afford himself.

Evan had moved on. After several visits with the Suttons' family doctor, he was back to his trumpet lessons and soccer practice, and to his grating, stupid telephone conversations with grating, stupid girls. There was no noticeable difference in how he treated Samantha—the fact that his little sister had saved his life had yet to come up—but Samantha was relieved that he was back to his old, aggravating self.

With the new school year just days away, Samantha had plenty to distract her. She was trying to catch up on all the trivia that her friends held so dear—the confusing lists of bands, brands, and boys. But even as the perils of Junior High loomed large, Chavín still haunted her.

Her departure from the village had been abrupt. After being escorted by her uncle to the hostal and helped into bed for a deep night of sleep, she awoke only to be whisked out of the courtyard with her groggy brother and into the waiting van. As they sped from the valley, she had caught sight of Alejandro and Isabel through the van's window, walking to the West Field with the rest of the town to attend the reburial of the Incan girl. Samantha had waved, but they had not turned their heads in time. She wondered if she would ever see either of them again.

Other memories were even harder to dwell upon. It was because of her that Gustaf and Anja Trautmann of Muri, Switzerland, were now in Peru's notorious Canto Grande prison. With Alejandro's help, she had interrupted a plan years in the making. Decades ago, and again this summer, Trautmann had amassed dozens of artifacts in the secret chamber under the Rio Mosna. Because of Samantha, these would never be sneaked out through the Ocllos' farm and over the mountains as he had planned. They would never reach Peru's vast shipyards at Callao, the anonymous warehouses of the Geneva Freeport, or the auction houses and fancy apartment buildings of New York, London, Tokyo, and Dubai.

The Madman could not harm her. But still, his fearsome image was with Samantha every time her mind wandered. She hoped that today's event at the university would give her the closure that she needed.

Jay still seemed distracted as he led them past the mournful statues of the university's Memorial Court, through the vast Main Quad, and beneath another archway to one of the university's busiest thoroughfares. He was deep in silent thought the entire way, returning to earth only as long as it took to maneuver his young relatives through the ceaseless buzz of bicycles.

The Anthropology Department was quiet, so quiet that Samantha thought they may have arrived at the wrong time. But the designated classroom was open, the lights on, and a projected sketch of the Lanzón snarled coldly on the whiteboard, indicating that a presentation was about to begin.

The classroom was a little one, and even with the very small audience of professors, the few seats remaining were in the very front row. They were close, too close, to the podium as the door swung open, the lights turned off, and a figure took his place behind the lectern.

Despite her uncle's warnings, nothing could have prepared her for her first sight of Adam.

His bus from Olleros to Lima was one of many that had tumbled off the road that summer, adding grievous injury to the insult he had suffered at the hands of the Suttons.

One arm, crushed in the bus crash, still hung in a sling, awaiting further surgery. The other was bandaged from elbow to shoulder, damaged by extremes of fire and cold. But most striking of all was the ghastly scar that hatched the side of his face and neck in a raised, red "x"—carved by the crossbar of the window as the bus had made its terrible impact against the valley floor.

Samantha had no doubt that he blamed the Suttons for all his misfortune—and perhaps rightfully so. It was Samantha who had caused the police to raid his room, after all, and Jay had sent him off as a fugitive in the night.

"Can I get started here?" Adam asked gruffly, and the small audience went quiet. At first, in the darkness of the room, she thought he didn't see them. But just before he began, he turned toward his advisor, directing his speech and his fearsome gaze into the front row. Samantha refocused her anxiety by trying to write down Adam's every word.

> I need to first express my gratitude to Dr. Sutton for arranging this talk today. You told me that it was the least you could do, and while I certainly agree with you [laughter], I feel like I'm expected to thank you. So I guess I will.

To her left, her uncle stiffened, but managed to smile and nod as if it were all a big joke.

> Real thanks go to my two informants, Chimay Fuentes and "Dijota" Vica, who provided much of the raw material for my

work. And to Dr. Sutton's nephew, Evan, who spent much of the season as my field assistant.

Now Evan shrank in his chair.

Everyone in the classroom was attentive as Adam began his presentation. He told them of an ancient priesthood, high in the mountains, who ruled not with armies but through the manipulation of the human mind. In their sacred Temple, the priests of ancient Chavín could harness the power of the sun and summon frightful, disorienting noises—feats performed with ancient mirrors, shell trumpets, and an ingenious acoustic water chamber beneath a grand stone staircase. They could even seem to disappear in thin air, only to emerge unexpectedly in another part of the Temple Complex or even far away, across the adjacent river. And the awesome effect of all of these illusions would have been magnified greatly by the powers of the San Pedro narcotic—powers that, after a summer of careful experimentation, Adam could attest to personally.

"Chavín's people were—as all people are—easily manipulated through confusion and fear," Adam concluded, a sly smile creeping over his damaged face. "Words to live by if ever there were."

Only a few people clapped as he marched from the room. But even the quiet rippling of the applause felt horribly familiar in Samantha's ears and lingered in her mind like thunder.

•• ● ••

The three Suttons sat in the corner of the university's coffee shop, sipping dolefully on mint-mocha freezes.

"So, Uncle Jay?" Evan asked. "You think you might go back to Chavín next summer?"

His uncle stared at him, trying to determine whether it was just a tasteless joke.

"No, Ev," he said. "Actually, Osvaldo has asked me not to."

Samantha noted the depth of sadness in her uncle's voice. He had left much in Chavín. His reputation. His nerve. And Professor Clare Barrows.

Samantha's heart ached for him. It seemed like he would never be the same.

And then, to her surprise, Jay's characteristic enthusiasm returned, and he dropped his voice to an excited whisper.

"But I'm making arrangements somewhere else."

Samantha allowed herself a smile. At least in this moment, Jay was his old self again, already planning for his next excavation. She felt herself get swept away, whisked along once more in the current of her uncle's zeal.

"In fact," he whispered, "I've been invited to go work in…"

SAMANTHA SUTTON

and the

WINTER OF THE
WARRIOR QUEEN

AUTHOR'S NOTE

What takes place in this story never happened. Ever. But because I have draped these fictional events over a real landscape, where real archaeology is practiced and where real people live and work, some further explanation is needed.

Today, the site of Chavín de Huantar faces major challenges. Poor drainage, for example, threatens to undermine some of its architecture. A paved road installed in the early 2000s destroyed much of La Banda's archaeology across the river, and drew condemnation from the international conservation community. Tourism, while a necessary source of income for the valley and its inhabitants, has carried with it its own detrimental effects.

But while the site may have many problems, looting is not one of them. This is no accident. The government of Peru, through its *Instituto Nacional de Cultura* and other agencies, takes every precaution to protect the site from the threat of illicit excavation. Because Chavín is a designated UNESCO World Heritage Site, Peru is helped in this endeavor by the international community, as well as by private organizations dedicated to cultural heritage preservation. Furthermore, the archaeologists who actually work in Chavín are far, far more competent than their fictional counterparts that I've created. Their relationships with local, regional, and national government agencies are strong; their consultations with Chavín's inhabitants are thorough and collaborative. They approach their work with the high level of professionalism that is expected of them. Most importantly of all, perhaps, is that the site is protected by a vigilant and knowledgeable local populace.

The finds and discoveries made by my fictional archaeologists are real—to a point. While I have taken liberties with precise locales, all but a very few artifacts discovered by Samantha, Jay, and the rest of the team have been uncovered at the actual site by actual archaeologists, at some time during the decades of professional excavation. I drew on the published literature for information on these artifacts, from archaeologists working at the site today, and from my own fieldwork at Chavín.

Also true are the various phenomena encountered by the team. The strange, terrifying sound effect exists and can still be triggered. The evidence suggests that the ancient manipulation of light with graphite mirrors is accurate as well. The galleries, too, are mostly how I describe them. The sole liberty I took with their arrangement is the continuation of the Lower Loco gallery as far as La Banda, though, as Samantha herself notes, such a design was reported by Spanish chroniclers. Several smaller sites are situated in the hills above the site, though none precisely match the one I described. Horribly, a devastating landslide did occur in the mid-twentieth century. Finally, the discovery of spatulas, snuff tubes, and other paraphernalia indicates that the ancient inhabitants of Chavín made use of the locally plentiful San Pedro cactus, a powerful hallucinogen. Knowledgeable practitioners still make use of this narcotic today for spiritual reasons and without calamitous effect.

While I have taken some small liberties throughout the novel, responsible archaeology demands that I own up to two instances where I have stretched the truth in more than just detail. There has never been an Incan mummy recovered at Chavín. During the 2000 field season, I witnessed the excavation of a juvenile female, possibly dating to the Inca period, from a hidden gallery beneath the West Field. But the remains were skeletal, not mummified—and she was reburied where she was found much in the manner I described. I stretched the truth in a similar fashion in describing the skulls that greet Samantha in the *Pasos de los Perdidos*. Human bones have been found throughout the complex, but not—to my knowledge—arranged in such a manner, or in such great number.

While individuals and businesses mentioned in this book are drawn loosely from my own experiences in Peru and elsewhere, they bear no resemblance to their inspirations. There is no Hostal Jato that I know of. No Osvaldo.

No Condor nightclub. No Ficho restaurant. And while there are galleries and monoliths in La Banda, they are not situated on land owned by the Ocllo family, who are entirely fictional themselves.

The madman himself is part of local lore, but not how I have described him here. Still, when I worked in Chavín, the prevailing sentiment in the village was that such an individual did once exist, that he was malevolent, and that he disappeared within the sinister gallery that now bears his name.

ACKNOWLEDGMENTS

Without the support and encouragement of many incredible individuals, this book could never have been written. My debts and my gratitude are huge.

Thanks first to my parents, Paul and Nancy Jacobs, who recognized a lifelong passion when they saw one. Their influence, understanding, and loving encouragement are on every page.

Thanks to Professor John Rick of Stanford University, who bravely leads a group of young archaeologists to Chavín most summers. I am one of a lucky multitude inspired by his exacting science, enduring professionalism, and constant, contagious enthusiasm.

Special thanks to my brave and tireless agent, Cathy Hemming; my gifted and considerate editor, Steve Geck; and to David del Ser, who, in addition to his nuanced knowledge of Spanish and kid-friendly Peruvian slang, provided a crucial early read.

Thanks also to Pilar Queen, Gabe Tsuboyama, Ben

Suter, Maya Popa, Liz Furze, Erin Curler, and Patrick and Lorette Gournay.

I am especially indebted to the people of Chavín and to the generations of archaeologists who have made the site the focus of their life's work.

And finally, thanks to my brilliant wife, Lindsay Pollak—heroine of my own life story.

ABOUT THE AUTHOR

Jordan Jacobs has loved archaeology for as long as he can remember. His childhood passion for mummies, castles, and Indiana Jones led to his participation in his first excavation at age thirteen in California's Sierra Nevada. After completing a high school archaeology program in the American Southwest, he followed his passion through his education at Stanford, Oxford, and Cambridge. Since then, Jacobs's work for the Smithsonian, the American Museum of Natural History, and UNESCO Headquarters in Paris has focused on policy and the protection of archaeological sites in the developing world.

Jacobs's research and travel opportunities have taken him to almost fifty countries—from Cambodia's ancient palaces to Tunisia's Roman citadels, Guatemala's Mayan heartland, and the voodoo villages of Benin. He now works as Senior Specialist at the Phoebe Hearst Museum of Anthropology at UC Berkeley.